The Teaching of Faith

The Teaching of Faith

Elizabeth Bruce

First published in 1994 by
Nexus
332 Ladbroke Grove
London W10 5AH

Copyright © Elizabeth Bruce 1994

Typeset by CentraCet Limited, Cambridge
Printed and bound by Cox & Wyman Ltd, Reading, Berks.

ISBN 0 352 32936 X

This book is sold subject to the condition that it shall not, by way of trade or otherwise, be lent, resold, hired out or otherwise circulated without the publisher's prior written consent in any form of binding or cover other than that in which it is published and without a similar condition including this condition being imposed on the subsequent purchaser.

This book is a work of fiction.
In real life, make sure you practise safe sex.

Chapter One

The soft buzzing was as if a light aircraft were high in the sky above her on a warm, summer's day, though the scents around her were not of hay and grass, but of . . . Faith awoke with a start, wide-eyed as her conscious brain identified the scent which reeked so strongly in her nostrils. Around her was a half-familiar room; a room which, in her dreams, she had seen as though through a mist. There was a good deal of glass about the place, not just in the mirrors which dominated most of the walls, but in the variously-coloured ornaments which proliferated on every available level surface.

With a soft gasp the young woman looked down at the whiteness of the silken sheets and the softness of the mattress on which she had been curled; rolling onto her back, her eyes became even wider, if that were possible, as she looked up at the ceiling. Ten feet above her, a mirror extended from the far wall to the nearer, then down the wall behind the bed on which she found herself. Still looking at the reflection of her nudity, Faith's mind recalled watching the rhythmic movement of her breasts as she had . . . She sat up.

Faith had been in this bed, naked; she smiled at the memory. Yet, as her fingers found the moistness between her legs, she strained to recall some detail as she ran her tongue around her lips. She could remember kneeling astride a man, though she found it impossible to remember anything about him. That was odd. Nothing about him remained, except the ache in her loins. That, and the wetness. The wetness! Faith bent forward, finding the damp patch on the bottom sheet, sniffing delicately: remembering.

The wet patch on the sheets was at the centre of the bed. Facing the mirror behind the bed, kneeling on the yielding firmness as she had done then, she had sheathed herself around the aroused flesh he had raised to her. The echo of her own wanting made her shudder just as a tiny movement off to one side made her turn her head slightly. She looked in the mirror at the man in a white towelling bathrobe who entered the bedroom, freshly barbered by electric razor. That explained the sound of the aeroplane, she thought.

He looked about thirty, but she suspected he was younger from his smooth lack of wrinkles; he was over six feet tall, and his fair hair was parted conventionally on the left, cut shorter than was normal these days. His smooth features looked lean and hard, as did his pectoral muscles displayed by the carelessly worn bathrobe. Her memory was of firm, tanned biceps which had lifted her effortlessly on and off his upright manhood. That, and of intense, pale blue eyes.

'Hello.' His voice was a well-modulated drawl as his face split into an assured smile. 'Glad to see you're awake at last. How are you this morning?'

'Fine. Thank you.' Her own surprised calm reassured her. Who *was* he?

Faith's first instinct was to cover herself; then she realised that, not only had he undressed her, seen her nakedness, but he had entered it pretty freely. Her mounting of him had been but the prelude. A stray memory reminded her of being on her back while he had eased his way energetically into her.

'No . . . regrets?' he asked, surprising her with the blush which flashed, all too briefly, across his face.

'Regrets?' she asked, keeping her expression neutral. She turned to face him, swinging her legs round so that she sat with her feet together, over the side of the large, comfortable bed. 'What are they?'

'Thank God for that,' he sighed, his expression so relieved that she wondered what else had happened.

'Should I have any regrets?' Faith asked.

'Well.' The man refused to meet her eye. 'We did rather, you know, get stuck in.'

'As I remember,' Faith said, 'we came back here from the party and . . .?' she paused, hesitating to admit her lack of memory.

'And fucked, yes.' He nodded his head while he looked away, but such was the proliferation of mirrors that he still looked at her, though from a different angle.

The sunlight streaming through the open, curtained window made the light-coloured walls almost glow; the rosiness reflected onto her skin by the mirrors made her look far more healthy than she felt.

'Did I give satisfaction?' Faith asked, trying to gauge his mood. Was he content, or would he want more? Who had initiated things? And what about Albert? Especially, what about Albert? He paused, smiling, looking directly at her.

'You gave more than that. You were quite wonderful.' He looked down again, for a moment losing his aplomb. 'I wondered if I . . .?'

'As I remember, you were quite . . . capable.' Faith had found that a suitably neutral term, especially with Albert.

Albert Cross, with whom she lived, was, at times, unpredictable. A professionally competent advertising executive, he had a very real, deep – and justified – inferiority complex about his bedroom performance. Faith had been attracted to him for his intellect, ability and position in Gibb McInley Gower rather than for his looks when she had begun working for the Agency. She needed someone with a thorough understanding of the business if she were to make progress.

Her progress had been from her desk to his bed, where his painful inadequacy had been apparent at once. Albert had persuaded her to undress, but had ejaculated prematurely in his underpants which, paradoxically, he had blamed on *her*. It was the first of several instances wherein Albert had proved himself to be rather less than adequate as a lover; hence her need for suitably neutral language, for he was senstive about the subject.

Faith had professed to understand, though how any virgin *could* was beyond her. It had been the first of the many white lies with which she had endeared herself to him. She had stayed the night and, it being a Sunday morning, had been successfully mounted by Albert in the warm, lazy atmosphere engendered by their sleeping together. By Wednesday – Albert was no gentleman – everyone at the Agency knew she had slept with him. By the following Monday, her desk had been moved to a better location and she was on her way. Three weeks later, after spending each weekend there, Faith had moved her things from her own single room in Enfield to his flat. It hardly endeared her to the others in the Agency; there had been several comments about her 'sleeping her way to the top' and 'giving head' rather than 'using her head', but she had expected worse. It had been a deliberate decision, one she subsequently regretted without showing just how much; but by then, she was trapped.

The tall man smiled, nodding his appreciation of her delicacy, his look of frank admiration making her feel uncomfortable as he asked: 'I hope I didn't . . . upset you?'

'Why should you have upset me?' Faith asked, though she knew that there *was* something that had, yes.

She remembered as he answered. 'Not everyone likes a finger poked up their backside,' he stated with confidence.

'There's a first time for everything.' Faith's quick riposte suprised him; her face was clouding, but she was unable to recall being treated in that way at all. A finger in her bottom! It should have worried her but, to her surprise, Faith found she accepted that it had happened; wondered what it had felt like. For a moment she thought of asking, but he was already hurrying the conversation past that.

'I thought you didn't like it. I'm sorry,' he said quickly, but she shook her head,

'No. It's not that. Honestly,' she answered, giving a weak smile, 'I was just wondering about Albert.'

'Albert?' the man asked, then nodding, 'Yes. Albert.'

'You *know* Albert, don't you?' she asked.

'Well . . .' He stopped, exhaling slowly. 'No. You mentioned him a few times.' He looked sheepish. He seemed ten years younger with that sheepish look, and she wondered whether he appeared that young when he made love. Albert lost *years*, but then, Albert had them to lose. This man would probably look like a schoolboy.

Faith conjectured that she must have mentioned the name when she was climaxing, but asked, 'You *were* at that terrible party, weren't you?'

'Ah,' his face cleared, 'yes. I wondered if you remembered that.'

'Albert and I went.' Faith held a hand up to her head, as if that would clear the fog which seemed to have obliterated much of her memory. 'It was in Belgravia, a terrible thing. One of Albert's clients. I remember Hartwell being there – he's another client – and someone called Mitchell. Albert passed out, I think. Yes; I remember now. Albert must have had too much to drink because he just . . .' She was beginning to recall other things, too.

This tall man with ice-blue eyes which seemed to bore straight through her had been there; with a slim, lithe, fair-haired woman of about thirty who had danced, very gracefully on a small onyx table, lifting her skirts in time to the music. Odd, for she hardly seemed the type; yet she appeared to be enjoying herself. There were plenty of men hanging about, enjoying her display.

'Knowing Jimmy Mitchell,' the man said in the silence which followed, 'I wouldn't be surprised if he didn't have something to do with that.'

'Really?' she asked, frowning as she looked at him. 'Why would he . . . why would anyone . . .?' she trailed off, aware of so many reasons for stupefying Albert that they would take all day to mention, far less explain. She had often felt that way, herself.

'And someone slipped me something, I think. Why?' She frowned at him as though he could provide the answer.

'Stand up, would you?' He lifted a hand, palm upwards, towards her, gesturing for her to rise, almost as though commanding her to dance at a very formal gathering. Yet he had a way about him, an assumption of control – that people would do as he said – not based on the fact that she was there, in his bed, in his home, in the nude, either. Faith frowned but complied, while the man smiled, then said, 'Come with me,' leading the way through the door from which he had emerged a few moments earlier.

The sterile bathroom was decorated more profusely than the bedroom with mirrors. He turned, pointing towards a clear space of wall where, when she looked, Faith saw herself full-length. Her dark hair was long, hanging mid-way down her spine and, even after an active night with this man, surprisingly untangled. She looked at herself directly, at her closely trimmed triangle of pubic hair through which her mound could be seen, and the peeking pink of her clitoris and labial lips. Her breasts were firm and well-defined, though the nipples had hardened into rubbery cylinders which seemed out of place amid those gentle curves. She stood two inches below six feet tall, weighing 135 pounds; her dark brown eyes were level, separated by her straight nose, whilst her complexion was smooth and creamy.

That smooth, creamy-pinkness covered her body; even her more exposed hands and calves retained the soft, youthful appearance which – it must be said – Faith had worked at. She was, she knew, a little vain, but felt that in her profession (as in the oldest) appearance was important. And Albert liked her to look nice; though more to gloat over than in appreciation of herself, she thought. At this strange man's suggestion, Faith turned full circle so that he could see the smooth, rounded globes of her buttocks and the long, slim thighs.

'Have you ever thought of being a model?' he asked quietly, startling her.

Faith began to smile, then something struck her; a faint memory of that very question. The edge of her doubt expanded and her eyes flicked to his concerned face as he asked: 'Did Jimmy ask you that?'

'*Someone* did, I think,' she admitted. She realised too, that he was not only taller than she was, but immeasurably stronger, and not just physically. His personality could overpower her whilst his manner and appearance told her that her proximity excited him. She was naked and he was nearly so. If he wanted to take her to his bed, to mount her in the position of his choice, there was little she could do about it, should she even want to. Even as she considered this, her mind rejected it. Faith recalled that her evening had ended happily in his bed, despite his strange sexual practices.

'Jimmy,' he nodded, reaching out a large hand to cup her right breast, making her gasp at his touch, his gentleness, the softness of his skin. He looked her directly in the eye then, as his thumb drifted across her firm, pliable nipple, his fingers gently teasing the flesh beneath, and said, 'He runs what he calls a "Modelling Agency". It's a con, though he does own a couple of "girlie" mags. Some of the girls appear in them, naked, of course, and pretty blatant. I've heard he's got a good business in porn, too. Seeing you, I wouldn't put it past him to have drugged the pair of you then hauled you off to the Mousetrap; he owns part of it, has a studio, I suppose you'd call it, there.'

'Are you trying to frighten me?' she asked, taking a pace backwards. His hand released her breast so that only the memory of the delightful sensations which had been beginning to arouse her remained. For a few seconds she wondered whether she had done the right thing, for the sensation still burned within her flesh.

'I wish I was,' he replied in a weary tone, shaking his head, 'but I'm not. Jimmy's a bit of a bastard.' Then, seeming to make up his mind, 'Do you want to shower? I'll see about breakfast.'

He was already turning away when she exclaimed

'Wait! No! Stop a minute; please. What . . . what should I do?' Her anxiety made him frown for a moment as he looked back at her, but then he relaxed again.

'Do?' he smiled. 'That depends on what you want to do. Won't Albert miss you? I would if you were mine.'

'I . . .' Faith licked her lips uncertainly for a few moments, pleased at the compliment but still uncertain; she looked him in the eye, surprised by the tone of utter honesty in his voice. He made neither move nor sound until she sighed, then nodded, grimacing at him in a gesture which turned into a smile. 'Shower; yes, I'm sorry. I don't even know your name.' Her embarrassment made her flush again. It was quite a solecism to have made love to a man to whom she had not been properly introduced; not introduced at *all*.

'Alex; Alex Pellew. Odd sort of name, I know,' he smiled, extending his hand.

For a moment she looked at it, then stepped forward and took the soft yet firm flesh; she released him again after a brief, wary pressure. This man was having an unusual effect on her; she found herself liking him more than could be explained in any rational way. Even discounting their unusual meeting this morning, he must have made himself very agreeable to her. That was probably it. Albert had been comatose; Alex had been pleasant, so he had brought her back to this place for some very rewarding, fulfilling sex.

'Have a shower, Faith,' he suggested again.

'You know my name?' She was surprised.

'Faith. Yes.' He nodded, starting as she moved closer to him. She found his knowledge intriguing, but accepted it. He, the sophisticate, knew *her* name.

'Faith Small,' she said, then laughed with him. 'Yes. That's a bit of a misnomer, isn't it? I was always called "Tiny" at school; and Oxford.' She still took pride in mentioning she was an Oxford graduate.

'So was I,' he drawled with a smile, nodding; then became serious as he turned away to leave her alone in the bathroom.

Carefully, Faith scrubbed herself under the hot shower, feeling the sweat being washed away, cupping her hand beneath her sex to fill it with warm, soapy water to try and remove as much of him as she could. She could recall the sensation of her cervix being flooded by him; quite unlike Albert, of course. If Albert restrained himself long enough to ejaculate within her, there was little fluid; hardly worth worrying about, though she religiously took her pill. This man, Alex. Yes, Alex. Alexander? Alexi? Alex. She'd have to remember that. Alex, now, had enough semen to *drown* Albert.

In the bedroom she could smell the toast and coffee as she tried to find her clothes. She found her dress, a pale tangerine shade Albert had insisted was apricot, her brassière (also tangerine) her stockings, suspender belt and shoes. Where were her panties? Had Alex kept them as a souvenir? It was likely enough. She didn't begrudge him that.

Dressed in what she could find, she quit the bedroom by the other door to find him in the kitchen just across the narrow passage, still in his bathrobe, an expression of concentration on his face as he bent over an automatic coffee percolator.

'Find everything?' he asked, smiling as he looked up.

'Everything but my knickers,' she answered, watching his face fall before he replied.

'You didn't have any on when you got here.' His voice commanded belief.

'What?' she asked, utterly surprised.

'Yes. I saw you when you first arrived at the party with a little man; was that Albert?' He paused while she nodded. 'Yes, well; I saw Jimmy Mitchell talking to him a couple of times, but I couldn't see you, until I was looking for a friend of mine. I went into the room overlooking the garden, and there was Albert, sprawled out at one end of a couch and you were at the other, with your legs splayed out. You didn't have any knickers. You looked pretty well gone.' He stopped, sighed, looking at her. 'Are you sure you want to know? I mean . . .'

'What?' she asked, her colour rising; this was something she *had* to know. Who had taken them? Where had they gone? And under what circumstances? Should she remember more about this party than she had done so far?

'Well,' he sighed, shaking his head, though still buttering the toast, getting the cups and saucers from the cupboard in front of him, 'Jimmy and his crew of hangers-on were there; looking as though they'd been at either the bottle, the needle or the straw, if you know what I mean?' He paused to look at her and, when she made no answer, continued, 'You were sprawled there; legs everywhere. That's when I saw you didn't have any.'

'Is that why you brought me here?' she asked. 'You thought I was a sure thing?' Faith tried to keep the edge from her voice, but failed.

'No. I heard them talking,' he replied. 'Jimmy wanted to take you to the studio. If he had, there'd be quite a portfolio of pornographic pictures of you by now. So I purloined you, shall we say?'

'Thanks.' She gave a tight smile which simply reflected her worry.

'When we came back here you . . . well,' he smiled, 'you were pretty willing. Surprised me, rather.'

'Yes.' Faith flushed. 'Yes, I remember that. Some of it, anyway. I'm sorry; that sounds awful.' Faith's features expressed her anxiety about recalling what sounded like a harrowing night.

'I'm surprised you remember any of it; and don't feel sorry. I rather took advantage of you, I suppose.'

'Perhaps we took advantage of each other.' Faith was willing to smile and compromise.

'Why don't you stay?' he asked abruptly.

'I live with Albert,' Faith said evenly. 'Can I use your telephone? I'd better talk to him. Tell him I'm all right. He'll be worried, I know.'

'Your friend won't answer. He collapsed on you at the party; passed out. He's still there, by the way. Kirkland's people have tried to wake him without success. What do you want with him anyway? With someone like that? You can do *much* better for yourself.'

'You mean with you?' she asked.

'Why not?' he replied. 'From what I hear, this,' he gestured around him with the toast, 'is better than West Kensington.'

Faith had to agree with him. The bedroom and bathroom alone would have been better than Albert's whole flat. Yet though it seemed an attractive idea, she hesitated.

'For how long?' Faith asked, her tone suggesting that he was likely to tire of her.

''Til you stop me making you want to stay,' he answered. It took her a moment to work it out.

He was offering her bed and board – mostly bed, she knew – for as long as she could convince him to keep her. A few months before, the suggestion would have scandalised her but seven months of working in the cynicism of advertising had blunted her sensibilities. Weeks before, she would have laughed; the memory of Albert, slumped on the couch at the party stopped that.

She recalled the other times when his uncertain temper had annoyed or upset her. His sexual inadequacy, now that she had learned better, loomed large.

'I have all my things at Albert's.' Faith shrugged.

'He won't be there for some time yet,' Alex replied, 'you could collect them before he gets back.'

'I could,' she agreed. 'Do I want to, though?'

She had arrived from Oxford with an offer of work and no entanglements the previous summer, having spent her time previously avoiding young men and women alike. Her father had lately died; a victim of his own success in the Diplomatic Service. He had spent so long in countries where the traffic drove on the right that, three days into his retirement, he had stepped off a kerb while looking the wrong way. Her mother had gone to live with her sister in a remote part of Cumbria, leaving Faith very much on her own.

For an answer, he closed into her, placed his left hand

11

on her right breast, his right on her behind. His tongue penetrated her mouth; he tasted of buttered toast. She could feel the desire at once. Her body betrayed her calculating mind, responding to his embrace by thrusting her pelvis into his long thighs, feeling the quickening male organ against her. When he broke away, Faith took a deep breath, her wide eyes looking at him as he picked up another piece of toast.

Everything was ready for the game and it was *her* serve. He made no move towards her, yet she could still feel the warmth and pressure of his fingers on her breast. Faith's seeping sex made her realise just how much he had aroused her; and from just one kiss.

'All right,' she breathed heavily, nodding, bending her flushed face and casting her eyes to the floor.

'Good.' Alex's pale eyes smiled. 'There's a party I should attend tonight, and I have no partner; you might like it. Not the same people as last night, of course.'

'I've had enough of parties for the moment.'

'Yes,' Alex agreed quickly, 'you must have; still, I think you'll like it. Here; I'll make some more toast, I've had all the rest. Do you want something cooked? Can't stand it myself, first thing, but you might.'

'No.' She felt awkward for refusing. 'I don't have much first thing, either.'

Though it was pleasantly warm outside, despite a wind blowing up the Thames, Alex called a cab from a nearby rank; then he escorted her downstairs to wait in the modern lobby until it arrived, wheezing like an asthmatic tractor. Faith formally shook hands with Alex as she stepped into the black vehicle, thanking him for his attention; she closed the door then waited until the cab moved a hundred yards down the one-way street before giving the driver the address of Albert's flat in West Kensington.

As the cab stopped at the foot of Albert Bridge, Faith quickly checked the internal rear-view mirror. As all she seemed to see was a view of the driver's grey coat, she kept both her knees pressed together and twisted sideways. Albert had warned her about cab drivers who positioned their internal mirrors to get a look up the skirts of their female passengers. She would be worth watching this morning.

Chapter Two

Sandwiched between the railway line and North End Road, the house had been designed by a Victorian building speculator who had made his mark on London; there were many such houses in the tangle of surrounding streets. The cab driver looked her up and down as he slowly searched for change, trying to prolong the performance in order to induce Faith to tell him to keep it. Faith knew that one, too, and waited, aware that she had little enough cash as it was, willing her expression into remaining neutral.

Faith could pack very quickly when pressed, and the mental threat of Albert's return was sufficient. Her case was still behind the high, old-fashioned wardrobe which Albert swore was a valuable antique he had picked up on North End Road. The fact that it was to hand convinced her that this was what she had intended all along. She had known that one day, she would abandon Albert. But for Alex?

Her initial reaction to his proposition had been favourable, but she wanted to be sure before she made the journey. Telephoning him, she asked if his offer was still open.

'Of course,' he drawled; she could almost see the slow smile.

'You don't know me very well,' Faith retorted, her case half-full. Second thoughts were her besetting sin, she thought; grab the chance while she had it.

'I know you,' he smiled, then added, 'in the biblical sense, anyway,' making her blush at the memory. She touched her lower abdomen, as though feeling him still there.

'I'll be about an hour; perhaps more. I don't know how easily I'll get a cab.'

'I have no plans until two, at least.' She checked her watch; it was eleven thirty.

'If I'm not there by then,' Faith promised, 'I'll be under a bus.'

'If you can't make it, call me again,' Alex said quietly. 'I'll change my plans.'

As he replaced the instrument, Alex smiled, his mind racing pleasurably. Yes, this might be just the thing; a change of plans. He liked Lillian very much, but they both knew that marriage would be impossible. Coming to an abrupt conclusion, he began to dial another number. This would require fancy footwork, but *just* might work.

'Rupert?' he said at once, as the connection was established. 'Alex! Your party still on tonight?'

'Of course it is,' the light voice on the other end said. 'Can't you make it?'

'No,' Alex said quickly. 'It's not that; it's just . . . Could you do me a favour? Are Pru and Colin coming? I thought you mentioned them.'

'Yes. Why?'

'There's this girl,' Alex said cautiously, 'I'd like your opinion of her.'

'Aha?' The interest in Rupert's tone increased with the rising note of his voice. 'What does she do? What does she look like?'

'She's rather stunning, as a matter of fact,' Alex answered. 'And, well, I'd like her to be Chosen.'

There was a silence on the other end of the line for several seconds while the man allowed his breathing to subside before answering: 'Really, Alex? Bad as that, is it? Do I know her?'

'No,' the tall man replied, 'you don't. You will tonight, if we can set it up. Are Lillian and Simon coming? And Max? I'd like their opinion, too.'

'Yes,' the man answered quickly, 'Julia and Harry should also be there. Do you, I mean,' he hesitated, then advanced a question, '*are* you going to nominate her? Tonight?'

'If I can,' Alex answered, his anxiety increasing. 'Do you think we could? I mean, I don't want to spoil your party or anything.'

'No, quite all right,' the man answered, then asked, 'Would she be suitable? Is she prepared for it?'

'I doubt it,' he answered. 'I'll call Lillian and tell her what I have in mind, shall I? Lillian and Max should be able to think of some way to get her going. She's staying with me, as a matter of fact. Lillian met her last night at Kirkland's thing. You were the lucky one, Rupert, you weren't there.'

'It's nice to know I didn't miss anything.' The man sounded as though he wished he had attended.

'I'll see you tonight, then. Right?' Alex asked, then rang off. There were quite a few people to call and arrangements to be made before Faith arrived.

Not having many clothes was an advantage, for Faith's suitcase, though capacious, had to be packed carefully. She gradually emptied her clothes out of the wardrobe on the far side of the bed from where she and Albert had lain together. Faith paused for a moment, recalling the Sunday morning when she had lost her virginity there, surprised that it had become just a dim memory. She changed into a jumper and skirt, putting her tangerine dress into a bag with her laundry. Once these were packed, she put her shoes into a few plastic bags, her make-up and various necessities into others, pushing them down into the spaces, spreading them out where she could, before fastening the case. It was still quite a weight.

With no feelings of regret she took her flat key from her handbag, stopping to realise that, if anything, she felt release. Placing the key on the half-counter by the telephone, she looked round as though fixing the flat in her mind; in fact, she was checking that nothing had been forgotten. Bowed under the weight of the case, Faith closed the door behind her.

Instead of simply pressing the buzzer to open the door, Alex also came down in the lift to help with the case, looking amused at the size of it, and asking: 'You didn't pinch the sink as well, did you?'

'No, of course not.' Faith flushed, stammering an explanation of the things she had to bring before finally leaving. How stupid she felt, and how terrible to be imposing on him. He ignored her awkwardness as he got both of them and the case into the lift, though he had an amused expression all the while.

Once in his flat again Faith hesitated, her flow drying up as she stepped across the threshold; it seemed she was taking an irrevocable step. Up until then, she could have returned to West Kensington and Albert without a thought. Too late, now!

'Will you have a drink?' he asked.

'I'll make it,' Faith said. 'It's the least I can do.'

'I was thinking of something stronger than coffee,' he answered. 'Though maybe not.'

'Sorry.' Faith bit her lower lip. 'I didn't . . . ,'

'Look, Faith.' He stopped, and then began to laugh.

It was such a relief from the tension that, without thinking, Faith joined in, leaning against the light-coloured wall beside the front door.

'I'm sorry,' he gasped, 'I've never been in this position before.'

'Nor me,' Faith confessed, happy that the ice was breaking.

'How about a Scotch? You look as though you could do with one. Your boyfriend didn't turn up, did he?'

'Albert?' Faith asked, surprised at the suggestion. 'No.'

He had thought he would be the sophisticate he had always imagined himself to be, but here, confronted by the reality, he knew he was at a loss. Faith looked every bit as lovely dressed in casual clothes as she had done lying naked beneath him, whilst he inserted himself into her. Then, with closed eyes, she had been arching her back to drive her hips into him in unconscious appreciation of his sexual technique.

'What . . .?' Faith began, but stopped, flushing.

Both of them were very aware of the fact that, twelve hours before, they had been intimate without the benefit of a formal introduction. It made for some awkwardness, for they had breached all the conventions by which they regulated their lives.

'I was thinking of going to this party.' Alex licked his lips in an uncharacteristic gesture of anxiety.

This was where everything could go wrong, he thought. If Faith refused, then he would have to start telephoning all the people with whom he had been in contact; it was as good as admitting failure. But at the same time, he had to tell her, give her some warning. If it was hazardous to prepare Faith for the night's events, it would be far worse *not* to prepare her. He could just imagine what would happen if she were suddenly confronted by Lillian. Later, part of the pleasure would be in the surprise, but not now.

'Do you want to come along? You needn't. It might be a bit . . . hazardous for you.'

'Hazardous?' she asked, surprised at the use of the term. 'How could it be hazardous? You don't jump off the fifth floor balcony or anything, do you?'

'No,' he answered slowly, trying to think of an adequate answer, 'but it could get a little wild. I thought I should warn you. That's all.'

'I'll go with you, if you want me to. It's the least I can do,' Faith said. 'You never know, I might even like it.'

'You'll like it all right, once you get used to it,' he answered. 'But it's a bit advanced, if you know what I mean?'

'Advanced?' She half-smiled, trying to penetrate the secret at which he was hinting.

'Sexually advanced,' he explained, looking her in the eye.

'What do you mean, sexually advanced?' she asked, intrigued and frightened at the same time. She had read somewhere, in *Cosmopolitan* probably, articles which hinted at various 'advanced' methods of sex. Some had sounded ghastly.

'We don't swing from chandeliers or anything.' He was unable to avoid grinning, noting with relief that Faith's smile almost matched his own. 'But I don't know what you're used to, you see? I mean it's none of my business.'

'I'm not a virgin, if that's what you mean.' Faith said, then added, a flush gradually creeping over her face, 'I mean, before last night.'

'Yes,' he agreed, 'I know,' and his flush vied with her own. 'But have you ever considered group sex?'

'What? No!' Faith protested, her eyes widening at the mention of it; even as her heart-rate speeded up however, a vestige of a smile decorated her face.

But Alex watched the pupils of her eyes dilate and, in a more confident tone said: 'It's not an orgy, but you'll see things you might not have seen before, that's all. I thought I'd warn you. Still want to come?'

'Yes,' Faith answered, and her tone gave away the fact that she found the prospect appealing.

'There are all sorts of advanced things,' Alex said, trying not to show his own interest, 'though you won't see all of them tonight. Bondage, for example.'

'Bondage?' Faith asked, her breathing catching, and giving away her desire. It was something she knew little about, but some of her dreams . . .

Alex wished Faith were older, more sophisticated; preferably with some experience of life. Faith was old enough to be his step-sister, but considering that he had introduced Helen to fleshly pleasure when she was seventeen, that thought only increased his desire. He remembered more about the night than she did.

Faith flushed, and said: 'I suppose there's a first time for everything.' She smiled at him as though trying to be everything he wanted of her; she was unable, however, to conceal her own ingenuousness from someone so wordly-wise.

Her answer seemed both to relax him and to bring him

to a decision, for he gestured down the passageway ahead of her, asking, 'Would you come into the bedroom, please?'

'So soon?' Faith asked. 'I thought you'd have waited.'

'I'm not going to . . . Trust me. Please.' He repeated his hand gesture, finally getting her moving. Feeling the flush rising from her knees, Faith preceded him into the airy room, where the curtains had been drawn back fully to allow the harsh, bright daylight to flood in. Entering, Faith crossed to the bed, turned and found that Alex had stopped at a dresser, pulled out a drawer, and was busily searching within. He looked over to her absently, smiled, then asked: 'Would you raise your skirt please, Faith?'

Suspicious despite his half-assurance, Faith raised the fabric high at the sides of her thighs to reveal her knees, then higher still on his instructions, until her briefs were revealed, and she stood with her slim thighs pressed tightly together as he approached her. He seemed to have something in each hand, but without speaking, he knelt before her, looked up then said: 'I'm going to remove your briefs, then I want you to lie on the bed with your legs apart. I've got something for you that'll increase your pleasure; both tonight and afterwards.'

'What?' she asked quickly.

'I'll show you in a moment,' he replied, then paused for four or five seconds.

Faith's worried eyes looked down at him, but he waited patiently until her tongue ran around her lipsticked mouth in an unambiguous sexual signal before he hooked a finger under the fabric high on her hip. Alex ran his finger down over her pubic mound to apply steady pressure vertically on the reinforced crotch; the back of his finger was in contact with the moisture within, his eyes on hers the whole time. The white briefs tugged a little, but slipped down her legs to her ankles as he said: 'In a couple of minutes you can put them back on. Or I shall, as I removed them.'

'What are you going to do?' Faith could feel herself flush for, as soon as her briefs had landed on the floor at her feet, she had stepped out of them; now she stood, splay-legged, before him. Faith had found herself changing since her arrival in London. Perhaps, she thought, she was just maturing. But this seemed an unusual thing for Alex to do.

She argued with herself that, with her briefs around her ankles, splaying her legs would have made her topple over, but she knew that she wanted to display herself to this smooth individual. Normally, she would have resisted this; would have felt a good deal of shame at doing it. If he had insisted on it she would have fought him, but it seemed natural enough after what she recalled of their previous meeting.

Alex looked at her eyes for a moment, lowered his own to her mound and the folds of skin which peeped beneath the shorn length of her pubic hair. The shroud protected her pink peeking clitoris but he knew that, with a little gentle pressure, he could have it standing proud and Faith gasping with lust. The outer lips of her labia were plump and willing; he could smell her faint musky aroma which he knew could bring him to a climax on its own. Later, perhaps.

'Lie down please, Faith,' he commanded, glad when she complied, though her legs were not separating as much as he wanted.

'What are you going to do?' she repeated, looking concerned as he brought her ankles together, holding them between his knees. He looked at her for a few moments then flattened Faith's knees out, spreading her thighs.

Automatically, Faith's hands reached down to cover herself, but Alex said: 'Put your hands behind your head, Faith, and keep your legs in that position until we're finished.'

'What are you going to *do*?' Her voice was becoming a wail, so he produced what his hands had concealed.

Faith's eyes widened at the sight of the small ball, just over an inch in diameter, whose silvery surface distortedly reflected the scene. She looked at it for a few seconds, then at his face. Although she knew the answer she refused to admit it, searching for some clue before asking, 'What are you going to do with that?'

'There's two.' He showed her both, then covered them again. 'I'm warming them up at the moment.' His voice sharpened, then he relented. 'Put your hands behind your head.'

'What are you going to do?' Her litany never varied, as he avoided the shocking answer she suspected.

'I'm going to insert them into your cervix,' he replied quietly. 'I'll push them up your vagina and, once there, they'll stay until you want to take them out.'

The young woman looked at him as though either he had taken leave of his senses, or she had. It was plain that she hardly believed the evidence of her eyes and ears. Seeing her distress, he explained, 'They're Japanese "Love Balls", sometimes known as "*rin no tama*" or "*hari-go*", and they've each got a tube of mercury inside them. When they're in position, you move; the tube tilts and the mercury flows to another position, which moves the ball again. It's something a friend gave me some time ago. They're very effective in arousing women, and the longer they're in place, the better. With us going to the party, I thought you might like some stimulation first. Get you in the mood.'

'What if they won't come out?' she asked, gulping at the thought of having something like this within her, but he smiled.

'He showed me how they should go. Watch.'

While her heart leapt to her mouth, Alex brought the ball in his left hand towards her; with the fingers of his right hand, he opened her labia to receive it, pressing the slippery surface against her. Despite his having held them, they were cool compared with her heat. She gasped a little as his finger pressed, pushing the ball within her, the shiny surface causing no discomfort to her opening. He pushed as far as he could, then pressed down firmly on her mound, making her gasp as she felt the ball move within her for the first time.

'Stand up, Faith,' he said as he released her feet and moved clear of the side of the bed, extending his hand to help her slip to her feet. Once vertical, Faith kept her feet apart, feeling the unfamiliar movement with her, coiling slowly and gently, like a snake. The sensation was hardly unpleasant.

'Tell me when it's still,' Alex said and, on being told, held one hand underneath her exposed vagina as his fingers gently probed her abdomen. She could feel the pressure through her flesh as he found, then pressed, the top surface of the ball, forcing it back down into his hand.

'There!' He held it between his fingers like a conjuror brandishing a card, sniffing her aroma with much appreciation, making her blush when she realised what he was doing. 'It goes in, and it comes out again. I'd like you to try it.'

It took him ten minutes to persuade her, being patient, answering as many of her questions as he could, and confessing his ignorance when she began asking about the long-term effects. Faith finally took a deep breath before she agreed to the experiment, for she was indebted to Alex both for her rescue and for putting her up. He intrigued her, too, though she thought it might be a good idea if she found a place of her own to stay; just to be safe.

She lay back a second time, spreading her legs wide. Alex bent forward, kissed the curve of her belly just above her pubic mound, then ran his tongue through the coarse hair; she gasped as he found her clitoris. His left hand unsheathed it to his moist, delicate embrace, his elbows digging into the soft flesh of her inner thighs as she tried to close her legs against this unexpected pleasure. But even as she was straining her hips upwards to meet him, she felt the first ball being inserted into her passage, the second behind it and, as she seeped oil at the balls and the following, propelling finger, she whimpered with the beginnings of pleasure.

Once he was certain they were both in place, Alex stood up, smiling, then crouched again to fit her briefs over her feet, which were still in her outdoor shoes. Faith brought her thighs together as he slipped her briefs up her legs, then allowed Alex to assist her from the bed as he settled them back into position. When he was satisfied he asked, 'Are they uncomfortable? The balls?'

Faith blushed a little, feeling the unusual sensations from her belly. 'I don't know, yet.'

'Now,' he became brisk, 'what will you wear to the party tonight?'

After looking through her wardrobe, his heart sinking at the sight though he maintained an equable expression, Alex gave her his opinion of the trouser suits she liked for work and the tights she wore with them, before he proposed an afternoon stroll. Anxious not to oppose him openly, Faith agreed, finding the stroll took her the length of Oakley Street – the widest street in Chelsea – from Albert Bridge to the King's Road where he turned towards Sloane Square.

No sooner had they turned into Oakley Street, with the wide prospect before them, vehicles parked nose to tail on both sides, than Faith began to feel the slow, subtle contractions within her abdomen. She tried to ignore them at first, holding herself rigid as she walked, suppressing the sensations which threatened to turn her insides to liquid. This lasted until they turned into the King's Road where, at the Town Hall, Faith had to swallow hard and, when Alex was looking across the street at the cinema, she pinched herself.

On the way towards Sloane Square at a leisurely pace, they looked at some of the shops while Faith struggled with the problem of her mounting arousal; at a shop opposite the Pheasantry Club, Alex bought a black dress for her. Alone in the tiny fitting room, Faith quickly rubbed her fingers against the wetness of her briefs, closing her eyes but keeping her mouth tight shut so as not to reveal her secret shame.

She liked the dress, as did Alex; the whole transaction was completed without her discovering the price in the time it took her to change back into her ordinary clothes.

As she approached the assistant with the dress back on the hanger, the woman looked her in the eye, making her wonder if her secret was known. But how could she explain that she was masturbating to obtain release from the most delicious feeling of arousal she had ever known?

As they left the shop, Alex took her right hand and smiled at her, raising her fingers towards his mouth, making her blush as he sniffed them. With his icy eyes on hers he paused for a few seconds before commenting, 'Lovely perfume, Faith,' as he kissed her hand then released it, whilst her blush deepened at the realisation that he knew what had happened. They walked a little further, to Royal Avenue where, seeing that Faith was flagging a little, he asked: 'Is something wrong? Are you all right?'

'Oh,' she breathed out hard. 'Can we go back please, Alex?' she asked.

He looked at her eyes, smiled, then asked in a gentle, understanding tone, 'The balls are working, aren't they?'

'Damn you, Alex, yes!' Her breathing was becoming a little ragged.

For a few instants he stiffened, then asked, 'Why don't you just press them out? Carry them in your briefs for a while?'

'Would that work?' she enquired. 'If you know where there's a lavatory . . .?'

'Hold the bag in front of you and press,' he suggested, but Faith refused. She was not expelling them in the street like that, so Alex hailed a cab and, five minutes later, they were back at Cheyne Walk.

Faith controlled herself until she was within the flat, pulling up her skirt in the hallway. She would have removed them there had Alex not picked her up and, almost effortlessly, carried her through to the bedroom, where he placed her on the bed.

'I'm going to undress you, Faith, then remove them if you want. Just lie still and be patient. If I turn you over, then accept it.'

'What are you going to do?' Faith asked, anxious again. The desire which had flared between her legs was lessening; the urgency within her was not quite so acute as it had been in the street, though the rumbling ride in the cab had been difficult.

'As I said, undress you completely. Then I'm going to rub you down with some oil; massage you, if you like. It'll tone up your skin.'

'Nothing else?' Faith asked. 'It won't *do* anything to me, will it?'

'If you mean, will it make you a raving nymphomaniac, no,' he smiled, 'but it will make your skin sensitive to touch.'

'Why?' she asked. 'Why should you do that?' Her suspicions were aroused.

'Between the oil, and the "Love Balls", you'll enjoy the party a lot more.'

'Will you . . .?'

'Will I what?' he asked, adding, 'Make love to you?'

'Yes,' she nodded.

'Undoubtedly,' he answered. 'The only questions are when, and for how long?'

'Soon?' she asked, trembling at the thought.

'When I've finished massaging you, if you like,' he answered.

Faith thought about the sensations which had coursed through her on their walk; she swallowed, hoping she could last that long without begging him to satisfy her; bring her to a release of the desire. She nodded her acceptance and was about to begin unfastening her skirt when he stopped her.

'No, I'll strip you, Faith. When we're together, you should *always* let me take your clothes off.'

'Why?' Faith frowned at him.

'Because – you'll have to trust me for this – I think you'll find it more stimulating.' Alex smiled at her as his hands moved behind her to lower the zip.

Before he made Faith lie face-down on the bed, Alex measured every aspect of her, from the maximum circumference of her breasts where they joined her body, to the width of her mound, and the length of her cleft, as well as all the more conventional measurements. To Faith, who asked for an explanation in vain, having her complete dimensions scrutinised seemed part of a strange fetish but, when finally he had finished, he piled up three pillows and told her to place her hips on them, lying face down.

Once Faith had complied, Alex said, 'Right. Now spread your legs wide apart, Faith,' whilst pressing on her inner thighs as he spoke.

'Like that?' she asked, spreading fairly wide, then realised that, standing directly behind her, he had full access to her sexual organs.

'That'll do to start with,' Alex answered with a mysterious chuckle.

'What's the matter?' Faith looked round to see him putting a mitten of some sort on his right hand, but he turned her face away, telling her to place her hands on the back of her neck and not, under any circumstances, to remove them. Swallowing, Faith complied and when he was satisfied he said:

'I'm going to caress you, Faith, before I apply the oil. And I think, before I've done, you'll be spreading your legs wider of your own accord. Let's see, shall we?'

The first gentle touch was to the small of her back, where the two 'losenges of Michaelis' were situated just above the beginning of the outswelling buttocks, though hers were usually invisible as she was so slender. The fine hair there – already stimulated from the slow arousal caused by the removal of all Faith's clothing – was gently stirred, and he heard the young woman gasp as her body reacted to this touch. Her genital muscles had clenched, moving the balls within her. As she moved, so did they, and the sweet, delicious pleasure was brought on yet again, even more strongly than before.

Faith forced her belly to distend into the pillows beneath her in order to hollow her back away from this delicate touch, but the feeling followed. Without a word, Faith pressed her palms down into the bed, forcing her chest clear of the pillows and, at the same time, spreading her legs as wide as she could manage.

'Excellent, my darling,' Alex remarked, pleased at this immediate reaction, then ran the chinchilla mitten up her spine to her neck. Before Faith could react, he brought the other one into play. With both hands encased in the chinchilla mittens, he then swooped around to cup her breasts, lightly stroking them towards the tips, which hardened.

Alex was listening to the cooing deep in her throat, paying attention to the whimpers which were becoming more prevalent until, long before Faith was likely to orgasm, his fingers within the mittens closed about the firm nipples and squeezed, very hard.

'God!' the young woman gasped, flinging her head back as the pain provided the perfect counterpoint to the sensations which had been welling up within her. She was too shocked to cry out, beset by the waves of pleasure which rippled down her belly, gripping the Love Balls then releasing them again, making the most wonderful liquid sensations within her.

With one hand fondling her bosom, Alex brought the other down between her thighs, letting the soft fur start at the backs of her knees then, slowly and surely, bringing it up the soft flesh towards the open sex at the join. Meanwhile, beside him, Alex readied the curved polished glass of the erect penis, knowing that within a few minutes at most, Faith would be begging, demanding release from those wicked sensations.

'No more, please, Alex,' Faith said softly, though her voice then rose in a wail. 'If you're going to fuck me, do it now, please. *Please!*'

'I haven't massaged you, yet,' he reminded her gently, his smile broadening. Already he could imagine using even more advanced techniques on her. She would like them, even though she might be frightened at first.

'Do it afterwards,' she answered, gulping air like a half-drowned swimmer, 'please, Alex.'

'How can I refuse you?' he asked, then brought the tip of the life-sized dildo, the '*harigata*', to the hot, gaping, pouting mouth of her vagina.

'God!' Faith gasped again at the smooth coldness of the glass as Alex said:

'Suck it in, Faith. Go on; suck it in.' He was urging her whilst applying only gentle pressure. This was perhaps the first and most basic lesson she had to learn. To accept the phallus, to seek it; to use it! Delicacy could come later, when she knew how to suck and hold.

'How?' she asked but, as her muscles contracted against a spasm which rippled through her, she caught the lower rim of the surrogate glans, drawing it within her, groaning loudly with pleasure.

The glass cock was cold. He had been quite deliberate about that, though another time he would have warmed it first. It was especially cold to Faith's overheated flesh so that to start with, after her first deep groan of pleasure, Faith gave a little scream, a mixture of surprise and fear; her muscles clamped hard on it, however, so that, when he tried to move it backwards again, he was glad that the craftsman who had made it had added the testicles. Tugging it against the power of her muscles, Alex tested Faith's ache, then released his hold so that she sucked it in again, gasping aloud. For a moment he considered pulling it out and releasing it again, letting her experience a rough parody of fornication until she stopped sucking on it.

But her taut thigh muscles, those of her whole leg down to the toes which supported them, were trembling with the rigours of her straining to withstand this terrible pleasure, which was stronger than any Faith had ever known before. She knew her body was responding to stimuli; that someone very clever had planned this, but that she was unable to help herself. In a corner of her mind she felt the shame of being so aroused, of masturbating herself in the fitting-room to obtain relief, and now of her abject groaning, whimpering surrender to this delicious pleasure; but there was nothing she could, or would, do about it. Greedily she sucked on the instrument, demonstrating to the watching, satisfied Alex how by relaxing her muscles the phallus dropped a little, only to be sucked back up as she tensed them again. Yes; Faith was either a quick learner, or a natural.

Alex waited until the sucking pressure on the glass cock had lessened before he removed it for a moment, listening to her satisfied moans. Slowly, he allowed the mitten to slip beneath the implement, making the tips of the hairs lightly caress her clitoris, whilst holding the smooth, heavy, slippery and now quite warm piece of glass at her entrance. He held it lightly for he suspected that she would suck again, but was unprepared for the almost-agonised scream of lust which Faith emitted, the tendons of her neck finally joining the remainder of her rigid body in supreme tension as the glass was sucked from his hand.

He cursed himself for not realising that it would happen so soon, watching helplessly while Faith climaxed, her hips working up and down on the pillows in a frenzy, the glass cock buried within her. He removed the mittens from his hands, waiting patiently as Faith's spasms continued. He could have denied her, stopped her even, but not yet. That would come later, when he was teaching her the techniques of denial in order to increase her pleasure; when she was used to being bound and then mounted; when she was obedient. He waited until Faith's irregular and harsh breathing began to grow quiet; maintaining a steady pressure on the glass cock, he knew as soon as her vaginal muscles released their grip, and withdrew it from her body.

Alex's first action on withdrawing the phallus was to cup his hand beneath her and, when her fluids ran into it, he smeared them over her clitoris and her cleft; obtaining more fluid from the seeping organ, he rubbed it over her perineum and anus, making her jerk and hiss at the unusual sensation. It struck him then that Faith, though sexually experienced, was perhaps not quite ready for such advanced techniques. She might possibly find the party too much.

Gradually Faith relaxed, first her legs, her bending knees a sign of her condition; he waited some minutes until her breathing was quiet before, in a quite matter-of-fact-way, he began to sprinkle oil on her back. His strong fingers began to massage the warm, clear oil into the soft, welcoming tissues. On his command, Faith had brought her arms together to form a support for her forehead but, after he had gone from her hairline, she replaced her hands on her neck. She waited until his hands had descended to the beginning of the natal notch, before she asked, 'Where are you going to . . .?'

'All over,' he said quietly, 'down by your bottom and then, after you've turned over, your breasts and your slit. Everywhere.'

'Why?' she asked, gasping as some of the oil was dribbled onto her buttocks, and tensing them uselessly against his touch.

'I'm stimulating your skin,' he answered, unwilling to tell her that much more would be stimulated.

'Like you stimulated my . . .?'

'Partly,' he answered, smoothing a thin trail of oil across her perineum towards her anus. He could feel her tension rising, and was smiling in anticipation. Soon, he thought, perhaps within the month, perhaps less, she would welcome this. Needing the terrible tension of the massage to achieve the aching release afterwards.

'Why . . . why . . . *there?* Aaaagh!' she gasped, as his questing forefinger touched the rim of wrinkled skin.

'Nice?' he asked, letting the oily tip of his finger run around the sensitive spot.

Alex knew what he was doing. This was hardly the first anus he had stimulated nor, he thought, would it be the last.

'Aaagh!' She could feel the catching in her breathing while Alex could only hear it, but both of them knew that Faith was feeling the stirrings again. The Love Balls were still at work.

'The first time we made love,' he said, 'I pushed my finger in there. Do you want me to do that again?'

'No. Please!' she gasped, gulping moisture from her tongue, trying to flood the dryness out of her throat. 'No more.'

'Then I'd better move on,' he answered, re-oiling his finger before pressing it onto her perineum, making her gasp again. For the first time since he had begun to oil her, Faith's back hollowed as she lifted her bottom to him, an indication of her excitement and arousal; his fingers idly brushed the bottom of her slit, next to her vaginal entrance. What a hot, liquid little hole, he thought. If this is what happens after a few minutes with the mitten and some oil, what will she be like after a spanking? Or a strapping?

While Alex had been concentrating his attention on the delicate orifices of her lower abdomen, his left hand had been working steadily, massaging the oil into the soft, yielding tissues of her rounded buttocks which, he suspected, would have tensed up had he not distracted her. They would need all the help they could get if she became one of the Chosen.

Alex carefully oiled the inside of Faith's thighs down to her knees then, when he was certain that her skin had taken all the moisture into it, said, 'Turn over, Faith,' standing upright to ease his own cramped back. Slowly the young woman turned but his sharp voice stopped her, cracking out like a whip:

'Don't move the pillows! Put your backside on them!'

'It's . . .' Faith, who was going to protest about the discomfort, the unnatural position in which she was about to be placed, stopped sharply. She looked at him, his taut expression, then placed herself as he had directed. Her head and shoulders were on the bed, her rear raised on the pillows and her legs spread wide, heels resting over the edge of the bed on either side of him. She looked as though she was thrusting her over-heated and aromatic sexual organ at Alex, who let his breath out slowly, concealing his relief from her. It had been a risk, snapping at her like that, but she had taken the instruction well.

Oiling his hands, Alex began to work on either side of Faith's throat, gradually spreading down over her shoulders; he listened to the sounds of her breathing as his hands kneaded her breasts, one at a time, working the oil into them, starting at the ribcage before proceeding towards her now swollen nipples. Before he had finished, her eyes were rolling wildly in her head, for the delicious stimulation she had already received found an echo in the sensations set up by his strong fingers.

As he worked lower down her abdomen, Faith's breathing began to tighten again as she faced the fact that he was about to approach her most intimate parts. She had already had those stimulated enough, yet there was no thought that she would close her legs, or protest at this treatment. Something about his calm assurance buoyed her up with the confidence to allow him to take what liberties he chose.

'What's the matter?' Alex asked, already working his fingers into her groin on both sides of her mound, and letting the slow pressure work as well as the direct stimulation had. Many young women had surrendered themselves to Alex after he had used them in that fashion; all had been satisfied.

'You don't know what you're doing to me,' she whispered, unable to find the energy to speak louder. Faith was conscious of the fact that, if Alex asked her to attend this party in the nude, she would comply without hesitation, for his technique of arousal had been successful. If there was bondage, so much the better.

'I'm making you feel good,' he said, 'and in such a lewd position, too. Look at you. Look up. Look at yourself.'

For the first time, Faith looked at the mirror above her, seeing herself as though she were a stranger. Faith lay across the bed, her feet dangling off the edge. Her hands were concealed and her legs spread so wide that there was no defence, nor any detail missed. She could have been bound in that position, yet she knew that it was entirely voluntary.

Alex asked, 'What do you see, Faith? A nice, well-educated, well-brought-up girl? Or do you see someone who has abandoned herself to lust? Someone who, even as I'm speaking, is coming, slowly?'

'Alex?' Faith's tremulous quaver sounded as his hand

reached down, the fingers opening her thickened labia to scoop up the thick, syrupy mucus which he then reached up to hold beneath her nose, allowing Faith to verify the truth for herself.

She had known it for some minutes; the slow seepage of fluid, which told her she was being aroused more deeply and steadily than she had ever been before. Faith looked up to the mirror, seeing again her abandoned posture, legs spread wide, her sex open, glistening with her own lustful moisture; and she felt a deep satisfaction. But her conventional morality returned, making her blush at the sight. Shame swept over her even as she experienced the electric satisfaction.

Then Alex said: 'This isn't unusual, Faith. You have desires and lusts the same as the rest of mankind. We're all subject to them, only some people seem to be able to satisfy theirs better, or worse. I suppose it depends on your standpoint.'

'Are you going to oil . . .?'

'Yes; of course,' Alex answered and, suiting his actions to the word, placed his oiled hands on her half-open sex lips.

Faith's rigid body bucked from the shoulders in a gentle, weary movement which complemented the hoarseness of her gasping whimpers. She made no attempt to close her legs, or bring her hands down from behind her head to prevent him oiling her whole vulva back to the perineum. Her eyes were staring up at the ceiling, watching him work, watching him stimulate her by coating her outer and inner lips in oil, then rub them together, slowly at first but with increasing speed, watching the blood which swelled them. The normally healthy pink of her inner and outer lips changed to a dull, engorged red as her body was wracked with sobbing gasps; then, as he finished off her inner thighs, the desire dwindled to a dull, moderated, but ever-present reminder deep within her. God, she thought, I'm ready to be fucked!

Chapter Three

Alex stood looking down at her for several minutes as he wiped the last of the oil from his fingers, whilst Faith looked at him in the mirror, seeing the top of his head and an attenuated view of his features. Deep within her, she could feel the twisting coils of desire beginning their sinuous dance through her system. That desire was something she had experienced very few times in her life, yet this man was able to excite her by touch alone. It gave her a new slant on what must have happened during the night when she had slithered up and down his organ.

'You're very lovely, Faith,' he said, 'very desirable. You must know that.'

'I'm what you've made me,' she answered breathily. 'I wasn't this . . . wanton, before.'

'Wanton?' he asked, nodding. 'Yes, perhaps I've awakened that. You must have known it was there. No?'

'No,' she answered. 'I had a normal childhood. Boarding school, university, that sort of thing. It was a scandal at school when one of the mistresses left very suddenly in the middle of term. We discovered she'd been molesting the girls; some of them, anyway. Willing ones. Some of *them* had to leave, too.' Faith shrugged. 'One of them was called "wanton" by our housemistress. I had to look it up.'

'Does that sort of thing bother you?' he asked. 'Female sexual advances?' It would be as well to know that before Lillian arrived on the scene. There were some women who would never even contemplate fondling another woman, and others who took to it like ducks to water.

The Chosen were a broad church; obedience came first, though.

'It hasn't happened to me. I can't see anything in it,' Faith answered, luxuriating backwards into the softness beneath her, and arching her back to push out her breasts and belly towards him. Would he mount her now?

'Would a female doing *this* offend you?' He brushed the back of his hand slowly up her labia, setting off the alarm-bells in her system as he touched her hair, not reaching the flesh at all, the most gentle and yet highly arousing caress she could imagine.

'I, I . . .' Faith bit off a groan. Her hips had responded at once and she transferred her gaze from the mirror to meet his eye, then said, 'I don't know,' in a tone suggesting shock, and not a little surprise. He took it as a good sign.

'Do you want to put something on? We don't have to leave until seven, and it's not far. I wouldn't want you to feel cold, Faith.'

'I don't feel cold,' Faith answered. She paused. 'Why didn't you make love to me yourself?' she asked, the hint of a tear in the corners of her eyes.

She knew how close she had been to crying with frustration at not having him lodged firmly within her vagina, or pounding away with hips pistoning. Either would have been preferable to the cold, hard, smoothness of the glass phallus, no matter how much it had roused her. Unless, of course, he was like Albert! They had made love at least twice during the night. That must be it. He was still recovering.

'If I had, I wouldn't have been able to finish the massage,' he answered. 'And besides, I'm saving myself for the party.'

'Will there be any of that, there?' Faith asked.

'Certainly,' Alex replied. 'Does that bother you?'

'How . . .? I mean, do they . . .?' she stuttered to a halt.

It was strange, Faith thought. She had agreed to attend this mysterious party partly on a sudden whim, partly out of curiosity, partly to repay him for his kindness in taking her in; but what did she know of him? He was a competent lover, he had bought her an expensive dress, yes. But he had also indulged in weird sexual practices, too. Not unpleasant, no; but really! Rubbing her down with thick chinchilla mittens. Inserting that, that *thing*, then oiling her all over. The tingling in her sphincter irritated her a little, yet it was just one sensation in a body suddenly aware of the other sensations coursing through it.

If he was preparing her for this evening, then it sounded like some party. She had felt very aroused when she had returned from her walk, yet that had now been released. So why was that soft, delicious sensation between her legs building up again? And more deeply than ever? Faith had little experience in the management of long-term arousal. Would this continue to build up to a full orgasm, or would it gradually dwindle again of its own accord? Some of her concern about the reason she was being prepared spilled over into her eyes, as Alex answered:

'You'll wear the dress, but without underwear. None of the Chosen women *ever* wear underwear to these parties, though they do at other times, of course.' He was looking into her eyes. 'And if you're wondering how it will all begin?' He paused, shrugging. 'It varies. But I'm sure you'll enjoy yourself; and others.'

Faith blushed at the thought of it. Not the enjoying 'others', but at the very real hint that the 'others' would enjoy her. Alex seemed to divine her thoughts, for he sighed, shaking his head.

'It's not what you possibly think,' he said quietly. 'At least, not often. Some people come for a drink and leave before anything happens, though they may guess what will happen. Sometimes it ends up with everyone in the centre of the floor; other times with people quietly pursuing their pleasures in private. That's usually the case, as a matter of fact. All these stories you hear about wild Chelsea orgies are just that. Stories. Inventions. Usually dreamed up by some journalist with an active mind, an over-active libido and an inactive social diary.'

'Who . . .?' she began, but he broke in.

'Who'll be there?' Shrugging, 'I don't know. Depends who's in Town. Why?'

'Who will I . . .?' she tried again, and this time, Alex seemed to understand what she meant.

'If you're worried about having to fuck someone you dislike, don't be,' he said. 'No one will force you to do anything repellent. The whole idea is for a group of friends, *close* friends, to meet and indulge in a little harmless pleasure. No one will give you a disease. If they did, it would mean certain ostracism, and that is something everyone wants to avoid at all costs. If you want any of the men to use a condom, say so and they will. They won't like it, but they will,' he assured her, bringing a smile to her face and then a look of anxiety.

'You said the Chosen?' she asked, frowning. 'What are they? Who are they?'

'The Chosen are a group of people – you'll meet some of them tonight – who have similar sexual tastes and pleasures, and who find and take as much of that pleasure with each other as they can. They're quite wealthy; they choose who will join their group, which is how they get the name, and they enjoy sex in all its forms. I think you'll like them. I only hope they'll like you equally well.'

'God!' Faith gasped as she lifted herself into a sitting position suddenly, making Alex back away in surprise both at her sudden movement, and her expression of alarm. 'I've forgotten to take my pill today!'

'Then I'd suggest you do it *now*.' He took a deep breath to calm his racing heart. Getting Faith pregnant at this stage would be a reflection on himself, more than on her.

While Faith donned Alex's towelling gown then went in search of her case, Alex also quit the bedroom, but to get some Scotch inside him. He now vaguely regretted giving in to his impulse to rescue the girl at the party. But, at the same time, he had no choice; she was very vulnerable. Faith was everything he wanted and yet, could he disappoint his father? The old man wanted him to marry within the Chosen – his choice had been Lillian

Brampton, of course – but something about her had always faintly repelled him. She was good, and good fun; there was no doubt about that. Lillian was probably one of the best lays he'd had. But Faith!

As he brooded on the future, he looked at the gathering dusk on the Thames, illuminated by the fairy-tale lighting of Albert Bridge, with the industrial complex in Battersea on the other side of the river. Downriver, through the trees in the quiet, green calm of Battersea Park, he could just see the Peace Pavilion, the pagoda built facing the river, whilst upriver, the industrial complex of Battersea lingered on, relieved only by the multi-coloured display of the Marina on the far side of Battersea Bridge. He was still there when he saw the reflection of Faith entering the warmth of the beige and brown room, where the good antique walnut furniture was complemented by the choice of wallpapers and hangings, and the comfortable leather couch and chairs.

Silently he watched her looking around with growing interest, standing close to the cabinets to gaze more closely upon the collection of *cloisonné* figures he had inherited from a relative. His heart went out to her as her unaffected expression showed her appreciation of the beauty; the same expression, he suspected, as had decorated his own juvenile features when he had first seen them twenty years before. Faith slowly toured the room, drawing ever closer as Alex inspected the traffic, multi-coloured vehicles which sped in either direction, blurred by the intervening trees in the narrow gardens which separate Cheyne Walk from the Embankment.

He heard her quiet gasp and smiled to himself at the thought that she had reached his collection of erotica. It had taken him almost ten years to amass; he was proud of it, too, explicit as it was. He had displayed some *shunga* prints by the Japanese masters, Moronobu and Nishikawa Sukenobu as well as some *makura-e*, the erotic pillow books. Some women turned away the first time they saw the collection, some even protested at it being displayed. They were hardly material for the Chosen. Not Faith. She hesitated, then shot him a sudden, illuminating glance which he caught in the reflection of the glass; he watched her covertly examine the paintings, statuary and photographs, becoming more interested as she neared him; then she was no longer looking at his collection.

'What's the matter?' she asked, coming up to stand alongside him, still in his white towelling gown.

He smiled, turning to look at her, keeping the gnawing anger and agony from his voice and features with difficulty. 'I was just thinking. Nothing very important,' he answered.

'What about?' she asked. 'You look sad.'

'Yes,' he agreed, taking some more Scotch, finishing the half-tumbler of Lowland Malt, 'I suppose I am. I *know* I am, in fact,' he added, not looking at her but at the dregs in the glass, trying to concentrate on whether to refill it or not.

It kept his mind from racing off over subjects best left alone. If this went well tonight, then he thought he would be more than just a little pleased. But the prospects were bad and the possibilities for disaster loomed everywhere, for there were so many things which all had to click together to make it work. If any one failed; if the others agreed; if Lillian consented to do as he asked; if Max agreed. If. If. If. Alex had no liking for that measly little word 'if'. He preferred certainties to speculation, though only in his private life. Professionally, he would on occasion take outrageous risks, but he always justified them by claiming them not to be risks at all.

'Why?' Faith asked, bewildered by the obvious pain he was taking such care to conceal. She could see that something was bothering him. Why did men always try to hide things from women? It never worked out for the best when they did.

'Faith,' he inhaled sharply and looked her in the eye, shaking his head but remaining silent.

She had been subject to a bewildering variety of emotions already, and this was yet another which turned her world topsy-turvy. She had woken up in Alex's bed with the memory of having made love twice. Both times – as far as she remembered – had been very satisfying experiences. She had left Albert, her stable platform in life, as well as GMG. Instead of drifting, Faith found Alex not only willing to give her shelter, but able to arouse her to a greater height of pleasure than she had hitherto known. She was still aroused, and had the prospect of an even more arousing party ahead.

At one stage, Faith had thought she would spend most of Monday on the telephone, looking for a flat. She would thank Alex very kindly for his hospitality and attention, perhaps get him something for his flat, something he needed; but that would be the end of it. They had both enjoyed the experience. She had learned something about men, and about herself, too, but she would look elsewhere for a lover. Now that Alex seemed to be saying the same thing without words, she felt the loss, a surprising sensation, a painful ache which dispelled the ache of pleasure and desire which had remained after the massage.

Alex looked down into his glass again, his chest rising and falling as he tried to put his thoughts in order, before he said in a quiet, earnest voice, 'I'm twenty-six years old, Faith. I work in the City at the moment; nothing serious, though it pays well. This place is mine;' he gestured around him. 'As I said, the Chosen don't want for much,' he paused, but Faith, the colour rapidly retreating from her trembling lips, her eyes fixed on his, remained silent.

It was as though she knew that what he had to tell her was so important and secret that, if he was once interrupted, he would never speak again.

'You . . .' he sighed, then looked her in the eye, 'you need to be educated, my darling girl.' He gave a grimace of a sad smile, his hand rising to caress the side of her face. 'Educated in the ways of sex and pleasure. You have a capacity for it, believe me. You called yourself "wanton" a little while ago. That's a convenient, though misleading, term.

'People use it in the narrow, restrictive sense of licentiousness; unchastity; lewdness. And they equate it with wilful immorality; with something disgusting. It's not that at all. Wantonness is playfulness; a gambolling, irresponsible, wild and unrestrained irrepressibility.' His voice was light, enthusiastic, as though visualising her in the role of a gambolling nymph; 'It doesn't mean anything lascivious or indecent, which a lot of people imply when they use the term. You too, I think,' he frowned, watching her flush as she confessed the solecism to herself. 'But you need to be taught, and,' he paused, sighing, 'I can't teach you much. Not because I don't want to, but because I don't *know*. There is a little I can pass on; I've already started, as you know . . . but there's so much more. So I'm just a stage in your development, if you like. I know; I suspect, that you'll move on one day. You'll find someone else to teach you, and believe me, there is a great deal to learn.

'Many women never, ever, discover one-tenth of their capabilities; sexually, I mean. Most think that anything other than the so-called "missionary position" is, well, indecent.' They both chuckled, Alex at his memories of bygone years, Faith at the afternoon on the bed. 'Some would consider their lover inserting his finger into their bottom during normal sex buggery. I suppose it might be, technically; I'm no lawyer. As for other, less widely-known practices . . .' he sighed, shrugged; 'but that's something I can't teach you. I know someone who could though. The chap who gave me those "Love Balls". In the Far East, some things they do . . .'

'Alex. I . . .' Faith tried to say she was quite satisfied with the present arrangements, but he prevented her, placing a hand over her mouth, looking her in the eye and smiling. Then he leaned forward, and kissed her forehead.

'It'll happen one day, my darling girl,' he said quietly. 'I know that, I think,' he sighed, keeping his hand over her mouth to stifle her protests. 'But until then, I'll look after you, do what I can to educate you and, even when you've gone, moved on to extend your knowledge, you can always call me. Promise me you'll do that.'

Faith was silent as he took his hand from her mouth, her dark eyes large. He found her height an added attraction, for he normally had to bend to see the expression in women's eyes. Alex could make out the turmoil within, the tiny facial tics and flickers as her muscles recorded the shifting emotions which beset her. It would do no harm for her to think, at the outset, that this was a temporary arrangement, something she could regard as a passing phase. Once he was her Master – which he wanted to be – she would find herself attached to him with bonds too strong to break.

Chapter Four

They dressed together, Alex complimenting her lavishly on her appearance, but checking to make sure both balls were still comfortable within her cervix. Faith could feel them as she moved about the flat; found, too, that her need to urinate increased. She could also, however, appreciate the slow, swelling surges of pleasure they engendered. Though she was nervous about this party for which they were preparing – and the more he told her, the more it sounded like an orgy – she occasionally found herself wishing that the hours would pass more quickly, for then she could obtain release. Alex had said that, before anyone made love to her, the balls would be removed; Faith found herself clinging to this as an indication of his regard. At the time, she would hardly appreciate the sensation of a lover thrusting himself within her, only to encounter those 'Love Balls' jostling for space with the sensitive tip of his erection.

When they were almost ready to leave, Faith put on her shoes before checking her appearance in the long mirror in the hallway, and Alex, coming out of the bedroom, hissed in annoyance at the fact that they were neither high-heeled nor black shoes.

'Alex!' she protested, 'I'm tall, I already feel gigantic. Everyone seems . . .'

'Is that why you hunch your shoulders?' he asked, his voice more sharp than she had previously known. 'To reduce your height?'

'Yes!' she admitted vehemently. 'Since I was fourteen, I've been too tall for my friends. I was half a head taller than anyone in my class. And at Oxford,' she sighed.

'High-heeled shoes make your legs slimmer and more attractive,' he said quietly. 'What size are you?'

'Seven and a half. Forty-one or two in these new Euro-sizes, I think. Why?'

'I'll try to organise something,' he answered with a shrug. 'Can you get away on Monday before the shops close? Or during lunch? It doesn't take long to buy a pair of black high-heeled shoes, does it?'

'Alex,' she protested, but he held up his hands in mock-surrender.

'Think about it,' he advised, 'that's all I ask.'

Faith waited in the entrance-hall to the block, where the imitation green-veined marble panels were plastic, and only the narrow column-like white marble panels were genuine. She wore a dark coat thrown, but not fastened, over her dress, feeling herself still trembling inside with the memory of how Alex had inspected her before they had left his flat. He had asked her to lift her skirt, then delicately pulled the front of the dress forward to look at her naked bosom, nodding when he saw her breasts. She wore the dress, suspender belt, stockings and nothing else.

Now she waited while he walked around the corner to fetch his car from outside the Holy Redeemer Church in Cheyne Row, the closest he had been able to park, even in the early hours of Saturday morning. That was the problem all over London: too many vehicles chasing too few parking spaces. Soon they would run out of space altogether, and drivers would be condemned, like the Flying Dutchman, to drive around for eternity. She was surprised when he returned with a new BMW 735, the glossy black body looking too luxurious even for this location.

On the way towards the fairy-tale lighting of Albert Bridge, Faith asked, 'How long do you think this party will last?'

'Until people decide they want to leave,' he smiled, as he steered up Royal Hospital Road, allowing the car to cruise gently. 'One party lasted from Saturday to Monday;' he smiled happily at the memory.

'*You* lasted all that time?' she asked, her head whipping round towards him with a mixture of respect and awe. She had heard at various times – mostly from young women at Oxford – of these tireless lovers and here, she thought, was Alex, giving the lie to her dismissive replies.

'No,' he laughed, 'and those still there were pretty satiated, too. No, I came to help the host clear up, never thinking anyone would still be there. Apparently people came in relays, you see? The original party would have petered out pretty soon, but there was always someone new arriving.'

'I see.' Faith felt happier about that. It confirmed her own judgment and also gave her a reference as to what would happen. It was unlikely that this party would be an endurance event, spilling over into Sunday. Already she was thinking ahead, to Monday; to returning to work where she would have to confront the problem of Albert.

'I shouldn't think this will go on beyond midnight, perhaps a little more,' Alex continued. 'It depends on two things. When the others leave, so that the frolics can begin, and whether Lillian's feeling frisky.'

'Lillian?' Faith asked, frowning. It was not a name he had mentioned before. She thought logically about it. She was unlikely to be his fiancée, otherwise he would hardly have taken her in. She might be his sister, of course; but 'frisky'? Would he describe his sister as 'frisky'? It had a sexual connotation.

'Yes; Lilian Brampton, Bill Brampton's sister. She can be outrageous, at times. If she's in the mood, she can get the whole thing going before anyone has the chance to leave. She's *really* been trained.'

'How?' Faith asked, intrigued at the implication. 'How can she get things going?' she amended, ignoring the other question of what he had meant by 'been trained'.

'I saw her at a party, once,' he replied. 'She came in, collected a drink and looked around. She was wearing a . . . I think they call it a kaftan. One of those long, loose dresses that can hide the fact that a woman's eight months gone. It had a zip down the front, I remember, and some kind of ethnic pattern. Next thing, she sees Gerry Kilmuir. You'll like Gerry; I hope he's there, actually; I want to see him. I'll introduce you.

'Anyway! Lillian spots him talking to some woman or other, so she goes up to the pair of them, asks the woman to hold her drink and does no more than get Gerry's "tackle" out. While he bends almost double trying to keep out of her clutches, she unzips this kaftan-thing. Starkers underneath, of course. Gerry was making all the noise then; you couldn't hear *anything* but him, except for a gasp that threatened to blow the windows out. Next thing, the majority of them were leaving like migrating wildebeest.' He thought it best not to mention his father's plans for himself and Lillian.

Faith found that, as Alex laughed at the memory, she too was smiling at the picture he described. Though Faith maintained a solemn expression under normal circumstances, she appreciated a good practical joke. This was reminiscent of several she had witnessed at Oxford. Lillian would be someone worth being friends with, she thought, if only in self-defence. But there was still that little nagging doubt about the term 'trained'; but she felt she was not yet sufficiently familiar with him to ask what he had meant.

Alex was right about it not being far. After passing through Sloane Square and heading north up Sloane Street towards Knightsbridge, Alex turned west alongside the Household Cavalry Barracks before turning south again, down the slope of Rutland Gate. On either side, the high buildings reached up, set back from the pavements which, as usual, were jammed nose to tail with vehicles of all makes and colours. The only unifying factor was the price which, Faith vaguely guessed, was greater than a year's salary for her. Albert drove a black Porsche, but it was a few years old, even though he kept it in good condition. He was forever moaning about how, in a decent agency, he would have been given a new one every year. Some hopes!

Towards the bottom of Rutland Gate some of the original houses remained; most of them were broken up into flats, although now and then there was a single occupancy. It was to one of those on the west side that Alex steered Faith, after squeezing the car into a convenient space in Ennismore Gardens Mews, ignoring the 'No Parking – Garage in constant use' sign.

The front door was opened by a man of medium height, whose smooth features, good looks and impeccable dress advertised him as the host. His hair was beginning to grey around the temples, but the surrounding corn-coloured fairness concealed it very well. There was a mischievous glint in his eye, which Faith took to be the usual excitement generated by such a gathering as he spoke.

'Alex!' His joyous drawl sounded through a smile which threatened to split his face in half as he stepped back, his light grey eyes already fastening on Faith. 'Good evening, I'm Rupert Brooks. Not the famous one, I'm afraid.'

Rupert's pale eyes, only of a slightly different hue to Alex's cold-fire-ice ran over her quickly, yet with the practised expertise of a man of the world. She knew she looked immaculate. Alex had approved of her careful preparations for the party, nodding when he saw her remove some make-up because she was dissatisfied with what she had done. She found his patience with her in this a welcome change from Albert's, who begrudged her every minute spent putting on her make-up. Yet he was critical if he found fault with the result she had achieved.

'This is Faith; Faith Small.' Alex eased the tall woman ahead of him as Brooks's hand was automatically raised towards her. Her own cool hand was enveloped in a strong, yet soft grasp. Rupert, like Alex, kept his hands in good condition, yet there was a surprising strength, too.

'I say, Alex,' the shorter man said after a pause, during which he looked keenly up at her, 'how did you get so lucky, you old bastard?' And before Alex could answer, he added, 'Don't pay attention to him, my dear, he's a born liar. I'm not what he's told you about me.'

'He said you were the perfect host, actually,' Faith answered, though Alex had omitted all mention of the man. Why? He had told her something about Lillian, yet nothing about their host and hostess.

'Just like him. Just like him.' Brooks's soft right hand was slipped from Faith's, his left coming round her back as he ushered her within. 'You can't even trust him to lie properly. The best thing you can do, my dear, is leave him at once. Come and live with me, instead; you'll be *much* happier, I *do* assure you.'

'And what would I do then, darling?' a woman's voice, indulgent as though she had heard this often before, sounded to Faith's left.

Faith turned to find a woman in her early thirties, long fair hair in an expensive, loose style which Faith had seen worn by several high-class models sporting the latest offerings of the most fashionable couturiers. Her blue eyes were large; she had a small, narrow nose and high cheekbones which hinted at her own former profession of fashion model. She wore a dark green cocktail dress with the hem exactly on her knee, figured with gold in a snake pattern which wound sinuously up from the hem until it flared out at its head, covering her left breast. It suited her slim figure; she carried herself well, speaking to Faith with an air of accomplished detachment.

'Pay no attention to my husband. He's incorrigible. I'm pleased Alex was able to bring someone. I'm Claire.'

'Faith,' the guest answered, taking the hostess's smooth and surprisingly cold hand, 'Faith Small.'

'I'm very pleased to . . . my! What a lovely dress!' as Alex slipped the coat from Faith's shoulders, revealing her new gown.

Two thin straps supported the tight-fitting bodice, whilst the fuller skirts which emerged beneath ended, like the hostess's dress, on the knee. Looking down quickly, Faith noted that Claire wore black high-heels, which meant that she must stand about five-feet three in normal circumstances.

'Are we too early?' Alex asked, handing the coat to Rupert, but looking anxiously at Claire. He needed people to talk to Faith while he made the final arrangements, and arriving before the others would waste time. Ideally, he would have liked most, if not all of the others to have arrived already, so that there would be ample opportunity to check that everything that could be done had been done.

'No,' her features split into a smile, though Faith could detect that the woman was a little nervous. 'Max just called to say he'd be here in a few minutes, but Colin and Prudence are here already. And some of our neighbours, of course. They're in there,' indicating the drawing room to their right.

Colin Hewer was a thin, saturnine individual in his mid-thirties, with a moustache which gave his fleshless lips perspective. He was of medium height like his host and with the same smooth, good looks; something of a 'force' in the City, Alex claimed, when introducing him to Faith, and mentioning that Faith worked in advertising. The man nodded slowly, his pale eyes fish-like, hooded slightly with caution, though he said nothing more than the usual platitudes about it being a tough business.

His wife, Prudence, a small woman who looked a year or two younger than her husband, had perhaps been drinking more than she should, but she smiled broadly when Faith was introduced, taking her arm to turn her away from the men as Rupert, Alex and Colin began talking.

'I think you're very brave. Have you been to one of these before, Faith?' she asked.

'No. I only met Alex the other day,' the younger woman answered, not keen to have the tenuous nature of her relationship with Alex advertised; 'Have you?'

'Oh, yes; lots.' She dismissed the question with a shrug of a shoulder. 'Are you staying?' Prudence asked, putting a wealth of meaning into the final word, a look of questioning doubt on her features.

'Alex wants to,' Faith answered, 'it's his decision,' trying to give the impression that she was as sophisticated as she would have liked to have been.

'I hope he's told you what's involved?' Prudence looked up as a figure appeared at her side; she broke into a smile. 'Hello Hector; have you met Faith, Alex's girl? This is Hector Vargas, one of Rupert and Claire's neighbours. Watch him: he's a bottom-pincher.'

Fifteen minutes later, whilst discussing the advertising business with Prudence, she suddenly stopped, staring across the room at a pair of dark eyes which were watching her openly and intently through a small gap between the general level of heads. Quickly she lowered her gaze and broke off, taking a sip of her white wine and asking: 'Who . . . who's the dark man across by the window. Dark eyes. He's . . .'

'Oh? That?' Prudence broke into a smile as she looked over, then back again, 'That's Max Hawes. Haven't you met him? I thought you came in together. He's a great friend of Alex's, actually. I thought you knew.'

'Is he? No,' Faith finished. She was sure she had seen him somewhere and was adding, 'I only wish I knew more . . .' when with horror, she saw Prudence gesticulating towards the man, beckoning him.

Before Faith could protest, flee or adjust her thinking, the dark, slim figure broke away from the general group to cross the room in a deceptively slow stride, slipping easily between the groups with a lithe, sinuous grace which ill befitted his stocky, robust appearance.

'Max!' Prudence exclaimed, 'this is Alex's new girl: Faith. Isn't she lovely?' She turned to beam at the taller young woman beside her; 'Quite stunning.'

'I was just thinking the same thing,' the quiet, lazy drawl sounded as Faith raised her eyes. 'Max Hawes.'

Max was about forty years old, five feet eight tall, broad shouldered, dark-haired and looking as though he had once played a mean game of squash. Yet he spoke with an accent which gave no doubts as to his upper-class origins, but very carefully modulated so as to make him appear ordinary. Though she had lowered her eyes to avoid his gaze, she was certain that his had never left her since he had begun to cross the room towards them.

'Faith Small,' Faith answered, trying to bring her breathing under control, for she was certain that she had seen this man before. But where?

In the normal run of affairs she would have been able to recall meeting someone so darkly attractive and yet, apart from his eyes and general build, she was unable to make any guess as to where it had been. Faith looked at the elegant, well-groomed figure in his perfectly-fitting suit with a certain amount of reserve, for she had a lively appreciation of his charm. His were the kind of looks of which she had always been suspicious; too smooth by half, her mother had called it. The kind of man who never gave anything away, either. Everything had its price, and he would know the exact value, too.

'Faith is in advertising. Don't you have contacts there, you naughty man?' The small woman, shorter than either, had all the self-confidence in the world, a confidence Faith thought she had possessed until this man appeared.

'I was just wondering where I had seen you before.' He nodded. 'Who are you with? Where could we have met?'

Max knew; had known from two steps into his crossing of the room that this lovely young woman was abashed by his appearance; it showed in the slight flush on her face and the set of her shoulders. Did she know what was planned for her? Alex would surely never be so stupid. He knew his reputation as a 'teacher of sex' often preceded him. Perhaps someone – that stupid Prudence, for example – had told her about him and his effective charm. Under normal circumstances, he would have used first one and then the other to bring Faith to his bed. Yet she was Alex's girl; the one he was in such a sweat about, who was 'out of bounds'. He could quite understand why, too.

'The only thing I can think of is the party at Kirkland's,

last night.' She tried not to give it any more weight than that. 'I was there with Albert Cross; my boss at Gibb McInley Gower. Kirkland is one of our clients. We'd just popped in.' She was trying to avoid having it known that Kirkland's party had been one of the high points in her short life.

'Yes,' he nodded, his jaw hardening, 'I have few business interests, but I do know Kirkland and, yes, I was there last night.' He tried to rack his brain to remember: yes; Alex and Lillian. They were both involved in this, he was sure. 'I must have seen you, though we were never introduced. I'd have remembered. Probably just glimpsed you through the crowd. Tell me . . .' He paused, looking up at the ceiling for a few seconds. The vague memory was returning, but only a snatch, of a slumped figure on a couch, for some reason. Could that have been this lovely young woman? Surely not! She would hardly have been so indiscreet. She looked as though she kept herself not just in good shape, but decorous, too. And would Alex . . .? Yes, Alex would. Off to one side, a new arrival was greeting people loudly. 'Were you wearing tangerine? A tangerine dress?'

'Yes!' Faith gasped, blushing, wondering whether he had seen her remove her underwear. 'I wouldn't have thought you'd have remembered me.'

'He always remembers beautiful women, don't you, Max?' Prudence's voice was a little less slurred than before, an indication that she was either sobering up or getting worse, but Colin was suddenly beside her and Max broke off to greet the newcomer.

Prudence took advantage of the arrival of her husband to go looking for a drink while Max promised to refill Faith's glass of white wine. This gave Colin the chance for which he had come, and he asked, 'Alex tells me you work for Gibb McInley Gower: is that right, Faith? Really?'

'Yes, that's right,' she smiled, glad to have Max leave, certain that her expression had given away her fears. Was she certain he had seen her matching briefs? In this company it would seem to be taken as an indication of sexual sophistication. Though Alex would have understood; would they? She was anxious not to have anything spoil the evening, for she was finding herself attracted to the tall man with the light-coloured eyes.

'There's a coincidence if you like!' Colin exclaimed. 'D'you know?' he asked. 'I'm seeing Barney Gibb first thing on Monday. Business meeting, of course.'

'Yes. Barney, of course, is the best man we have,' Faith answered, recalling that she had only seen him three times since she had been there; twice when he was getting into his car and once when he was donning a coat in reception.

'I was told he built that from nothing. I know he's run some tremendous campaigns.'

'Yes. He has brilliant concepts,' Faith replied, finding Albert's favourite phrase about his own work useful. 'Have you seen his adverts for that new French mineral water? The one that just features the bottle being poured out, then the frog jumps into it. The one with the caption: "Frogs know what they're doing when it comes to water"?'

'Yes,' Colin nodded, his lips a downturned line, 'had it run by my people for hours. That's the kind of thing we're looking for.'

In the far corner of the room, Max turned as the tall, fair-haired younger man reached his side, a soft smile in place as he asked, 'You've decided then?'

'Yes.' Alex nodded, feeling the trembling in his chest. 'It'll upset the old man, but I have to.'

'I agree,' Max said. 'She's lovely. And you were right to request changes in tonight's arrangements.'

'Will you be . . .?'

'I can't stay,' Max shrugged, 'but Lillian should get things going. I've spoken to her; she knows what to do. A fortnight, you think? Down at Marigold's place?'

'We can't use the Hall,' Alex agreed with a worried shrug. Keeping it from his family at Pellew Hall until Faith was more suitable was his main concern. Max smiled.

'Then I'll talk to people for you. Cheer up. It won't be as bad as you think.'

'The Stables, do you think?' Alex asked.

'Yes.' Max looked over to where he could see her alert, laughing features through the crowd of heads, and his expression was grim. 'I'm afraid there's no option; she wants discipline. But you mastered Helen, which wasn't *too* difficult. You have more experience now, so you should be able to master Faith; she could be something of a problem. Anyone can teach her discipline, but sex – and the pleasure to be had from sex – she can only learn from her Master. You *do* understand?'

'Of course.' Alex nodded. 'But I don't think she'll have any problem in that respect. She's had those two "*hari-go*" in since about two, and they've worked. I used the mitten on her this afternoon, and she took the "*harigata*" without any problem. Sucked it out of my hand!'

'Good.' Max's voice was enthusiastic, his face lighting up into a satisfied smile. 'I'll tell Lillian. Wonderful.' He delivered a controlled punch to the taller young man's shoulder.

'I want her, Max,' Alex said seriously, his mind now completely determined. 'It's . . . it's important to me.'

'I can quite understand, Alex; and have her you will,' the older man said. 'I must get back.'

Chapter Five

Faith and Colin were interrupted by the return of Prudence and Max, but to Faith's relief the smaller man avoided the subject of the Kirkland party. Instead, she found herself being gently interrogated by the three of them about her background, her attitudes, even her taste in music and art. They avoided politics and social issues. None of the questions seemed to be overtly prying, yet she had the feeling that they were delving into her background. But she knew that as she was a stranger there, they would obviously want to know something about her.

'What would you say was your greatest weakness, Faith? Vanity?' Colin asked.

'You've got every right to be vain,' Max interjected. 'Hasn't she, Pru? Show me a lovely woman who isn't vain and I'll show you someone who's blind.'

'You're certainly lovely,' the older woman agreed and, to Faith's surprise, her small tongue ran quickly around her lips, moistening them. Slightly disconcerted by this obvious sexual excitement, the young woman hesitated for a few seconds before she answered.

'I can't resist a dare. I dived off the twelve-metre board at the school pool once, even though I was scared of heights, because someone dared me to do it.'

'But did it cure you of being scared?' Colin asked.

'No.' Faith answered, her dark brown eyes glinting uneasily at the memory, 'but then, I didn't do it for that. It was just the dare, you see?'

She knew that revealing something so personal on such a short acquaintance was stupid, but they had asked, and they seemed such nice people; their acceptance of her was due mainly to Alex, of course, but she felt no qualms about the revelation.

'Faith!' Prudence admonished. 'The truth, now! What kind of men do you like?' Her shrewd eyes pinned her like a butterfly in a case.

'Men?' The girl blushed, looking in horror at the older woman, 'I've never thought much about them. I mean, they're all right. Don't get me wrong!' She flushed that either of the men or Prudence, whom she suspected may be bi-sexual, could take that as an invitation; 'I prefer them . . . to women.'

To her surprise all three nodded, as though the answer was only to be expected, and had resolved a doubt in their minds. As abruptly as it had begun, the flow of questions ceased. Faith found herself thinking that she had either imagined it, or suspected their motives for no good cause. Alex joined them while Max moved away, and Faith breathed a sigh of relief.

She found his presence disturbing, then realised that, at the back of her mind, she recalled Alex telling her – almost casually – that Max had studied sex and pleasure to an almost amazing degree. Yes. It could have been Max who had supplied Alex with the 'Love Balls' which, she knew, were still at work within her, for she could feel the heavy swelling desire there.

Gradually, the neighbours and the peripheral members of the party drifted away: some to the West End's more fashionable restaurants, or to a dozen other dinner parties. As the numbers dwindled, so the groups amalgamated and condensed; fewer groups, and larger. Max, who seemed to have no partner, was the odd man out, though no one paid any apparent heed. He knew everyone. Watching people talk to him, Faith found she could spot those who would be staying by the way they deferred to him, as though the rest were disinterested in his speciality.

Faith was seated on the arm of a couch, one of only two discussion groups, while Alex made himself amusing in the other, on the far side of the room. Claire stood beside Faith, almost holding court with the men: Vargas – who had pinched Faith's bottom within moments of their being introduced – and Colin Hewer, who was holding a small glass of clear liquid from which he occasionally sipped. Prudence had seated herself at the other end of the couch, but was taking no part; like Faith, she was listening to the opinions of two of Claire's neighbours about the nature of excitement.

Their hostess, whose former occupation was evident in her graceful movements and poise, turned her head and, in a quiet voice, asked, 'You're applying for admission, are you? I hope you know what you're doing.'

'Sorry?' Faith frowned, looking at her in surprise. Even seated, she was on a level with the woman.

'You're applying for admission to the Chosen,' Claire repeated, without impatience. 'You show a lot of good sense, but I wonder if you know what you're doing.'

'I'm afraid I don't know much about them,' Faith began.

'No. Rupert says we're rather like the Freemasons, in a way.' She shrugged. 'Secrets and all that; though none of it's very secret. If you're admitted, you'll need never work again. You'll never want for friends, money, or somewhere to stay, and with your looks, you'll marry well, too. But there's a price for all that, Faith: discipline. Self-discipline for the most part. Has anyone told you that? It's very important.'

'Yes.' Faith nodded gravely, swallowing. 'I remember Alex said . . .' Faith fought to recall exactly what he had told her. Was the hostess trying to warn her off, or was she preparing her? It was a fine point.

'Alex is really rather fond of you, isn't he?' The woman smiled in the direction of the tall young man. 'You *do* realise what will happen here tonight, don't you? I shouldn't say too much, but I wouldn't like you to be under any illusions about it. Unless you're prepared, you might not . . . well . . .' The woman shrugged.

'What?' Faith asked, feeling her apprehension rise. Had she gone white? She felt pale.

'You're going to be fucked, possibly by everyone; by all the men, certainly. I know I shall enjoy you, or you'll enjoy me, one or the other.' Her perfectly calm face, beautifully made-up, convinced Faith that she was serious.

'I . . .' Faith was about to protest when Claire placed a hand on her left forearm; a warning expression filled her eyes as her voice dropped below the general tenor of the conversation.

'It's the beginning of your "acceptance", if you like to think of it as that, Faith. By the Chosen. Alex asked that you be considered, so please don't shame him by making a public scene. I'm sure he told you something of what would happen tonight.'

'Yes,' Faith gulped and would have continued, but Claire said:

'You're very young, Faith; possibly the youngest we've ever considered. I was twenty-five and married, when I was accepted. This is only the first stage, and not an unpleasant stage, either. After tonight, if you find it repulsive, then that will be the end of it. But remember; once you reject the Chosen, you can't be re-admitted. Just as, once accepted, unless you are wilfully wicked, they can't reject you. And I must say, everyone's sex life is much improved.' She looked knowingly into Faith's wide, dark eyes.

Yes, thought Claire, this is one we not only want, but *must* have; bend the rules for if need be! This young woman would be excellent if trained as a Pleasure Slave. She hoped that Lillian had thought of something interesting to bring her out of her shell, though from Alex's description, she was ripe for awakening. Yes. She was glad now that Rupert had agreed to alter the arrangements for the party, just looking at those firm young breasts which filled the dress so deliciously; Julia could improve them, of course, but they looked good enough without.

It was almost eight-thirty when Lillian Brampton arrived, strutting into the large lounge to pose by the doorway barefoot; she was wearing a long, dark cloak which reached beyond her knees and carried a coiled, black leather whip in her hand. She stood about five feet nine, with a cropped thatch of blonde hair, cut in a *gamine* style which showed off her neck to advantage. Her pale colouring gave her the initial appearance of youth, but Faith put her age at somewhere in the late twenties, with large grey eyes which swept the room in a single, knowing pass. Vargas saw her and tried to ease past, but Lillian turned, bringing the coiled leather down on his flabby buttocks with a ringing comment.

'Begone, lecher! Leave these poor people to their pleasures!' She drew a laugh from the men and some derisive cheers from Claire and Prudence. The only other woman there was a petite, dark-haired, dark-eyed, elegant and graceful woman who moved well. She had been introduced as Julia, whose slim, almost boyish figure was sheathed in scarlet.

'Because I'm a scarlet woman, my dear,' she had insisted to Faith. 'I live with a man who isn't my husband;' Faith though had understood this to be something of a joke in modern Britain.

Julia's partner was Harry Hood, a small, portly man with a short neck, a prominent nose and spectacles. He looked fifteen years older than Julia's thirty-five, but was pleasant and unassuming. She found his jewellery surprising: a medallion at the very point of his open-necked shirt, heavy gold chains on his wrists, but no rings, though from the pale tint and slight indentations in the skin on the backs of his hairy fingers, they had only recently been removed.

As the door closed behind the fleeing man, Lillian beamed at the others, asking, 'You all know Simon, don't you?' gesturing with the whip towards a dark-haired young man of about her own age who had followed her. Conservatively dressed, he exuded the confidence of someone who reaped the rewards of life without having to make much effort to earn them. There was a chorus of nods and familiar greetings as Lillian swung round, asking, 'Darling, get me some champagne, would you?

I'm parched. Max! What are *you* doing here? Staying?' There was a speculative look in her eyes.

'Only for a short while,' he answered with an amused acknowledgement. 'I'm here as a technical adviser,' he ended, drawing a chuckle both from the newcomer and some others. Faith found herself smiling at his wit, giving the knowledge of his field of interest. It sounded as though they all knew about it, too.

'Then you can hold my whip for a while.' She handed the black coil of leather to him, asking, 'Everyone here?'

'Hector was the last to leave, as usual,' Claire announced. 'I don't know why he doesn't bring someone and stay. He might even like it.'

'Then why don't we start?' Lillian asked.

While she had been talking, Lillian had been unfastening first the neck of her cape, then the middle and, as she finished, her hands withdrew into the slits in the sides; it was wrenched aside to reveal her standing with legs splayed, and naked. Her sparse pubic hair was the same shade as that on her blonde head, so she was either naturally blonde, or careful about matching.

Faith was glad that her gasp was shared by several others, though she noted that no one, not even Max commented on the fact of her nakedness. They were too used to Lillian Brampton's spectacular ways to find this more than a momentary surprise. Simon placed the champagne in her hand; she sipped as she acknowledged his gesture with a smile and blown kiss, then looked round again, stopping as her eyes met Faith's.

The younger woman went cold as their eyes met, and held. While Lillian slowly sipped her champagne, the room remained silent but gradually, heads were turning to look at her. Faith found herself unable to remove her eyes from those of this exotic creature, whose breasts showed only a slight sagging; but the fullness of them, and the hard engourgement of her nipples, amazed Faith.

'Who have we here?' Lillian asked, holding the glass to one side while Simon refilled it, her eyes on Faith.

'It's Alex's girl, Faith, Lillian.' Max had uncoiled the

whip and stood holding it where the stock joined the long, plaited leather of the remainder. It dangled in front of him, so that the plaited boss was held at a height which might have been taken for a long, limp, black, woven penis.

'What do you look like under all that frippery, Faith?' Lillian asked, sipping again.

'She looked beautiful enough dressed,' Max answered for her, but Faith felt herself flush as the attention of the whole group was concentrated on her. Then Alex was standing behind her, his hand already on the zip at the back of the bodice.

'Shall I undo it, my darling?' he half-whispered, speaking loud enough for everyone to hear.

For a moment Faith hesitated, her heart pounding with expectation at the thought that her dress was to be removed, then collected herself. Her surprise at Lillian's arrival had caused her to clench her muscles and the 'Love Balls' had moved eccentrically within her again, setting up a series of pulses of pleasure that were spilling through her abdomen like ripples, each of them in turn giving birth to new ripples which eddied back and forth within her. She knew now why Alex had insisted on her keeping them, for under normal circumstances, she would have either buried her face in her hands, or fled.

Now Faith rose from the arm of the couch while Rupert fussed about in a corner, her fingers displacing Alex's, her eyes still fixed on Lillian as she lowered the long zip to the bottom of its range. Bringing her hands diagonally across her chest to her shoulders, crushing her breasts momentarily, Faith slipped the straps from them, then lowered her arms to her sides, feeling the weight of the skirts begin to drag the fabric against the upper slope of her smooth breasts. They ought to be smooth enough, she thought; Alex had oiled them pretty freely. The memory of that delicious torture sustained her as the bodice broke free of its last restraint – Faith's erect nipples – and with gathering speed, the dress fell in a heap about her widely-spread ankles, as the appreciative inhalation from the others told her the gesture had gained their entire approval.

Faith's only garments were her brief suspender belt and the white stockings which encased her legs, whose feet were stuck into the now invisible shoes as Lillian, having handed the champagne glass to Simon again, approached. She had an admiring smile on her pale face, and she stopped close enough to Faith to allow her to see it clearly, as she frankly admired Faith's full breasts. Very faintly, the sound of the initial tapping of Ravel's 'Bolero' began, the insistent rhythm seeming to be pitched at an almost subliminal level. Close up, Faith could see that Lillian wore a very pale lipstick which enhanced her *ingénue* appearance.

'You're right, Max,' Lillian said, not taking her eyes from Faith's breasts, 'she *is* lovely, isn't she?'

Then Lillian leant forward and, even as she started to move, Faith knew exactly what was going to happen. Lillian had made no secret of her interest in the round, hard buds which faced her, so there was no surprise – though a shiver of ice rippled up Faith's spine – when Lillian's wide mouth gently closed around her right nipple, the pale lips spreading wide to permit her tongue to caress the outstanding flesh. Faith felt a little dizzy; it was the first time a woman had ever touched her sexually. She could feel her equilibrium leaving her for a few moments as, in an equal mixture of fascination and horror, her eyes remained on Lillian's mouth.

'Her nipples taste as good as they look, too,' Lillian said, as she removed her mouth a little way. 'Alex is a lucky man.' Then she fastened on her left nipple.

But Lillian, despite being overtly intent on Faith's nipples – her left hand was caressing the blood-engorged right nipple – had interests in another direction. Before Faith was aware of it, a smooth hand had snaked between her thighs, pressing quickly within her defences. The sharp inhalation and sudden movement of her thighs surprised even Faith, especially as, instead of moving together, they moved apart to allow Lillian more access. Her body had betrayed her again!

Flushing once more, feeling more embarrassed than she had ever done, Faith took three deep breaths as Lillian finished caressing her nipples, then stepped away, bringing her right hand up, two fingers now glistening with the oily fluid from Faith's vagina. Watching Faith's eyes intently, Lillian deliberately held her fingers beneath her nose, inhaled, then put out a delicate tongue to taste the fluid, before pushing her coated fingers into her mouth, clearly indicating her desire. There was a silence as Lillian considered; her eyes locked with Faith's, and a smile slowly gathered as she asked: 'That doesn't taste like Alex, does it? No; that's you. You taste wonderful. I'd like to drink some more of that, but later. Later;' then she turned, smiling to the others. 'What a lovely girl. Isn't she, Max?'

'I said so before, remember?' he asked, looking at Faith with a smile slowly breaching the severity of his normal expression. Faith felt a hand snake around her body from behind which came to rest beneath her right breast, the thumb just touching the fullness of the underside.

'Magnificent,' Alex's voice whispered in her ear. 'I'd ditch the rest and step out of the dress, my darling. The fun's going to begin, soon.'

'Did I do it right?' Faith asked, uncertain.

'You were perfect,' he answered warmly.

Faith looked to her left to where Prudence already had her dress around her hips, her breasts looking absurdly full; the areolae were raised as though swollen, the tiny nipples in the centre erect, but dwawfed by the surrounding tissue. Alex saw the direction in which she was looking, and slid his hand higher to support her breast.

'Look at Claire,' he said softly. Their hostess had removed her dress, but the sight of another naked female was not what made Faith's breath catch: as Claire turned towards them, her hands raised above her head in a pose similar to a naiad supporting a fountain, Faith could see the decoration.

From her shaved crotch, where only a few stubby fair hairs remained about the delicate area of her clitoris and the long slit which vanished beneath, there emerged the long, sinuous figure of a golden snake. Frankly staring, Faith followed the length of the snake's body up the left side of Claire's abdomen and stomach until it broadened out into the wider, kite-shaped head, which faced forward so that her left nipple provided the odd-shaped tongue.

'Claire!' Alex called, attracting her attention as, all around them, women and men were undressing. Some were undressing others, none were hurrying. There may have been passion in the air like a warm, heavy scent, but there was no haste or fumbling.

Claire walked over with the poise and deportment for which she had once been famous, a proud smile on her face as she stopped before them. She knew from Faith's interested expression that her body decoration had provoked yet another mixture of admiration and excitement.

'Like it, Faith?' she asked while, behind her, Lillian was standing, one hand on her hip while she sipped her champagne, watching the preparations.

'I've never . . .' she gulped, '. . . seen anything like it.' Faith felt her excitement rise, but with a certain horror, for the snake looked tattooed on the skin. Each separate golden scale was edged with a deep blue, looking so realistic that, from across the room, it looked part of the tattooist's work.

'Claire's artistry.' Alex sounded amused behind her, his forefinger and thumb now rolling her nipple gently between them.

'Is it a tattoo?' Faith asked.

'God; *no*!' Claire laughed, throwing back her head. 'It's paint, body paint. Rupert has a cousin in California who sends some over every so often. Takes forever, of course.'

'I liked the one where you had your nipples done as eyes, a nose on your stomach and a pair of large, red, vertical lips beneath,' Alex remembered. 'Possibly the best you've done.'

'I remember that one!' Claire laughed. 'Everyone wanted to kiss me, all of a sudden.'

A slightly more penetrating conversation made Claire turn to where Colin was seated on the leather couch, naked, talking to Lillian. He looked and sounded defensive as Lillian, in an amused tone, asked, 'What's the matter? Won't Percy perform, Colin?'

'Help me off with these, would you, Faith?' Alex asked, opening his shirt. While Faith's attention had been on Claire's bodypainting, he had removed his jacket and tie whilst easing off his shoes. Faith turned to face him, nervous again at such intimate contact, though she knew it was silly. This man had made love to her, he knew more about her body than anyone else, now; yet she felt nervous about removing some of his clothing.

She unfastened his trousers and tugged them down, then pulled his pale blue underpants down to release the semi-erect penis, which stood out from his body at an angle towards her. Then she knelt in front of him to tug them lower to his ankles, trying to ignore the swelling flesh beneath her chin, keeping an ear open to Lillian's conversation, startled when she heard her exclaim, 'God; that Faith's a fast worker! Are you the "crumpet who's going to blow his trumpet, strumpet"?' The sheer volume and excitement in her voice silenced the room. Faith flushed, frowning as she tried to understand what the far more experienced woman meant. She thought it had some sexual connotation, but failed to appreciate what it was. Beyond Lillian, she could see anticipatory expressions fading into doubt.

'I'm sorry. I don't know what you mean.'

'Are you going to give him a blow job?' Lillian asked with gusto, still enjoying the situation, even as she began to understand that something was wrong.

'Sorry?' Faith found herself uncertain, gulping and aware of the slight tremor which was invading her lower limbs, and rapidly spreading upwards. Lillian was using terms which Faith had only heard whispered before.

'Fellatio, my dear. "Smoking his pole".' Lillian tried

again, but her enjoyment had now vanished; it was only determination which held her. From Faith's expression, obviously neither of these terms was familiar, and indeed, she realised that the whole concept was foreign to her.

Lillian cast an anguished look, not at Alex, but at Max for some reason, while the silent room looked on. The urbane figure at first showed little emotion in the face of silent entreaty; then he commented, 'Faith needs to be educated, Lillian. You must remember that this is only her first visit. It is neither the time, nor place, for that education. I'm sure she *will* be educated, in time. Why not accept her as she is?'

'Yes.' Lillian's face cleared into a smile. 'Of course; we all had to learn, didn't we?' She turned back to Colin, who looked no happier, though Prudence had taken one of his hands and was using it to squeeze her right breast.

Alex acted as though nothing at all had happened, in helping her to collect their clothes and fold them neatly, then place them against the nearest wall. Already Claire had Rupert's hand between her thighs while with the other he was fondling her right breast. Faith could see the steady rise and fall of her chest.

'Come on, Colin!' Lillian protested. 'I'll arouse you.'

'Sorry,' he shrugged, 'I don't think anyone can. We nearly didn't make it tonight.'

'Why? Prudence been sucking you dry?' Lillian asked, then turned to where Max perched on the broad leather arm of a chair. 'I could revive him, couldn't I, Max?'

'You could revive the dead,' he answered pleasantly, still fully dressed. 'You could arouse anyone here. Even me.'

'You couldn't revive this,' Colin sighed and shook his head, opening his legs to reveal a poor, shrivelled, shrunken worm emerging from a bed of coarse black curls, his scrotum slack and pendulous beneath.

'Lillian could, Colin,' Max advised him. 'All she has to do is press the right buttons. And Lillian knows all the right buttons to press.'

'She doesn't know Faith's,' said Julia, whose slim,

androgynous standing figure with wide-splayed legs was being caressed from behind by one of Harry's hands, whilst the other seemed to be behind her. Her voice held a throaty quality which Faith was beginning to recognise at last: a passion was stirring within Julia. It flashed through Faith's mind that she had never heard or felt that kind of passion when she was with Albert; but Lillian was turning to look at her again, smiling.

'That's not fair.' Lillian looked directly at Faith, then back to Julia. 'Faith's half-aroused already.'

'Go on, Lillian.' Colin's eyes were alight. 'Rouse Faith. I bet you can't.'

'If I do,' Lillian answered, 'then I'll rouse you, too.' She looked directly at him, all the while sipping her drink as elegantly as though she were wearing a new Paris gown.

'You can try,' Colin answered, shaking his head.

'Come on, Faith.' Lillian looked round to her, then crooked her finger, beckoning her into the open space in the centre of the drawing room. 'Let's see what you can do.'

Chapter Six

Faith suddenly felt reluctant to move; her legs remained still while her heart fluttered in her chest. It was only the gentle pressure of Alex from behind, that pressed her slowly and reluctantly forward. She swallowed convulsively a couple of times as her legs began to work of their own volition, yet as she approached Lillian, who was handing her glass to Simon again as the quiet, perseverance of 'Bolero' quickened slightly, Faith looked round the room.

Not to Alex, though, but to Max, whose quiet, calm features, studied almost to severity, belied the fire and interest in his eyes. She opened her mouth slightly to ask for his intervention, for she had no experience of this kind of stimulation, but Max was well ahead of her.

'Don't go mad, Lillian,' he said, 'Faith may not have felt a woman's touch before. Have you?' He directed this last to Faith who shook her head, for her throat had constricted, preventing her from speaking. She looked anxiously at Lillian, whose smile had lost much of its voluptuousness, being more compassionate and benign now. It was as though she realised Faith's extreme nervousness, yet when she looked at Max, her whole expression changed to one of irritation; as though she blamed him for Faith's being there.

'Kneel down, darling.' Lillian made a patting movement with her right hand. 'Simon. Would you bring me your scarf, please?'

'Sure,' he answered, turning and vanishing from sight.

Reluctantly, her eyes on Lillian the whole time, Faith knelt on the soft, sheepskin rug just in front of the blonde woman, trying all the while to keep her eyes from looking slightly below her line of vision at the sparsely covered pubic mound, with the ruddy line of her sex showing through. From the musk catching at her nostrils, Faith knew that Lillian was excited and strangely, despite her own reluctance, Faith felt a thrill of pleasure running down from her sternum to her navel.

'Bend forward on all fours, my darling,' Lillian instructed, the only voice in the room. Faith obeyed, glad to look at the rug rather than Lillian's groin, and well aware now of the liquid heaving in her own.

'Now, put your knees and ankles further apart. A little further; that's it.' Lillian's voice was low and gentle, for she was kneeling too, now, just by Faith's right shoulder.

A white, silken scarf with a fringe of tassels appeared on her left just behind her arms, the fabric touching the side of her breast and ribs, sending a shiver of delicious pleasure through her bosom. She saw Lillian's arm sweep beneath her, then raise the tassels so that the scarf was slung underneath her. Lillian was in no rush; she knew the power of anticipation as well as urgency, and she gradually raised the scarf until it touched the bottom of Faith's ribcage an inch or two below her breasts.

Lillian began moving it gently from side to side, letting the smooth silky fabric slip gently across the soft skin. Faith gasped a little at the first, slow, sensual touch, licking her lips in anticipation, as her breathing became slightly heavier.

'That's right, darling,' Lillian said softly beside her right ear, 'whenever you feel the pleasure coming, tell me. Lick your lips or stick out your tongue. That way, I know just what to do for you.' The slow movement continued. Faith now knew that Lillian was in complete command of the situation.

Yet though it was slow, this touching was never boring, for Lillian varied both the pace and the point of contact. She was holding the tasselled ends of the scarf and, when it was pulled higher at one side, she would adjust her grip to allow the long, loose end to dangle down on Faith's long, unprotected back. The first time it happened, Faith gasped in surprise, arching her back to escape the touch. Then a second, quieter gasp as the pleasure took her up another notch on her scale of arousal. Again she licked her lips, wetting them as the tassels which had touched her were withdrawn. But she knew, as did everyone watching, that Lillian would do more than just slip this soft scarf around Faith's stomach.

Gradually the scarf was worked higher until the edge delicately touched the underside of her pendulous breasts, evoking a quiet groaning sigh from Faith and another lip-wetting from her tongue. With the scarf hanging beneath her, it felt as though her breasts were being filled from a reservoir higher in her body, the pressure pushing down towards her nipples, making them swell to new heights, tingling as they did so. The feelings were so new to her that she found them impossible to describe, even to her rational mind, as she experienced them on a basic, sensual level.

The scarf retreated for a few moments, then again approached, mounting higher as it began to gently stroke the swelling breasts, stopping short of the tender, tingling nipples, slightly pressing the fullness of the upper unrestricted flesh, tilting her nipples towards her stomach. Lillian worked while the music increased both in stridency and pitch. 'Bolero' ran for just three seconds over fifteen and a half minutes, but Rupert had, by juggling with his machine, produced a version three times as long, layering the recordings so that the gradual pounding took longer to swell into the full development.

Faith sighed again as the tassels touched her, this time at the base of her spine. She could feel the burning shame, her belly curved outwards, towards the softness of the long, soft sheepskin pile, at this, her pent-up groaning, letting them all know of her arousal. Her tongue, now obedient to Lillian's insistent encouragement, was poking out of her mouth without moving, while her chest heaved. She had never felt so much lust. Faith let her hands slide forward on the rug, splaying them out, lowering her shoulders, bringing her back almost level again. She looked up where, directly ahead of her, Claire was seated on her husband's lap in a large, leather armchair.

Her hostess faced the same way as Rupert, her feet drawn up to the cushioned seat, her knees widely separated, allowing Faith to see the long, open cleft of her sex which fanned out; Rupert's right hand meanwhile gently trailed up the inner surface of one lip to the clitoris Claire was exposing by pulling back on her mound with her hand. There Rupert ran the tip of his finger lightly around the little pearl, before slowly drawing it down the other lip, across her perineum until it vanished briefly within the slightly pouting anus, only to reappear again. On the way back up, Rupert's finger slipped gently into the distended vaginal opening to collect some of her liquid warmth, which was once again drawn up the soft, inner lips towards her clitoris. From Claire's facial expression, eyes closed and slack-mouthed, she was thoroughly enjoying the attention.

Faith could feel herself being aroused, both by the sight before her and the treatment to which she was being subjected. After drawing the scarf down her body again, this time almost to her hips, making Faith spread her legs wider apart, Lillian took the tasselled end and, while she gently slipped it loosely back and forth across Faith's lower abdomen, she dangled the tassels down the cleft between Faith's globular buttocks.

Once again Faith groaned, her tongue licking around her full lips, her breathing becoming harsher, far more strident as she desperately fought for oxygen; but Lillian was not content. Instead of moving the scarf up Faith's body as she had in the past, she held the tasselled end horizontally and, very slowly, carefully and above all, lightly, she let the soft strips of silk touch Faith's slightly-open vulva. The touch electrified her. Where before she had been well aroused, now she could feel the fire rushing through her veins, seeking escape in some direction.

This time there was no mistaking Faith's reaction. Both her groaning and the licking of her lips was accompanied by a further depressing of her belly, in order to present her buttocks to this delicate touch. As the gentle, insistent, terrible stimulation continued, the flesh of her stomach and thighs began quivering, tremors running through her as the passion was raised up to a different plane.

But Lillian was nothing if not thorough. She had been asked to arouse this young woman, so she would do so. If in the process Faith entered a different world to any she had previously known, then so be it. Lillian knew the agenda planned for Faith, as, slowly, she slipped the tassels up one of the lips and back down the other, before moving away downwards towards the soft flesh of the inner thighs. From the reaction so far, Faith would train beautifully as a Pleasure Slave. Alex would be so pleased.

Faith no longer felt ashamed of her reactions; that feeling had vanished beneath the urgent need within. She was gulping air more noticeably, her chest almost heaving, tiny whimpers coming from her in response to the waves of pleasure which were sweeping through her deepest recesses. These waves surged down her hard, out-thrust belly to explode within the inner walls of her vagina, where they added to the musky aroma which by now, she was certain, most of the group could appreciate.

Lillian watched the tension in the inner thighs until she saw the indications for which she had been searching. Suddenly, without any warning, she dropped the scarf, and reached both hands beneath Faith to grasp her stiff, engorged nipples. They felt to Faith as though the whole substance of each breast had been filled to overflowing; they tingled and ached with a sensation previously unknown, even in her most passionate encounters. With a determined expression on her face and an almost savage strength, Lillian's thumbs and crooked forefingers closed around them, and squeezed. Hard.

Faith was at the point of release when this sudden, unexpected and painful sensation surged through her, bringing her body back up to the vertical; with head thrown back, and eyes closed, her mouth opened in a silent scream of protest to the high ceiling as Lillian crooned into her ear, 'Not yet, my darling. We have only a little way to go, now. Just a little way. I can't let you come just yet. But don't worry; Lillian knows when to release you. Lillian will help.'

Obedient to her mentor's instructions, too shocked by the treatment to protest, Faith lowered herself into the same position again, arms splayed out and bottom raised as Lillian called, 'Simon, my champagne, please! And the ointment in the black tub,' as she took up the scarf again.

Faith waited with the patience of a well-schooled horse as the ends of the scarf were once again picked up and adjusted loosely around her stomach. This time, Lillian slowly moved the scarf up towards and then over her breasts, keeping it slack, carefully adjusting the tension so that, as she moved it, the scarf only just brushed the fine hair on the skin.

The young newcomer groaned again as the fabric finally found her nipples, wondering why, when they had felt so sore a few moments previously, that pain was transformed into a source of heat which seemed to radiate through them. Back and forth the scarf moved, growing gradually tighter until the breasts were enclosed in the soft fabric which was not yet sufficiently taut to distort their pointed cone shape. As Lillian moved the scarf gently across her nipples, Faith's pleasure returned, more insistent than before; she could feel her sex-lips swelling and then something cold and wet dropped onto the small of her back.

She gasped at the sensation, but Lillian's voice was soft in her ear. 'It's only a little champagne, my darling. Would you like me to lick it off?' and before Faith could reply, her warm mouth was applied to the spot between her shoulderblades where the cold liquid had touched. Lillian's soft, moist, hot tongue followed the trail of champagne down towards where her sacral dimples showed as very faint outlines. Yet all the time the scarf was moving across her nipples, rousing her again.

Faith was moistening her lips once more when another

slight splash of the chilled champagne landed, this time lower down. As she gasped, aware of the conflicting tensions within herself, Faith found her voice. 'Please, no! No more,' she managed to gasp; but she was too new to these games, too ignorant to realise she could not yet be released from the delicious arousal. The wanting within her was like an explosion which she could only contain by tensing the muscles in her abdomen into a hard, rounded shape which Lillian noted, nodding to Simon. Had Lillian given way to her plea, the others would have complained. Faith's performance was the reason they were there; to judge it, to sample her, to decide whether she should be admitted to the Chosen. That would never be done if Lillian gave way to the desperate pleas Faith was sending to her, and Lillian knew that, more than anything in the world, Alex wanted Faith to be Chosen.

'Just a little more, my darling. You'll like this, especially,' she said, tipping champagne from her glass onto the base of Faith's spine.

The young woman whimpered softly, then moaned as Lillian drew her finger from the pool of wine on her back, down to the depression which rapidly became the 'natal notch', the groove between her buttocks. Under the slight pressure of Lillian's forearm, for her hand still held the champagne glass, Faith raised her belly a fraction and then gasped as the pool of champagne began to trickle downwards towards her anus. As it found its way, the wine flooded over the tiny hairs there, imparting such a sensation that Faith's tongue poked out, large and round through her permanently-open mouth. To Claire, now thoroughly roused by her husband, Faith looked sufficiently depraved for anyone; she wondered how long it would be before someone displaced Lillian to mount the young woman; she looked as though she would appreciate a hard ride. Would Lillian spank her, first? No; it was too soon for that; she was too undisciplined yet. She had probably never had a spanking before.

As the wine hissed passed her anus, imparting a fizzing, tickling sensation, Faith's groan was even more pronounced. Her deep breathing had become dangerously shallow, the tension in her body and limbs imparting a tremor which most of them knew only too well. Lillian dropped the scarf, swung her right leg over Faith's back then let herself down onto the naked skin, facing her rump.

'There,' Lillian said as Faith gasped. 'Not long now, my sweet, I promise you. You've been very good. Hasn't she been good, Max? So very good.' But there was no answer from the expressionless man who watched.

Max moved to stand behind Faith, looking directly at her rear, watching the muscles of her thighs and crotch carefully. He could see the tiny, pink, palpitating anus and the deep red of her sex, and he nodded to himself as the latter throbbed. He had taught Lillian this technique; it was quite basic and perfectly proper for someone as uneducated in these ways as Faith. It would be a useful introduction to the ways of arousal, and the deferring of satisfaction until the proper time.

Yet that proper time was fast approaching, by the sounds she was making as Lillian worked. When she was more experienced, more trained, Lillian could prolong this with Faith for an hour or more. He had worked Lillian for most of one day before giving her release. He could still remember her high, keening scream as she climaxed.

Faith could feel Lillian's sex on her back; knew it for what it was, knew the heat within it. She could feel the slippery softness of the oily, shiny, open sex lips which gently massaged her spine as the blonde woman bent, gently touching Faith's open sex. Faith groaned instantly with a long, warbling wail of pleasure which Lillian dealt with firmly. With her thumb and forefinger she pinched the delicate, damp skin around Faith's anus, instantly stopping the warble as Faith's flesh retreated from her touch.

'You haven't educated this little opening, have you?' Lillian asked no one in particular. She expected no answer and got none, for she was starting on the last stage.

Lillian felt up beyond the clitoris, pressing the bump she found, expelling one of the 'Love Balls' which she laid on the carpet between Faith's legs. Then she removed the second, listening to the sound of Faith's reaction before exchanging her champagne glass for the black pot of ointment Simon held out to her. She was glad she had been told about the balls in advance, for it was important for Faith to be mounted quickly after her arousal. Removing the balls at this stage – the last chance of a rest for the young woman – prevented any delays. The balls had done their work, for Faith had been halfway aroused before she ever laid eyes on her.

While Lillian carefully took some of the white ointment from the jar on her finger, her other hand was caressing Faith's right buttock, testing the tension within the smooth contours. Once the ointment was in place, Lillian stepped clear of Faith, crouched beside her and with slow gentle stokes, applied the ointment first to the outer lips of Faith's sex, then refilling her finger, touched the clitoris lightly, and pressed her finger slowly into Faith's vagina. Just the touch alone would have been sufficient to have started another paroxysm of lust, but the added sensations which were beginning to flow from within her added to the response.

Faith's groan brought Lillian's other hand into play at once, digging a thumb directly into Faith's inner thigh to suppress the pleasure which was sweeping through her. For the third time, Faith's pleasure had been reduced, but the older woman was too experienced to believe that it was permanent. This was just a temporary expedient to stave off the inevitable. Faith's pleasure was going to come sooner or later. Lillian knew that she had done well to hold her this long, but she was unable to work miracles, not without much sterner methods which were totally unsuitable in this context; with a strap she could have prolonged it far more. None of the Chosen would have objected, of course, but it would have frightened Faith, which was not the object of the exercise. Faith was here to be gradually introduced into the ways of the Chosen; to be chosen herself, albeit without her full knowledge.

Dipping her forefinger into the pot again, Lillian smeared ointment gently around the swollen nipples which shook and shivered as Faith's body strained. With another smear of ointment on her finger, Lillian remounted Faith in the same position as before, facing backwards. She knew she had only a few seconds before the ointment began to work and positioned herself carefully. Lillian brought her legs round outside Faith's, planting her feet against the inner sides of her widespread knees; her limbs were intertwined with Faith's, holding them securely apart. By that time, Faith no longer cared about her position or the circumstances in which she found herself. All she wanted was release from the dreadful, lustful longing within her. With careful precision, Lillian applied the tip of her finger directly to Faith's anus without penetrating it.

The warmth the ointment imparted had been slowly seeping through Faith's tissues, gradually gathering pace. The young woman's sensations had been battered to the point where she thought that it would be some time before she felt any pleasure again, but suddenly it struck. Immediately the hot, stinging sensation in her vagina and clitoris began, Faith tried to close her legs against it, but found that Lillian was stopping her.

'Tongue out, darling,' the woman whispered to her lovingly, glancing round to where Simon was watching Faith's face. He nodded as, automatically, Faith's tongue extended.

'Now! She's ready for release, Alex!' Lillian called sharply as Faith brought her head up and back, mouth open in a whimpering croon as 'Bolero' blasted forth in time to Faith's mounting desires.

Ahead of her, Rupert's erection was firmly embedded in Claire's body, the fair, fringe of her short pubic hair offsetting the long, shiny-wet flesh. She could see Claire's abandoned expression, her mouth still open though no sounds were emerging, her eyes now wide and staring, her hands rubbing down the sides of her labia to add manual stimulation to her pleasure. Rupert's hands were on her breasts, the nipples being gently caressed. Claire meanwhile was wondering whether she had ever seen anyone look quite so abandoned as Faith, whose expression of desperate desire made the older woman melt.

Just as Faith felt the air move behind her, before she felt Alex at all, Claire found her voice in a long, low moan of release, her hips working a little, her muscles clenching frantically at the embedded organ. Faith could see the seepage from Claire, running thickly past her anus onto the leather, then she lowered her own head as the first touch of Alex's penis at her entrance took her grateful attention.

Lillian never moved. She remained on Faith's rump while her feet held Faith open and Alex quickly knelt behind the imprisoned young woman, his erection looking too hot to last long. She reached out her arms and, as Alex placed his penis against Faith's vaginal opening, Lillian drew Alex to her, rubbing her breasts against his smooth chest, calling out, 'Your lover, darling! Suck, my darling, suck!'

And Faith sucked; how she sucked! To the stridency of Ravel's music, Alex was drawn smartly within her, his tight scrotum slamming against her clitoris; further pressure on the abused organ brought another gasp from the frantic young woman imprisoned between them. There was no backward and forwards movement from Alex at all, for Faith had gone beyond that point. Her vaginal muscles, uneducated as they were, squeezed hard on the invader of her sexual organs. Alex, already kissing Lillian deeply, their tongues fighting like snakes, gave a grunt. Lillian knew what that meant, and slid her body backwards to press her clitoris against Faith's spine, still taking her weight on her legs.

While Faith milked Alex's penis, Lillian rubbed her clitoris against Faith's spine, the bumps of the bones alternately pressing and releasing against her. Faith climaxed violently, bucking her back up and down, her voice rising to a scream of sheer pleasure which was torn from deep within her. Even the pleasure Alex had provided that afternoon was as nothing to the extremity in which she now found herself. Prudence raised her head from Colin's crotch, her mouth dripping with seminal fluid to look in wide-eyed wonder, and not a little jealousy, at the explosive nature of the release.

Claire, her honeypot now seeping her husband's fluids too, looked benignly at the scene before her, whilst Julia simply smiled as Harry replaced his erection in her bottom, took hold of her tiny breasts then sodomised her again. Simon, the odd one out, knelt, cutting off Faith's cries by kissing her; it seemed the best way. He had seen her reaction to the suggestion of fellatio and thought it would be best if someone else took the risk of being bitten first. His erection was complete, so full that it ached. He was looking around for someone in whom to plunge it.

In the hallway, Max smiled as he closed the door on the scene he had done so much to set. Faith was a good choice. If that was how she reacted to Lillian's ministrations, then she would indeed be worth educating. Lillian was, after all, his best pupil, but he thought that with a little care, Faith might just be almost as good. Discipline would be a problem; it always was with someone coming to it so late in life. Yes, the Stables would be best, but getting Faith there without trauma might be difficult to arrange. There would have to be some very careful planning.

As Max closed the street door quietly behind him, Alex withdrew his flaccid penis from Faith's still-writhing opening. Lillian stood up to go with him, laying the length of her body along his, feeling the wetness against her abdomen. Simon spotted his chance; moving quickly in behind Faith, he inserted himself deeply within her before she was aware of him. The young woman had lowered her face to the carpet, resting her forehead on her forearms; her throat was making crooning noises at this new intruder; she was now careless of who it might be, taking such liberties. She wanted a stiff penis within her. She wanted to feel that boost again. Often.

Simon's hands sought and found her breasts and as he began to move within her, Faith moved her body in sympathy with his. If he was mounting her, then Faith was more than willing to be mounted. The ointment on her sexual organs, anus and breasts was firing them up for the occasion and, long before Simon obtained his release, Faith was climaxing gently. Each wave was stronger than the last, though nothing reached the epic proportions of the one Lillian had induced.

In a distant, neglected corner of her mind, Faith thought that she would never let Alex go; and she would worship Lillian. This woman had brought her to a pitch which she had never known existed, and which she would have doubted had she not experienced it. These people might have odd ways; they might seem slightly perverted, to some. But of one thing she was certain. Faith was never going to return to Albert. *She* had Chosen.

Chapter Seven

Faith became aware of a different mood in the party. Her head felt light and yet, thick. As though she had cotton-wool where her brain normally resided; her mouth too full of it. She had lost count of the various sexual mountings, had hardly been keeping score, in fact. It seemed that, no sooner had one man exited her than another replaced him. Yet there had been periods of calm and quiet. Periods when she had lain back on the rug with closed eyes and focused on the semi-dark room around her, listening to the blood pounding around her system, to the liquid slappings of passion all about her.

The men had approached individually; she recalled words being spoken, but nothing of the content. What they had asked, whatever they had suggested, she had complied with. She had lain on her back; she had knelt on all fours; they had penetrated her hot, aching sex with their hot, hard erections. They had climaxed within her after a longer or shorter time, their harsh breathing matching the urgency of their frantic movements. None had offered her anything but the most considerate attention; there was no attempt to force her. Not that she would have objected. Faith felt that any of them could have suggested something much more different and she would have complied readily.

Yet there were other approaches, less direct, less demanding, more insidious. Claire had been first, a hand stealing across her flattened breasts as she lay looking sightlessly above her, adrift on her own cloud of euphoria. A soft, gentle hand which caressed her burning breast, a mouth which nibbled and sucked at her firm nipple, wetting it. It felt so hot to her that Faith thought she must be steaming gently but, on opening her eyes she saw nothing, just the tranquil features of Claire, her lips still encompassing the coral nipple, a vacant look of passionate surrender in her blue eyes, heavy-lidded like a religious statue.

When Claire realised Faith was watching, she smiled, and raised herself to kiss Faith's still-swollen mouth gently, her lips almost as dry as Claire's own; then she eased her hands down Faith's stomach to her pudenda. While Faith groaned softly, only slightly more violently than a sigh, her legs parted automatically before the approach. Claire's fingers carefully opened her wet outer lips and flicked gently against the inner lips, exciting them in an unusual and yet, very pleasant manner, before two fingers gently probed her hot, moist passage.

With those fingers placed deep within her, Claire's thumb began a dance up and down the soft external tissue, gently touching without pressure, never remaining in one place long enough to be noticed; yet attracting blood back to the outer lips. The tingling which Faith had felt so strongly, deep within her, began to surge again, starting from a multitude of diverse points. Her breasts contributed a substantial share of the early tingles, the electric threads leading down through her abdomen to unite with those radiating from her clitoris which, despite being left alone, throbbed with desire.

The moisture began to seep again, and Claire's thumb transferred it from her vagina to her hot, eager and willing clitoris; tenderly applying the juices, she revived the battered little organ. Deep within herself, Faith could feel the wanting begin again; the monster with the apparently-insatiable appetite inside her acted as though it had hardly been fed at all.

Claire felt the first tremors in Faith's breasts with her lips, the trickling tension which she recognised from her own desires. In response, she took all of Faith's right nipple into her mouth, sucking deeply, using her tongue to jam the rubbery tissue against her upper teeth, letting the discomfort work on quieting Faith's unappeased monster. It was important – not just to Claire, but to the others – that Faith should not be brought to her climax too soon, for there were others to be satisfied yet. Alex would probably want to mount her again; she knew her husband would.

But Faith was not so easily stilled. Lying back with her eyes closed, her pink tongue poking out from the swollen lips, she tried to quell the ache of desire within her; she was more than happy when Claire kissed her mouth, her teeth trapping her tongue in place. As she kissed her, Claire's restless hand soon had Faith panting again, thrusting her hips forward into the embrace. Albert had been a quick fumble man, followed by an even-quicker mounting. Unable to sustain intercourse for long, he had persuaded Faith by sheer repetition and personality – along with a lack of knowledge on her part – of the myth that this was satisfying sex. Faith knew better, now. Before long, Claire's head vanished between Faith's thighs.

Claire knew what she was doing with her tongue around Faith's vulva. She held open her labia with her fingers while she slowly, carefully and, above all lightly, caressed the soft, moist ruby-red skin. The delightful salty taste of the young woman stimulated her tongue to flicker higher, barely touching the glossy skin of the swollen clitoris, then down, changing shape to penetrate the hot moisture of her tunnel. Faith's hips were beyond jerking high against this torture; her exertions filled her limbs with a gentle fatigue which drained her. Though she slowly moved her hips up and down, her autonomic system was sending out uncertain messages which were being reinterpreted by her body. Faith rested her hands in the blonde hair, moaning softly as Claire, misjudging Faith's responses, climaxed, her breath shuddering within her chest.

The young woman, legs apart, eyes closed and mouth opened, arched her back against the sensations which threatened to engulf her perceptions. Her rump lifted off the carpet, balancing her body lewdly on her out-spread feet and her shoulders as she offered herself to Claire's insistent and experienced tongue and fingers, her juices spilling over the fair woman's chin. Faith's open mouth, with nothing to fill it, gaped; the swollen lips held apart as much from passion as from fatigue, emitting noises she was sure she had never made before.

Rupert looked over from the bar to where Claire was sitting, half-turning away from Faith's fleecy crotch, chest heaving with her deep breathing as she tried to regain her composure. Claire knew that she was able to arouse both men and women, yet she had never come across anyone so uninhibited as Faith. There was something wild, yet terrifyingly innocent about this young woman; something she found difficult to understand. Faith had looked thoroughly attractive and normal when she had arrived with Alex, a little awed by the occasion maybe, but others had been the same before her; Alex had that effect on young women. Yet once she had been roused, her reserve had fallen from her; she had become as lascivious as any of the much more experienced women present.

Lillian, attracted by Faith's moaning, returned, and her tongue lapped up all the emissions she could get, covering Faith's entire vulva while the young woman tried to regain her composure. Lillian however would have no truck with such weakness and, within a few minutes, Faith's breathing grew faster and deeper. Lillian's tongue was both an energetic, mobile, soft, moist snake which explored deeply into Faith's sex, and a firm, round spear which shot back and forth. At other times it was a broad, waving leaf which scooped the oily, salty fluid from her very walls.

Carefully, Lillian inched her fingers up Faith's buttocks, separating them gently and moving on until, as Faith lifted her hips to her in ecstasy, Lillian slipped a finger into the optimum position. As Faith's lips returned to the carpet, Lillian's forefinger gently pressed against the wrinkled rim of Faith's anus. Faith felt the touch immediately, but found the sensation not unpleasant. Rather, it enhanced the other sensations her body was producing.

This, she thought, must have been what it was like when Alex inserted his finger into her, or nearly. Then, his erection had been within her, forcing her vaginal passage back against her rectum. Perhaps *that* made a difference. She would have to try to find out, but later. Later. Now she was being stimulated very thoroughly and well.

Slowly, fraction by fraction and with gentle care, Lillian introduced her forefinger into Faith's bottom hole; she watched the expression of awed pleasure on Faith's face, and listened to the catches in her voice as a guide for when to push gently, and when to wait. And, like Claire before her, Lillian's tongue was working, moistening Faith's sexual organs, bringing the younger woman to an extremity of pleasure. That was something they all had to get across to this new addition; the fact that sex was pleasure. Sex was fun! Sex wasn't something to be hidden from the light of day; it was not just furtive fumblings in a darkened bedroom. Sex and pleasure could take place in the open, in the light. With friends.

Quite half an hour after Lillian had begun, the pleasure was finally delivered. Lillian's forefinger could be inserted no further; Faith's hips were raised as she whimpered with pleasure. Already the web between her fingers was pressing on Faith's perineum. But Lillian had no desire to penetrate further; bringing on Faith's pleasure like that had satisfied her. That, and the emissions at which she had lapped, with every expression of delight. Faith had been an inspired choice. She was sure Max would agree with her, and that everyone there would give a good account of her performance. Faith had been Chosen.

Eventually, when Faith's head cleared enough for her to see and think straight, she found she was being caressed by Alex, lying with her back to him whilst his hands smoothed over her young body from shoulders to crotch. Her legs were splayed out, displaying her gaping orifice, but so were Claire's and Prudence's. Claire sat on top of Harry, his short, thick erection pressing against her anus.

In a few moments, Claire knew, her control over those muscles would be overcome.

Then she would slip onto his shaft and Harry would enter her as he had been entering Julia – as he *always* entered Julia – who was kneeling before Colin, her mouth around his rising member. Prudence was sprawled on Simon, who held her sex open with two fingers of his right hand; his middle finger meanwhile gently stroked up her cleft, carrying the moisture she was emitting up to her sharply defined clitoris, which stood proud of the surrounding flesh.

Rupert and Lillian arrived with drinks, a concoction in which champagne had been mixed with ginger, lemon, guavas and a couple of drops of a green liqueur Rupert kept well out of sight of Lillian. He usually denied there was such a liquid to be had, though he had desperately importuned Max for it, until finally he had been given a small bottle with the injunction to use it sparingly. Now they handed out the drinks, Claire glad to rise to collect hers, for her muscular control had been slipping and she knew Harry had distended her opening. It wasn't that she disliked Harry, or being sodomised, for Rupert often obliged her like that. It was just the combination she disliked, though it would have been rude to have refused him.

'Lillian said she'd do the beads,' Rupert said cheerfully, handing round the drinks, making sure that everyone, including Faith, had one.

If anyone deserved one, Faith did. He would be interested, too, to see what effect it had on her. Max had claimed that, administered properly, it would perk up the most jaded palate and, from the look of exhaustion in her eyes, Faith's palate was the most jaded in the room. But then, most of the party had already enjoyed her.

'She'll never do that!' Alex snorted. 'Not now.'

'Who said I won't?' Lillian asked sourly, turning on him from her prone position on the carpet where she had placed herself next to Simon. 'I could show you a thing or two.'

'I agree; you could,' he smiled. 'But you couldn't do three, now. You're too far gone. You'd be lucky to get them *in*, far less out again.'

'No I wouldn't!' she protested. 'Fifty says I could.'

Before Faith was fully aware of it happening, some of the party had begun trying to organise bets on the outcome, the loud and contradictory conversation making any attempt to understand the proceedings impossible. It was at this point that Faith asked in a plaintive, almost querulous voice,

'What's going on, Alex? Betting on what?'

'Lillian's going to do the beads. I've seen her do five. I've even seen her do seven, though that was some time ago. She won't do three, tonight. Not after the rogering she's had. Two's as much as anyone can expect.'

'Oh.' Faith found the explanation less explicit than the comments which had prompted her questions, but Rupert was already marking names on a sheet of paper.

'Alex?'

'Two.'

'Claire?'

'One.'

'Pru?'

'Two.'

'Simon?'

'Four.'

'You'll be lucky,' Rupert grinned. 'Faith?'

'Six.'

'Six? What do you think Lillian's made of? Brass?'

'Six!' Faith insisted, irritated into sullen obstinacy by his superior air, though she had no idea what she was doing.

'It's your money! Harry?'

'If Faith says six, I'll go five.'

'Four,' Julia said without being prompted, digging her teeth into Colin's tender shaft so that his howl had to be repeated.

'Three!' Julia smiled at the response. She would keep him aroused like that until Lillian began 'doing the beads', when she would let him release his pent-up seed. That was what he needed to cure his drooping member; lots and lots of mouth massage.

When all the bets had been marked down – Lillian bet seven – the woman lay on her back on the long-haired sheepskin rug on which Faith had been roused and pleasured, her legs spread wide. In one hand she had a bead necklace which Claire had provided. Each white bead was oval, about one and a half centimetres long, and about half that at the widest point. She unfastened the clasp and, with the necklace in her right hand, used her left hand to open her sex, unable to resist running her soft fingers up and down her swollen, blood-engorged sex lips. After she was calm again, while the tension in the room mounted, Faith – who was still lying on Alex in a position where she could clearly see every detail of Lillian's anatomy – was suddenly surprised to see the woman introduce the ring of the clasp into her vagina then, shifting her grip to the first bead, push gently upwards.

To Faith's mounting amazement, Lillian slowly introduced the beads one by one, not moving quickly, but steadily pushing them, one after another, into her vagina and, after the first three or four, twisting the beads as she pushed.

'Why is she twisting them, Alex?' Faith whispered.

'The string is securely knotted, so they're held rigid. As she turns the beads, the string turns too, and further up, they move. Remember the balls? Remember how you felt? Lillian's feeling that right now.'

'God!' Faith gasped softly, her heart going out to the gasping, flushed woman who was nearing the end of the string, and pressing the beads within her much more slowly.

When she stopped, Simon knelt between her thighs and passed a leather thong through the ring-clasp at the protruding end of the necklace, drawing it through until the knotted end prevented it moving any further. Once done, Lillian pushed the remainder of the necklace deep within herself until she came to a stop, her breathing too deep to continue. Then Lillian released her hold on the thong, placing her hands beside her hips and pressing down while she cleared her mind, trying to ignore Simon.

Simon opened her outer lips and laid the thong up her cleft and across her clitoris before closing them together again, pressing them tight, holding them like that until Lillian tapped his hand. Immediately he withdrew, moving away from her as Lillian took charge. She paused for a few minutes to allow herself to regain normality, her eyes closed, not looking at anyone. She took the free end of the thong in her right hand and tugged it gently, holding her lips closed with the fingers of her left hand all the while.

The thong slipped across her clitoris but she held it away at an angle, so that it made no contact until Alex called, 'Clasp in sight!' which made her stop and recover her composure.

'She's going to pull that thong and bring the beads out again across her clitoris,' Alex whispered in Faith's ear. 'And she'll count them out while she's doing it. She can't stop; she has to keep pulling, so there's no chance of a rest in between them to give herself a break. And she can't just rip them out quickly; Lillian *has* to bring them out slowly, one by one. She thinks she'll get to seven before she comes, but she's too aroused to make three. Your fifty pounds is as good as lost.'

'Fifty pounds?' Faith asked, wondering what he was talking about. Who had said anything about fifty pounds?

'Yes. Your bet,' he answered. 'You bet fifty pounds she could get to six. Remember?'

'Yes. I . . .' She paused. 'What if she reaches eight?'

'Anything above six means Lillian wins,' he said sourly, shaking his head, 'but she won't.'

Faith's eyes grew large and round as Lillian's right hand began to move steadily while, if anything, her left held her sex even more tightly.

'One!' Lillian said with smiling confidence as the first white bead slipped wetly into view.

'There goes your bet, darling.' Rupert hoisted his glass

to Claire, who shrugged, her breasts wobbling provocatively.

'Two!' Lillian's voice was a little more strained as the second appeared and Alex sighed, shaking his head. He had guessed wrong again.

'Three!' Lillian had found a new confidence; the announcement upset Colin, who was on the verge of spilling his seed into Julia's mouth.

'Four!' Lillian's confidence was waning again, the catch in her voice a sign that her pleasure was being brought on quickly so that, 'Five!' sounded shaky, even to her, but her hand never stopped the same, relentless pressure until, 'Six!' As Lillian's hips jerked upwards, her head tipping back as the waves of pleasurable pressure broke within, and she surrendered to the sudden desire inside her. Without waiting, she began to move her hips up and down in a parody of love-making, as she continued to remove all of the beads. Simon knelt to kiss her mouth, while Claire fastened her lips around her left nipple and sucked hard.

When order was restored, Rupert looked around and into Faith's languorous, half-open, heavy eyes, smiling at the sated young woman who had previously performed so beautifully.

'You win, Faith. What made you choose six?'

'Alex said he'd seen her do five and seven,' Faith answered slowly, thinking carefully about the words, unsure whether she was speaking, or dreaming she was speaking. 'I just took an average.'

'You bastard, Alex.' Rupert looked at him in surprise. 'You might have told me!'

'I didn't think she'd make two,' came the unworried answer, and they both laughed.

Chapter Eight

There was no possibility of Alex driving back to Cheyne Walk, so they called a cab at twelve-thirty and, with Faith's winnings stuck in Alex's pocket, they were driven back to the flat. Feeling as though she had been put through the wringer, Faith was almost doubled over when she got into the lift as Alex asked, 'What's the matter? Are you ill? Something you drank?' His concerned expression was turned to her. At the back of his mind was the thought that, twenty-four hours previously, he had brought an almost comatose Faith back to his flat. Was this reaction to alcohol something that happened as a matter of course? If it was, then he hoped that the Stables would cure her of it.

'I'm sore,' Faith answered, not knowing how to stand. She was too sore even to hold herself, but Alex's expression seemed puzzled, as he asked:

'Sore? Where?' His voice held a tender, concerned tone she barely recognised. Albert, in similar circumstances, would just have shrugged and probably told her to stop complaining.

'My fanny!' she answered sharply, glaring at him. How was it that men *always* asked embarrassing questions like that?

Once the pleasure had seeped from her body, when the alcohol and aphrodisiac-induced euphoria had released its hold on her pain-centres, Faith had become aware of the painful pounding she had received in that most sensitive region. Albert's dimensions meant that during sex with him, her vagina had never been properly stretched; until she had bedded Alex. Albert had been fortunate to deflower her. The anxieties of the day had led her to ignore the discomfort, but the steady penetration and various erotic ministrations had almost bruised her sexual organs.

Alex's concern became obvious at once, for his arm encircled her in support, and, once the door of the flat was opened, he almost carried her to the bedroom.

'Just lie flat,' he said, 'I'll get your things off and get you a cold compress, or something.'

'Not cold, please. Not cold,' Faith answered, but Alex was already rolling her onto her side so he could reach the zip.

Once the dress had been slipped off her legs, Faith spread them a little to relieve the pressure on her aching flesh. When he returned from the kitchen, adding a couple of ice-cubes to a washing flannel, Alex separated them further, applying the flannel gently to her mound. Faith drew her legs together, pushing the flannel away, placing her hands above her mound to protect it.

For a moment he looked at her closed eyes, sighed, then nodded to himself. He went into the lounge, and removed the silken ropes which controlled the movement of the curtains there; they were simple to replace and he needed something immediately. Back in the bedroom he fashioned a slip-knot and loop at one end of one rope, and eased it gently over Faith's right ankle before moving her leg outwards towards the side of the bed.

Faith was already in a state of semi-awareness; her breathing shallow, she made no movement to prevent him. He laid the rope down the side of the bed, around the corner of the bedpost, across to the other corner, and up again. Alex moved Faith's left ankle to meet the rope, which he fastened around it with another slip-knot. Then Alex did the same with Faith's wrists, moving her gently and slowly, fastening them to the supports of the headboard, spread wide, so she would be unable to prevent him touching her, or to touch herself.

From the bathroom he brought the rubberised mat which he covered with a thick towel, then lifting up her behind, he slipped it beneath her. Faith moaned when he applied the cold compress to her battered labia, now open to his caress. He could easily have toyed with her, but was more concerned about reducing the pain she was suffering. Her entire crotch looked a dull, angry red, reminding him forcibly of what it would look like after a sound whipping. Yes, my dear girl, he thought, you'll experience that, too, before much longer. But by then you'll be fully trained and have taken your place in the Chosen.

For Faith, the sensations around her hot, sore sexual organs were so similar to those she had just been experiencing that she opened her eyes, thinking that she was dreaming. Yet there was Alex, his concerned expression no dream, and delicious sensations of cold liquid in her crotch. Then her memory returned, the coolness of the liquid reminding her, and she tried to lift her head to peer down her body past her breasts. Then she recalled the mirror.

Looking up, Faith saw herself spread out on the bed, the restraints making the sensations in her ankles and wrists comprehensible. Alex was adding more ice to the flannel. Realising what he had done, she knew she should be angry at being tied in this position, but the gentle easing of her pain brought a smile to her face.

'Alex?' she whispered. His face turned to her at once, though he kept the compress against her flesh with his right hand as he brought his head close to hers.

'What is it, darling?' he asked quietly.

'I didn't know you were like this. Tying girls up at your age. Do you wait outside schools, too?'

'Only for you,' he smiled, wondering where her mind was wandering. Perhaps she had some fever, or maybe this fitted with a dream she'd been having. Waiting outside schools? What could she be thinking about?

'It feels good.' She was able to move her hips a little, pressing her vulva into the pad to show that she appreciated his ministrations.

'I'll leave it alone for a bit,' he said, 'and see how you

are in the morning. It may take a day or so to settle down. You took quite a lot of punishment, one way and another.'

'Are you going to untie me?' Faith asked, her voice not carrying any of the agitation he had expected. There were some women – Prudence was one – who came out in spots just at the thought of being tied like that, while others preferred it that way.

'Do you mind being tied?' he asked. 'Only, it'll stop you pressing your legs together; or playing with yourself,' he added, making them both smile. His other reason was to test her reaction to being tied up. Despite the earlier mention of bondage, this was the first chance he'd had to try it out on her. They might have to spend a good deal of time and trouble at the Stables, training her to be fastened. And even if she enjoyed the sensations of being tied, would she like to fornicate in that position, too? It would be as well to find out, he thought.

'I don't mind,' she sighed, smiling at him. 'Are you going to fuck me, now? I've never . . .'

'No.' He found a smile. 'Not tonight.'

'In the morning?' She sounded anxious.

'Haven't you had enough?' he asked gently.

'Did they all do it?' she asked.

'All but Julia and Prudence, I think,' he answered, then asked: 'Are you disgusted? About the women?'

'I don't know,' she answered, 'I can't think. Ask me tomorrow.'

When Faith moved and felt the restraints, her dream of riding a horse across a flat, deserted beach, vanished, only to be replaced by a dim awareness of her position. With her eyes closed, she allowed herself to think, building slowly on each successive sensation. She was lying on her back on something soft; a bed? But not a bed she could remember; it was *much* softer than any bed she could recall. Her legs were spread wide; wider than any position she would normally adopt. Funny! She could remember Miss . . . Miss Glover! Miss Glover, who had that small moustache which came and went, from time to time. She could remember her standing in front of the class, reminding them that 'nice' girls didn't spread their legs too wide apart, or cross them whilst wearing short skirts. There were several such lectures on what 'nice' girls did and didn't do. From the sound of it, she thought, 'nice' girls didn't have such a good time.

There was something firm around her ankles, too. She tried to close her legs fractionally, but the discomfort in her ankles increased. She tried separating them and, while the discomfort eased, she could feel a distortion in her hips, and she stopped. Her wrists felt the same restriction, and why were they spread like that? Thinking about her position, she imagined herself lying on a pile of warm, soft, newly-mown grass, her arms and legs spread wide, luxuriating in it.

Was the park-keeper watching her from the bushes? They all knew that when he spotted a group of girls, he would prowl around, trying to get a look at their mulberry-coloured knickers. Some of the girls claimed that he was paid by the Head to spot any girl wearing white, non-regulation knickers, but Faith thought that unlikely. Janice Becket had often said that, for a dare, she would take hers off and see if it gave him a heart-attack, but no one had dared her. Was that it? Was she showing her mulberry cotton knickers to the old man?

And yet, there was a strange feeling, down there, between her legs. It was like the time she had slipped in the gymnasium and fallen astride the bar. Luckily the bar had not been high, otherwise she could really have been hurt. The girls had all laughed and said she was lucky not to have been a boy, which made Mrs Tiller red-faced and furious. But there was an ache, as though she had cycled a long way on an uncomfortable saddle. Like the time when Albert had first penetrated her successfully.

Albert! The name caused her to open her eyes as she remembered him; they widened as she looked up at the ceiling. Above her was her reflection. Spread out on a bed! Naked! Wrists and ankles secured at the corners.

Just as, in her imagination, she was being carried off by white-slavers, her memory returned, and with it, a measure of peace. She was lying on Alex's bed and the ache in her crotch had been caused by the effort that had been put into it by, was it five men? Yes, five men and two women; or was it three.

Faith found she was very uncertain about some details, but she could remember the release when Alex's erection had slipped into her burning-hot orifice. Even just with the memory, Faith could feel her breathing altering, as the last vestiges of passion gripped her. If that was what sex was like, if that was true passion, then she wanted as much as she could get. And from the way she remembered the party, it seemed that there was plenty of it to be had. Alex had mounted her twice, after that.

She lay quiet, looking up at herself, half-smiling at the thought of the position she occupied. Would Alex take advantage? She hoped in some ways that he would, for she could feel the stirrings within her again and, for a moment, thought the 'Love Balls' were back in place. But as she concentrated, alternately tightening and then releasing her vaginal muscles, Faith could feel nothing untoward in that region. She moved herself a few times, arching her back to lift her hips to a new position then stopped, waiting for the slow, sensual, lascivious effects of the movement within her. Faith was almost sorry when she felt nothing. The 'Love Balls' had been removed by Lillian before Alex had entered her.

Faith finally called out Alex's name, twice, not loud enough for the passing drivers in the cool, sunny Sunday morning to hear, but sufficiently loud for him to appear a few moments later, tousled, unshaven and surprised, his eyes appearing small in the morning sunlight.

'Hello,' he smiled at her, advancing to stand by the bed. 'How are you this morning?' His whole stance softened at the sight of her.

'Better than you, I hope,' she answered. 'You look as if you've spent the night on the floor.'

'The couch in the drawing room, actually,' he replied,

rubbing his head and trying to ease his back. He still wore his shirt and trousers, but his feet were bare on the thick carpet.

'Oh!' Faith felt ashamed. 'I'm sorry. I didn't mean to take your bed. You should have let me . . .'

'How are you, here?' Alex interrupted, then laid the back of his hand on her sex, watching her face wince slightly at the light pressure, noting the still savage heat.

'All right,' she lied, trying to force her facial muscles to revert to the bland expression she preferred to adopt.

'No you're not!' he answered at once, sharply. 'You're still hot there, for one thing. Too hot. I should cool that down before you do anything else.'

'Untie me, please, Alex,' Faith urged, 'I have to get up.'

'I'll put another compress on that, first,' he warned her, already turning away.

'I can sit in a bath,' she protested, 'the warm water will do it good,' and, when he gave her a jaundiced look, she added anxiously, 'I need to pee.'

Faith had more control over her bladder than that, but she knew that it was a risk he dared not take. He could argue with her about the state of her injuries, but something as basic as this knocked all his rational thinking sideways. Alex knew when he was beaten, but he looked her in the eye, adopting a stern expression.

'Okay,' he agreed, 'I'll unfasten you. But when you've had your pee, and your bath, I want you right back here, again.' His expression was so serious that she felt herself obliged to challenge it on principle.

'Why?' she smiled. 'Do you like looking at my fanny?'

'Faith,' he sighed, shaking his head, 'I was up until two-thirty this morning putting cold compresses on you there.' He gestured to her open sex. 'Now you act as though it's cured. You know it's not; I know it's not, so why be silly? You can come back to bed for a while and lie there with your legs apart. You don't need pressure on it right now. I can get your breakfast to you and everything.'

'Do you want to fuck me, Alex?' she asked. 'I don't mind if you do.' As far as Faith could see, it was the only reason for keeping her in this impossibly erotic position. A tentacle of her mind wondered what it would be like to be kept like that permanently, or at least, held like that while someone penetrated her. She felt the stirrings within her abdomen as he replied:

'Have you forgotten what you felt like when we got back, last night? You could hardly stand. You certainly couldn't *walk*. You don't cure that with a cold compress, two aspirin and a night's sleep.'

'All right,' Faith sighed, seeing some of the sense he was trying to make. 'I'll lie down again. I promise.'

'And I'll make sure your legs are kept apart,' he promised her, 'with this.' He unfastened the silk from her right ankle.

Alex ran the bath while Faith used the lavatory, ignoring her blushing protests that she didn't need him there. She had never had anyone present when she had used the lavatory before; not since she was old enough to go by herself. He turned away, getting on with what he was doing, then helped her into the bath, added some salts to the water, and left her alone.

He returned ten minutes later with a strong cup of tea, and a smile so broad that she was forced to return it. Despite her misgivings, she had to admit that it was pleasant to lie back in the warm water, allowing her thoughts and body to drift. Her hands found her vulva, and she ran her fingers lightly over the flesh, feeling the areas which still seemed sore. The ache was centred around her vagina, so her memories had been true. Several men had penetrated her last night.

Thinking logically, she should have been angry; not so much at Alex or the other men – she was a woman and men had, if not a right to penetrate her, then at least an inclination – but at the memory of Claire and Lillian! Especially Lillian! The blonde woman had played her like a violin. She seemed to know every fibre of her body, and her mind. She had known, before Faith, the precise state of her arousal, and how to bring it about. She had been able to tell Alex when he should mount her. God! His erection had been *so* welcome. It was large and hot and strong, which was just what she needed to scratch the terrible itch she had felt, high within her.

To her surprise, Faith found herself gently caressing her clitoris, then quickly stopped. That was no way for a properly-brought-up young woman to behave. If she started doing that, who knew where it would end? Sitting more upright, she began to plan for the day. Sunday. Was it only Friday when she had left work with Albert, dressed for the party in Belgravia where her life had changed? She could remember the excitement as Albert had tried to impress upon her the range of people whom she would meet, what to do and what not to do. She had been tempted to tell him that her education had included manners, that she knew when to speak and when to hold her tongue – which is more than she could say for him.

Now, Albert was a strange little man with a small penis and an uncertain temper, whom she worked for – or thought she did. She would have to see about that on Monday. Not Albert the Provider. Not Albert the Lover. Not Albert the Sex Educator. It was Albert the Redundant, as far as Faith was concerned. Yet, as she dried herself, looking into the mirror, making sure the ends of her hair were dry too, she wondered what would happen on Monday. Did she go into the office and act as though nothing had happened? Why not? She had a job, she liked it, and if Albert wanted to be funny about it . . . She'd cross that bridge on Monday. She had shown that she knew what she was doing, despite Albert's help. Gibb McInley Gower wasn't going to collapse if she left, and she knew that she could get another position in advertising with what she had learned there. So she had something to thank Albert for, although the knowledge had been won at a high price.

Alex was waiting in the bedroom when she arrived from the bathroom, sitting on the bed; he looked up from his business papers. Faith was going to say something when he rose, indicating the mat and towel which he had placed in the centre of the bed.

'Alex . . .' but he cut her short.

'I'll apply the compress again,' he said, 'you have a rest. After our visitor arrives we'll take a slow walk, all right? If you just lie about you'll stiffen up. Or I will.'

'Visitor?' Faith asked. 'What visitor?'

'Julia,' he smiled at her. 'She's got some things for you, I hope.'

'Some "things"?' Faith repeated, frowning at him. 'What kind of things? Alex, what are you talking about?'

'A surprise.' He laid a finger alongside his nose, smiling again; 'I've got a surprise for you. Julia's bringing it with her.'

'Alex!' she protested, but then grimaced, shook her head and, seating herself on the edge of the bed, moved back onto the towel.

It reminded her of her first night with Albert. She had told him she was a virgin and he had put the towel beneath her in case she bled all over the bed. It had failed because he hadn't penetrated her enough and, when he did rupture her hymen, the towel had been forgotten. That was her fault, too, apparently.

'Spread your legs, Faith,' Alex said, then fastened the loop around her right ankle, pulling it wide into position. Within a few seconds, both ankles were secured.

'You just like tying women up,' she accused. 'Haven't you got a gag to put in my mouth? Or are you going to put something else in there?' She had seen what Julia and Prudence had been doing, and remembered some of the girls discussing whether boys preferred that to normal sex. Would Alex? And would he tie her up and make love to her? Even with a pain in her sex, she found the prospect enticing.

'There are times when I feel like gagging you,' he agreed, but he was amused and she found herself laughing with him.

He brought the flannel and ice cubes, gently running the cold fabric up the soft skin on the inside of both thighs to get her used to the idea of the compress, but Faith's breathing rose again and she asked him to stop.

'Please, Alex!' she protested. 'You don't know what that does to me.'

'Tell me,' he suggested, holding the compress just short of her vulva, looking up at her. There seemed to be waves of coldness coming off it, a gentle zephyr which was sending prickles of delight through her again. One of these days, he thought, I'll have to try that suggestion Max made, about putting an icicle up her anus whilst taking her from behind. It was supposed to tighten up the muscles, which he could well believe. Remembering the grip Faith had taken of his erection, he thought she might break it.

'Just put it on my fanny, Alex. I can stand the cold, but I can't stand you tickling me like that. Oh, God! That's freezing!' she gasped, as he took her at her word; she strained to escape up the bed, but she was held securely by the silken rope. After a few seconds, still gasping, she nodded to him and lay back on the pile of pillows he had prepared for her, allowing her system to adjust.

'Now. Breakfast in bed?' he asked.

'Naked? With a cold compress on my fanny?'

'What would you prefer,' he asked, 'an icicle up there?' but he was already on his way out of the room. Alex was uninterested in bondage, apparently. At least, she thought, he hasn't retied my hands.

Chapter Nine

Julia arrived at twelve-thirty, being ushered into the bedroom as Faith's expression of panic signalled to Alex that lying in this position was *not* how she expected to receive visitors. He might at least, she thought, have thrown something over her, even just over her hips. Instead, Julia walked elegantly into the room, smiling brightly, a small brown case in her hand.

'Faith, darling.' She leant over the bed to kiss Faith's cheek, then looked down at the nude, helpless figure, asking, 'Is something the matter, Alex, or are you already training Faith in restraint? I must say it's a . . .'

'Faith was a bit bruised, last night,' Alex replied, his eyes flashing warning signals to her.

'I'm not surprised.' Julia turned to face her again. 'All those men banging away at you like that. What's that? A cold compress? Best thing for it.'

Faith's surprise at Julia's acceptance of her position was compounded when Alex unfastened the rope from her ankles as Julia laid her case on the bed. She seemed to accept as quite unremarkable the fact that Faith was spread out like this, and Faith wondered about her comment 'already training her in restraint'. Then Julia was opening the case, asking, 'Has Alex told you what I've got for you?'

'No,' Alex shook his head, 'just; a surprise.'

'What do you think of this?' Julia asked and, from her case, brought out a pair of knickers.

They were small and white; the waistband was white, from which white suspenders hung, but the rest was so sheer that it hardly had any colour. Julia held them up, showing that the elasticity was sufficient.

'Try them on,' Julia urged as Faith asked:

'Where did you get them?'

'Julia makes them,' Alex answered. 'Last night at the party, I gave Julia your measurements and asked to have a couple of sets for today. Thanks, Julia.'

'It was a pleasure, Alex, dear boy,' the older woman answered, as Faith slipped the garment up her legs. Once in position, Faith looked at herself in the mirror marvelling that the line of the leg went precisely up her groin, yet it seemed there was only a thin haze of fabric across her skin.

Every detail of the mound and pubic hair could be seen and, hardly thinking of what she was doing, Faith separated her legs so that she could see the hot red line of her labia beneath.

'Try this, too.' Julia brought out a brassière, holding it in front of Faith for her to put her arms through the straps, then pulled it on and fastened it.

Faith winced, for there seemed to have been some mistake in the measurements. It was made, like the knickers, of white fabric with the almost transparent gauze between, but it had been made too small for her. Her breasts felt as if they were being squeezed, and there was no point to the cups, just circular holes. Before she could say anything, Julia placed her fingers on the upper surface of her breasts one after the other, depressing them in turn, and bringing the hardening nipples poking through the holes into the open. Instantly she could feel them swelling, the slight constriction of the fabric around the areolae making them thrust outwards.

'It's . . .' Faith hardly liked to make an unfavourable comment, but Julia intervened with:

'You think it's too small, don't you? It's meant to be. This strap around the circumference of your breast is slightly smaller than the breast itself, so it compresses the flesh, pushes it out and provides *some* support. It squeezes the nipples, though I think, you know, Alex, Faith would benefit from nipple rings. She has such lovely nipples. What do you think?'

'I think she looks amazing,' Alex answered, looking Faith's reflection in the eye.

For a few moments Faith looked at him, then back again, unable to believe what she was hearing.

'You want me to wear this?' she asked.

'Yes,' he nodded. 'It enhances your figure.'

'It makes my tits poke out!' Faith exclaimed. 'That's what it does.'

'And what's wrong with that?' Julia asked. 'I wear nothing else, normally. My breasts are flat and small; I was always flat-chested. But I've gradually forced them out until now . . .' Julia opened her neat, cream blouse to show Faith.

Julia wore the same type of flesh-coloured brassière, its smaller holes entirely filled with her nipples, its shape clearly enhancing the size of her breasts. For a moment Faith stood irresolute, shaking her head, then asked, 'Doesn't it hurt?'

'A little to start with,' Julia agreed, 'but then, your period hurts for a little while, too. It's no worse than that and, after a few days, you won't even notice. I'd suggest those nipple rings, though. Enlarge your nipples, Faith. They're lovely now but, just a *little* larger and they'll be magnificent.'

The frankness of the advice quite took Faith's breath away as she looked at her reflection again, then looked at Julia, protesting, 'I look naked.'

'The best foundation garments try to achieve that,' Julia replied. 'A natural shape without all the straps and bones. In your case, you could tie two silk handkerchiefs together to cover your breasts, and they'd still look good.'

'What about the stockings, Julia?' Alex asked. 'Did you manage to get those?'

'Yes; only in white, though.' Julia turned back to her case. 'It was all I could get at such short notice. Even then, my friend had to open up specially for me.'

Neither would be satisfied until Faith had donned the

white stockings, who, rolling them up her legs, wondered when they would ever stop. They were edged with lace which ended a mere inch from her crotch, held by the short suspenders hanging from the waistband of the knickers. They made Faith's already long and slim legs look even longer. Gazing at her reflection, the young woman swallowed, knowing that what she was seeing was a new Faith, a different Faith to the one who had taken refuge with Alex. More sensual and sophisticated.

'Do you like it?' Julia asked, cocking her head on one side, looking at Faith's reflection.

'I have to say yes, thank you.' Faith lowered her eyes while her throat worked, then looked at Julia again, watching the dark eyes sparkling with appreciation.

'They come in several colours,' the older woman said, 'ivory, peach, black, red, and flesh, of course. And I'd suggest a different style, too. French knickers, in case you're worried about VPL.'

'VPL?' Alex frowned, looking at Julia with a puzzled expression.

'Visible panty line,' the small woman smiled at him. 'You wouldn't know anything about that, would you?'

'No,' he agreed, smiling again at the thought.

'Are you telling me it wasn't you who ran a finger down the edge of my knickers the other night at Betty's?' Julia asked. 'You wicked boy.'

'Ah!' He flushed. 'Well . . .'

'Next time, I'll expect you to take them off,' she said gently, smiling up at him, then swung back to Faith. 'Happy with them, then?'

'Well,' she gulped, shrugging, looking for help to Alex, who just grinned. 'How much do I owe you?'

'That's all been taken care of, hasn't it, Alex?' Julia asked, turning to the tall man.

'Yes!' he said quickly. 'Actually, it has.' He wished he was elsewhere.

'Alex!' Faith protested, but between the two of them, they quelled her.

Julia asked what colours Faith wanted and, when she

was unable to make up her mind, said that she'd make a selection and deliver them – with matching stockings – as soon as she could. Refusing the offer of a glass of wine or anything else alcoholic, Julia left the other items on the bed, closed her case and, clucking like a hen, made her way out.

When Alex returned to the bedroom, Faith was still standing admiring herself, twisting this way and that.

'She's going to make some crotchless knickers,' he leant on the doorframe, 'so you'll be more accessible.'

'Is sex all you ever think of?' Faith asked.

'It's the single most important thing in our lives, next to breathing and eating,' he answered. 'Sex is what makes us what we are: we're born a particular sex. What we make of it determines our jobs, pleasures, our lives sometimes. Bad sex impoverishes families, ruins marriages and can bring down companies and governments. Good sex can make life worth living, and it needn't be like last night, either.'

'I never realised that something like last night could happen to me. I thought it was something that the *News of the World* reported. That it happened to someone else. That things like that were . . .'

'Depraved?' he asked. 'Is that what you think?'

'Yes,' Faith answered reluctantly, 'something like that.'

'Do you feel depraved?' he asked quietly, trying not to allow his expression to guide her answer.

'You're asking me?' Faith found the question amusing. 'Last night I took on all comers. I had more pricks in me than a pub dartboard. I had women, *women*, licking out my cunt! And I ended up on that bed, *tied*. My legs apart. And again today, Julia came in and found me like that. What do you think I feel like?' Her amusement was eroding as she recounted the litany of what had happened, her voice rising gradually to a higher and sharper level, but still she looked in the mirror.

Her nipples were firm and some of the soft, pink, surrounding coral behind them was pushed through the circular holes. Unconsciously, she was standing with legs splayed and, as she sighed, Faith reached down and through the fabric, parting the lips of her sex, letting the outer lips spread on the soft white, fine gauze.

'Now,' she sighed, nodding at his reflection, 'I feel depraved.'

'How do you feel, down there?' he asked.

'Why?' She looked at him. 'Are you ready again?'

'No,' he answered in a tone which she recognised as quiet irritation, 'but there are some things I'd like to show you.'

'Sorry,' she nodded, swallowing hard. 'Really. I suppose that after last night, I thought that all you wanted to do was fuck me.'

'I would love to,' he said, 'but later. Tonight, perhaps, if you're feeling up to it.'

'What do you want me to do, then?' Faith asked, sighing at the thought that soon he would be resuming his former attentions.

'Why don't we see if what you've learned so far is effective, Faith?' he asked, smiling as without any protest, he closed in on the young woman.

Faith stood transfixed, her eyes widening as she watched their reflections. Alex, after slowly removing her only two garments, ran his half-open mouth all over her breasts, her stomach and thighs, particularly the soft, inner aspects, before coming to rest on her hot, aromatic vulva. With gentle, supple fingers he opened her and began, with tongue and lips, to stimulate the liquid musk which oozed from her quim, proving that Lillian was not the only one who knew how to bring her to a long, shuddering climax.

Long before she reached this stage, her senses assaulted not only by the actual sensations from her body, but also by the visual stimulation of watching him do these things, Faith ceased to stand quietly. Her hips jerked and she was sighing, groaning, crooning with delight as he practised his skill on her. Not bad, Alex thought as he worked, at least the experience of the party hasn't made her feel disgusted or repelled by the sensations. He tapped

Faith's anus, pressed it and would have gone further, but his memory brought him back to the present.

Alex had intended to teach Faith something about the more reasonable and useful aspects of advanced sexual techniques in that morning's lesson, though her overstimulated crotch was now a setback. Still, there was time to introduce her to something vaguely familiar, something he knew she would enjoy because it was similar to what Lillian had been doing the previous night.

Faith was off on a cloud of her own; her breathing was fast and harsh as the desire he had stimulated sought an escape, and Alex had to bring her back by flicking a leather thong across her arm and back, stinging her flesh into paying him complete attention.

'Faith, this is serious,' Alex said, when she was focused. 'We can do that later tonight, if you want, but not now. I'd like to show you something important. Do you know what this is?' he asked holding up the cord he had used on her.

She was prepared to swear it was a whip he had used and, though some of the stinging had gone off, she could still feel the tender flesh on her arm. It had assuaged her longing, that hot, liquid yearning within her body which, if left too long, would begin to seep from her without her being able to prevent it. Yet Faith knew that he would never allow her to reach that stage. He may have strange ideas about sex and pleasure, but he was hardly cruel to her. If she was stimulated, she would be relieved of the ache.

Dragging all her concentration to the fore, Faith studied the item he held out to her. It was a simple leather thong, knotted in places with a loop at one end, which ended abruptly some two inches after the last knot. In all, it comprised about eighteen inches of thin, square-sectioned leather.

'No; looks nasty,' she replied, wondering if this was where he whipped her. She had no evidence that he would, of course but, after the previous night, when she had found people doing the strangest things to each other, anything was possible. If he suggested that she lie still while he took a whip to her, would she leave? A frightened little voice within her told Faith that she would not.

'This will bring you absolute ecstasy,' the tall young man smiled at her. Then, checking the lights, he said, 'Lie down, Faith. On the bed, legs apart.'

'Legs apart, of course,' she answered, but she was smiling at him. While she moved from the mirror onto the bed, Alex was removing his clothes so that he was naked when he joined her, his warmth taking the chill off her skin. Holding the thong before her, he asked:

'Have you seen this before, Faith?'

'No.' Faith's eyes focused on it; there was a vague memory of something like it. A thong, yes, but her mind was unable to place it.

Alex sensed that there was something at the back of her mind, for he spoke quietly and calmly, reminding her of the previous night's party.

'Lillian used something like this to bring the beads from her cervix, remember? Only that one wasn't knotted like this one. Yes?' Seeing her eyes clear as the memory returned, he went on, 'This is very similar, only it's much more simple, and the knots act like the beads. They're much smaller, of course; rougher, too. But they perform the same function. They stimulate the clitoris. I'm going to push it up inside you, Faith,' the young man said, while Faith stared at the well-used implement with eyes as wide as he had ever seen them. She remembered Lillian's carefully-controlled spasms as she tried to reach the level of seven beads. Lillian had been using beads for some time and if that was what it did to *her* . . . but Alex was talking again, his voice a quiet, confident monotone as he continued to explain what he intended to do.

'There's nothing to worry about, my darling. I'm going to use my fingers to push it up your vagina and into your cervix so that only the loop hangs out. You won't feel all that much, actually. Not for something as small as this.'

While Faith lay with a surprised and partly frightened look on her face, Alex opened her hot, moist vulva, feeling her jerk beneath him as he touched her again. Inserting the loose 'tail' first, Alex placed his finger on the first knot and pushed upwards, slipping three or four in behind it as he turned his attention back to the young woman.

'When it's up there, it should nestle just around your cervix.' He paused, checking to see that what he was doing was right, then said, 'When you've had it there for a minute or two – or even longer, possibly – I'll pull on that loop that's hanging out.'

High above her on the ceiling, Faith could see every detail of what he was doing, and felt the distraction of the divergence of her senses. Her sight was telling her one thing, but her sense of touch was giving an altogether different impression. Her body could feel the thong, and her mind was telling her that this was going to overload her pleasure circuits.

'It'll come out very slowly,' Alex said, 'one knot at a time. It's a very delicate balance, you see. Not everyone is made the same, or reacts the same, and of course they react differently to this than to the beads. I won't get it right first time, darling, but eventually, we'll both get the hang of it, timing it right. And when we do, you'll be absolutely dripping, I promise you. But I've got to use one of those thin dildos, because I can't push it far enough in, and I want as much of it in there as I can get.'

Red-cheeked, Alex finished the task a few moments later, aware that slipping such an item into Faith's vagina was not what she had expected him to be doing.

'Now; why don't you have a rest for a moment, and we'll carry on where we left off later?' Alex asked.

Alex had been correct. It took him three attempts before he got the speed just right, pulling the loop at the right rate, adjusting it to her breathing and the little excited cries she was giving out. First, as she had seen Lillian do the night before, he laid the loop up across her mound, then closed her outer lips around it; he held them tightly closed with his fingers before he began to pull on the loop. As each knot was freed from within her, the comparative roughness of the knotted leather, giving a scratching sensation as it emerged, was slowly drawn across the surface of her clitoris, with predictable results. The process seemed to send waves of agonisingly pleasant sensations thrilling through her entire body. Faith's hips flailed about, which finally convinced Alex that in Faith's case, restraints might be needed if he was to repeat this stimulation.

Alex gave Faith three attempts, varying the speed while he tried to judge it right. Each of them was arousing, while on the final one, Faith was begging him to stop and do it again, crooning endearments to him in between. Smiling at her reaction, more confident now of her eventual success, he sat beside her, stroking the side of her face until she had calmed down again. Then he asked, 'Would you like me to show you something else, Faith? Or have you had enough for one day?'

'Could I have a drink?' Faith asked, running her tongue around her parched lips.

'Certainly.' He sounded contrite for not having suggested it before. 'Champagne?'

'Champagne?' She looked surprised, her expression doubtful.

'I'll tell you what I'll do. I'll get you something you'll like. Just stay there and rest, darling.'

'Like this?'

'Like that,' he grinned. 'Don't move. Unless, of course, you're cold?' His smiling expression clouded over, but she reassured him.

'No! I was just . . .' But Alex, having heard the first word, was already heading for the door to the hallway.

Faith could hear him in the kitchen; there was a rattle of china and the familiar 'pop' of a champagne cork, then he was back again with a tray. A tray? Faith struggled up onto her elbows as the tall man placed it on the bed beside her, asking, 'Had this before? Cornflakes and champagne?'

'Cornflakes . . .?' Faith stopped, looking at the two bowls on the tray where she had expected to find the more familiar glasses. Each was piled high with the familiar cornflakes, and, as Faith watched in amazement, Alex poured some of the clear, fizzing liquid into the bowls.

'Don't make up your mind until you try it,' he said, handing her one of the bowls.

'I can't see . . .' She stopped, shaking her head.

'Just try it,' he urged, 'and then we'll shower, and I'll see about teaching you some more, if you're up to it.'

After a few moments of silence, Faith reluctantly nodded, looking at the tense, expectant features of the naked man beside her. Before she spoke she considered him carefully, noting the half-aroused state of his member. Unless she was stupid, that would be slipping into her again. The thought thrilled her as she said, 'Not bad. I didn't think it would go together, but it's not bad at all.'

'It's a mild aphrodisiac,' he replied, 'probably based more on the champagne than the cornflakes. They'll give you some energy, of course, but I'm glad you like it. It's just what you need as a "pick-me-up" in the middle of a session like this.'

'Do you . . .' Faith finished her mouthful. 'Do you often have sessions like this? Times when you just lie around fucking and sucking?'

'Faith!' he protested, closing his eyes, worrying her.

'What's the matter?' she asked.

She had thought that she was being sophisticated in asking about it so openly, but she had offended his sensibilities.

'Faith.' He stopped again, taking a few breaths while he pondered the best way to answer her. 'I . . . it's like this. What happened last night with Lillian was unusual, but Max *taught* Lillian. She was a great pupil, his best, he says. And most, if not all, of the women there last night have been taught some of those techniques. Not just by Max, but by their husbands and lovers. We all, at some time, acquire that knowledge, perhaps the way monkeys learn. By watching others.

'It's at times like this, lazy Sundays, that we have a chance to practise them, or put them into practice. Sexual proficiency isn't something you're born with, although from the age of puberty, any young couple can physically have sex. The physical ability is innate, but the more advanced practices aren't. They have to be learned. You could have gone through life and never known about any of this, and been very happy, too. But the fact is that we all happen to believe that there's more to sex and pleasure than just mechanical, animal coupling.

'We respect our bodies and our minds; we don't abuse them with drugs or dangerous practices, although some of our friends do. There's room for quite a diverse selection; the Chosen come from a very broad church. And while it's permissible to talk about "fucking" in moments of passion – and to use quite a lot of the other terms, too – here, like this, I don't think it's necessary. Do you?'

'I'm sorry, Alex.' Faith was blushing. 'I thought that, you know, I should. I was only trying to be . . . well . . .' She stopped, took a deep breath and would have stuttered her way through an explanation had not the smiling man made a suggestion.

'Why don't you eat up? Do you want some more?'

'No.' She shook her head. 'This is fine,' she said as she spooned some more into her small mouth.

'Right,' he nodded, '"Sufficient unto the day is the evil thereof".'

Alex waited until Faith had finished her bowl of cornflakes, then from the dresser where she knew he kept his 'kit', brought out what she took to be a necklace. The individual plastic beads were just the right size, though more widely spaced than was usually the case; the necklace would not have been out of place on a 'flapper', being three feet long, though there were no catches holding the ends together. One bead was three times the size of the other. With vivid memories of Lillian in her mind, Faith was in no doubt about the purpose of this strange device.

'Oh, God!' she gasped, her breathing immediately

beginning to deepen. She had seen the effect they had had on Lillian, a far more experienced woman than she was.

'What's the matter?' he asked, looking at her with a mystified expression. 'This is just another device like the knotted thong. You saw Lillian use one yesterday evening. What's the matter?'

'That's just it,' Faith breathed. 'I saw what happened. I couldn't . . .' She shook her head, but he was already talking again.

'In Japan, they use four slightly larger balls on a chain and call it *konomi-shinju*: "Pleasure Pearls", though they come in all sizes and numbers. There, they're used by either sex and they're pushed into male and female rectums; or is it "rectae"?' He paused, looking at her with a frowned question in his eyes. 'Anyway, at the moment of climax, they're withdrawn, slowly. I'm going to push as much of this as I can up into your vagina like I did with the thong. Do you think you can take it?'

One look at his hopeful expression was enough for Faith. Even if it hurt her, she thought, she was going to take as much of this as she could stand. Alex is taking a lot of time and trouble to do this for me, she told herself, so the least I can do is co-operate.

Starting with the end furthest from the largest bead, he did his best to insert it, gently and patiently pressing and turning, trying to avoid over-stimulating Faith; finally, he had to give up when there were still six inches protruding.

'Now.' He laid a hand flat in the centre of Faith's abdomen, which was slightly distended from the beads within; he could feel the slight bumps of firmness, and knew that it was as packed-out as he could contrive. 'Are you all right?'

'Yes, thank you, Alex.' Faith's answer was soft for, despite the knobbly beads within her, she felt very aroused. She had found inserting the 'Love Balls' something of a trial; the intimate touch had made her tremble at first. The knotted thong had been another, but she had survived, yet the cold slippery feeling of the beads now set her up for what was to come. She knew now why Lillian had paused between the insertion and withdrawal; it was to give her body time to recover.

Alex too was pausing, looking at her flushed expression, trying to judge when it would be practical to begin. Both of them expected that, quite soon, Faith would be gasping, her hips writhing with delicious pleasure as he drew the beads, warm and moist, from her body and across her clitoris.

'I'm going to pull gently, Faith. Steadily. Like you saw Lillian do last night. I'm not going to press too hard on your little "bud". I'll leave that for another time, when you need to be shown that stimulation. For now, removing them from your moist little mouth there will be about enough. All right?'

'Yes.' Faith licked her lips, swallowing to relieve her parched throat. 'Thank you, Alex.'

'I'm going to give you some stimulation,' he said in a warning tone, then began to pull gently on the largest bead.

Holding her stiff sex lips closed around them with the fingers of his left hand, Alex controlled the tension of the beads across the straining surface of her clitoris, watching as that small organ began to swell again. Long before the beads were all out, Faith's hips were heaving, her gasps and cries of sexual arousal filling the room. Her musk pervaded his nostrils as he nodded his recognition of the efficacy of the treatment. Yes. When she was more experienced, he thought, when she returned from the Stables, perhaps, he would use this method of arousal again.

As the last bead was removed, Alex, who wanted to clamber up between Faith's legs, laid the warm, sticky string aside. His erection had risen with the aroma of her musk so that he was ready for her, but he knew he should check the state of her vulva, and enjoying himself within her was hardly an option. Her gasp of delight and satisfaction at the first touch of the tip of his tongue in her vaginal opening was enough to convince him that she was ready, too. He wanted to ignore everything, to concentrate on working his member deeply into Faith, then on riding her firmly until she climaxed, but it would have been needlessly cruel. Besides, there would be other times.

After satisfying *some* of Faith's desires with his tongue and fingers, whilst being careful to avoid the tender flesh around her cleft, he asked, 'Do you want to walk? We could go over the river to the park. Or up the King's Road again, if you'd rather.'

'Are you going to put those balls in again?' Faith asked, feeling that if he was, then she would stay in bed.

'No, not today. One tomorrow, though.'

'One?' She frowned. 'Why one? Why only one?'

'Because it'll be a long day and two would have you screaming before the end of it. As it is, I expect you to take it out and bring it back in your handbag.'

'You don't think I can take it, eh?' She smiled, then shook her head, rising from the bed.

The first thing she saw, draped at the bottom of the bed, were the white knickers and brassière, both of which made her smile a little.

'I suppose I'd better put these away and get my other things on,' she said. 'I can't very well go out walking on a Sunday in those.'

'There's somewhere I have to go,' he said. 'You could come with me. It's not far; a walk. I have to check on a friend's property, in Old Church Street.'

'Why do you have to . . .?' she began, but the expression he turned towards her stopped Faith in her tracks.

'You always want to know why, don't you?' he asked quietly. 'You can't accept things as they are.'

'I'm sorry, Alex,' she said, 'but I'm new to all this. I don't have any experience of what to do. How to go about things. I'm trying to learn.'

'Yes,' he smiled his apology, 'I know; I should have realised. Kim's off on his boat and his house is empty. I have keys and I check it every so often for him. Pick up the mail and the free papers that every fool sticks through the door. Stops it being burgled.'

'When do we start?' Faith asked, more brightly than she felt. She collected the knickers and brassière brought by Julia and would have put them away had he not asked:

'Why not try them?' he said as he rose from the bed. She had not thought of an answer, had made no sign she had heard, when he laid a hand on her wrist.

'No, Faith. As a favour to me, if nothing else. Put them on.'

'Why?' she asked, turning to look at him, surprised by the strength and firmness of his hold on her. 'Would you get a thrill thinking about what I've got on underneath as we walk?'

'And seeing your nipples poke out through your blouse,' he answered with a boyish grin, releasing her. 'That's the bit I like.'

'You . . . you kinky devil!' She smiled at him, shaking her head. But knew she would do as he asked.

Faith wore a white skirt and blouse of a light fabric, both of which buttoned up the front, and white shoes which made a clacking sound on the hard marble floor of the entrance hall as they left. Alex and Faith strolled up past the Holy Redeemer Church, stopping to admire the burgeoning wisteria which was gradually flowering as it sprouted from the front of various houses, the scent heavy with the promise of a hot summer. Mid-afternoon in Chelsea on Sunday, even with a bright, warm sun on the pavements meant quiet; apart from tourists, there were few others about.

They crossed the King's Road, where traffic approached mid-week proportions. Faith was surprised at seeing just how busy that semi-fashionable thoroughfare could be. They continued down the leafy avenues of Carlyle Square, the gardens bursting with greenery until they turned left then right into Old Church Street, heading for Fulham Road.

The house was set back from the road, with a small front garden which had been reduced to a few overgrown beds amid the flagstones. Alex waited whilst Faith preceded him through the stout door, having to push hard to gain access. When he closed it, Faith was already crouching to pick up the pile of papers which had been pushed through the ornate, tarnished letterbox. Most of the mail was addressed to 'The Occupier'. Between them they separated the genuine mail from the circulars and free newspapers, Alex dumping the latter in the small dustbin hidden behind the pillar of the gateway at the front.

When he returned, Faith was looking around her at the decorations in the hallway which ran directly from front to back, half-panelled, with a series of coloured sporting prints from the eighteenth century on the walls above the dark wood.

'Do you want to see the place?' he asked. 'I don't suppose Kim would mind. He's rather proud of his house. Says it's the most degenerate place in Chelsea, and I believe him.'

'No.' She flushed. 'I was just curious. Why degenerate?' He smiled at her.

'Actually – ' He stopped, his smile broadening. 'There *is* something I'd like you to see. Come on.' Alex took her hand, pulling her gently after him.

The house had been closed up for some time; dustcovers concealed much of the furniture on the ground floor, but when Alex led the way upstairs, Faith was surprised to find that, apart from drawn curtains, most of the furniture in the rooms was uncovered. Leading the way into one room, Alex indicated a canopied bed with a flourish, asking, 'There! What do you think of that?'

'A four-poster bed,' she laughed. 'I've never seen one before.' She crossed to examine the delicate slender uprights supporting the canopy above.

'It's too stuffy here for this sort of thing, don't you think?' Alex asked.

'I think it's lovely,' Faith answered. There was a bare mattress on the bed, looking as though it had seen good service. 'And so wide.'

'Yes,' he agreed, 'but when you entertain your mistress in bed, you need room to manoeuvre.'

'Mistress . . .?' She looked at him, then flushed. 'That's me, isn't it?'

She had never given it a thought, before. She was Alex's mistress. Just as she had been Albert's mistress before that, though she had always preferred the term 'living together'. She couldn't imagine Albert having a mistress. A mistress was something exotic. A 'kept woman', her mother had always said, lowering her voice, too. Something not very nice, and yet, she rather liked being Alex's mistress. She was proud of the fact, too. Walking to this house, she had thrust her naked nipples against the fabric of her blouse, daring the world to look, thinking that anyone could tell at a glance that she was a 'kept woman'.

'You look hot,' he said changing the subject. 'Are you?'

'Yes. How long are we going to be here?' Faith asked. 'I'm looking forward to getting my stockings off.'

'Stockings?' He looked down to where Faith held out her right leg for his inspection. There was the familiar white sheen of a stocking.

'Why bother in this weather?' he asked.

'I can't not wear them, Alex,' Faith protested, 'not after you bought them for me. I'm almost too hot to take them off.'

'Do you want to?' he asked, but she shook her head.

'No,' she answered. 'You can take them off when we get back. You've done just about everything else.'

'Why not do it now?' he asked. 'You *do* look a little like a well-cooked lobster.'

'I'm not used to the heat this early in the year,' Faith agreed.

Dropping her handbag on the dresser just inside the door, Faith crossed the room to the bed; turning and sitting on the end, she looked at him for a moment, regaining her composure. With all the windows closed, the room was very warm, the smell of mustiness and old furniture like a scent. Alex could feel the sweat prickling his skin as Faith placed her hands alongside her hips on the mattress. She slid backwards onto the bed, laying her back down, looking up at the canopy for a moment. Above her, the fabric hung about the edges of the four posts, suspended from rails, for there was no central canopy; she could see the ceiling. It was some seconds before she asked, 'Are you going to do that for me, then?'

'Of course,' he answered, placing one knee on the bed.

A metal fitting had been added to each of the fluted posts at the foot of the bed, at the level of the mattress. Into the wood had been screwed a circular loop of metal, hinged at the post so it could be opened into two halves. The top half was received into a slot in the lower where, by twisting the rounded end, it could be secured. Alex turned back to Faith, whose relaxed eyes were on him, her smile still in place. Without any show of the whirling thoughts which were running through his mind, he began by unfastening the buttons on her skirt, not hurrying, but taking each one at a leisurely pace until he saw the white of her briefs.

'Why don't you just haul up my skirt?' Faith asked. 'Or reach up? I don't mind.' But he ignored her, holding the two sides apart then letting them fall.

Lying there, Faith's legs and crotch were displayed, the white stockings and the narrow, white suspenders attached to the waistband of her panties. She smiled in silence as he looked at her then, almost casually, whilst quite gently, so as not to worry her, he lifted her right ankle complete with shoe on her foot. Unfastening the catch on the ring, he opened it, then placed Faith's ankle within it, snapping it closed again and twisting. Faith's leg was secured as surely as though it had been in concrete.

'What are you doing?' she asked, too surprised to be alarmed. Had it been in the bedroom of the flat, Faith would have lain back, watching him in the overhead mirror, but now her mind asked a question her mouth found impossible to frame; how did he know it was there?

'This,' he said, placing her left ankle in the same position on the opposite side.

Faith was pulled down the bed by this movement, for though the rings were on the inside of the posts, they were still some distance apart. Her opened skirt had ridden up to display just how brief her briefs were, and with her wide-legged position, her flesh was pressed against the fabric. There was a sudden look of understanding on Faith's face, a look compounded by excitement and interest; hope and desire.

'What are you going to do?' she asked, but her hoarse voice told him that, if Alex had no idea, Faith would be quite keen to tell him.

'What do you think I'm going to do?' he asked, running a hand up the inside of one of her thighs.

'You were going to remove my stockings.' She propped herself up on her elbows.

'I will; eventually,' he answered, still stroking her thigh. He could see the tremble in the muscles there, pleased that the previous night's activities had not dampened her ardour.

'Eventually?' Her voice lifted at the suggestion that he had something else in mind, first. 'Then you'd better make sure the door's locked, downstairs,' she said. 'We don't want anyone coming in. What if some of the neighbours saw us and called the Police?'

'Okay,' Alex agreed, rising to his feet. It might be no bad thing to have her relax for a few moments.

Later, he carefully unfastened the cuffs of her blouse, then the front, starting from the top and working down to expose the short white slip, pulling the last button from the waistband of her skirt. He then eased the blouse from her shoulders, laying it across the back of the well-stuffed armchair beside the bed. Next came the slip, a short thing which barely reached beneath her waistband and which peeled off easily.

For some half a minute, Alex looked at Faith in silence, wondering whether he should go through with this. Lillian had suggested that he try securing her before they made love, just to see what her reaction would be. She had made an impression on Lillian. As she lay propped on her elbows, as silent as he was, he could see the interest in her eyes, and the gradual increase in her respiration. Just having her ankles secured apart like that was making Faith feel horny.

Faith's brassière was unfastened at the back, then removed so she could lie down again; all the while her eyes were on him, pupils dilated. He was about to continue when, on an impulse, he slipped out of his casual trousers and open-neck shirt and stood alongside the bed, looking down at her. The young woman's eyes were on the rising erection as he glanced at the corners of the bed, but in vain. Kim used to have short chains with bracelets on the ends here, he thought. What has he done with them? The rings were still in place, so he hadn't totally given up bondage. He found a stainless steel bar running cross the bed beneath the uncovered pillow, along with two familiar objects which had been concealed beneath it.

More rings held two chains to the bar, allowing them to be slipped along into any desired position. Each chain was about eight or nine inches long, ending in a stainless steel spring-catch like a dog-lead. Faith was looking up at the ceiling, trying to quell her mounting excitement as he brought the first chain into view; she placed her wrist across the bar in readiness. With a minimum of fuss, Alex wrapped the chain around her wrist and fastened the catch to one of the links, securing first her left and then her right wrist. The simplicity stunned him. He could appreciate that, even with a struggling victim, these could be easily applied by one person and the thought made him tremble. What *was* Kim doing?

'What's the matter?' Faith asked as he sat beside her on the bed. He looked at her, aware of his own desire showing in his eyes. He was silent for some moments until in a quiet voice he asked:

'Comfortable?'

'Yes, thank you, Alex,' she answered, deliberately forcing her breathing to obey. 'Does your friend do this often? Tie women up like this?'

'Who? Kim?' he asked, finding a smile.

Faith lay stretched out, half naked; she knew that, come what may, she was going to make sure he entered her before she was released from this position. She owed it to Alex; she owed it to herself. Why was he shaking so, though? What was wrong with him? It seemed that something had struck him about all this and he was getting cold feet; and *that* would never do.

'Yes,' Faith said, 'Kim.'

'Sometimes,' he answered. 'He doesn't like them struggling too much.'

He knew that, like Kim, it pleased him to have a woman fastened to his bed, legs spread wide, unable to prevent him doing what he liked to her. But there the similarity ended, for Alex knew how corrosive that pleasure could be; it was to be indulged sparingly. She tried to shrug, but the distance had been worked out too well, there was hardly room to ease a cramped muscle, far less shrug. Yet it was not uncomfortable.

'Does he hurt them?' Faith asked.

Suddenly, he saw that one wrong word could cause untold problems here. What should he say to her? What should he conceal? Kim was also quite fond of spanking and strapping these young women, sometimes on their sex organs. If it was done to promote their orgasm, Alex saw nothing wrong in it, but he wondered whether Kim saw it like that. That was something Faith would learn at the Stables: the pleasure to be had from a sound strapping on her vulva; but not yet. Not while he was trying to determine her attitude to sex and bondage.

'Not much, no,' he answered. Then he diverted her with, 'Aren't you going to ask me to take the rest of your clothes off?'

'How much is not much?' she asked, ignoring his change of subject. She was beginning to know him; know the way he changed the subject when an answer was what she sought.

'Now and then one or two of them will get spanked,' he said frankly, unhappy that Faith was asking him. That was the trouble with her, he thought, she had a good mind and an insatiable curiosity. She might become less curious and accept more, after she had been to the Stables. Yes; she would accept more. She'd be more disciplined, for one thing.

'Spanked?' She frowned. 'Is that all? Spanked?'

'Yes,' he said, 'I think I told you. There are people who derive a lot of pleasure from spanking, or being spanked. Kim does. That's why he's got this set-up.' He gestured to the bed.

It was important to keep that uppermost in her mind; that there was pleasure here, and no undue cruelty. She too, in time, would learn to appreciate the beneficial effects of a strap across her behind. And not just her behind, either. He looked forward to seeing her vulva deep red from a sound thrashing.

'Lillian, too?'

'Lillian, too,' he answered. 'There are times when Lillian behaves badly, I know; though she isn't punished for it in the usual sense. And Claire.' He shrugged. 'There are times when Claire likes a little rough treatment. They all do, sometimes. More than that, some of them.'

'Such as?' she asked.

'Such as?' He stopped, thinking. 'I can remember when Claire had an affair. Just a brief fling. Little more than a one-night stand, in actual fact. Rupert knew about it; she hadn't done much to hide it, after all. She wasn't trying to deceive him. So she asked him if he would take a strap to her backside. He did; and took her from behind, afterwards.'

'Why?' Faith frowned. It seemed an unusual thing to do, but these people were unusual.

'Why take her from behind?' Alex asked, his expression amused. 'Because, my love, Claire's backside was a deep shade of red from the strap. With him banging into her with every thrust, Claire was getting another instalment of a reminder not to 'flaunt her fanny'. According to Rupert, it was the best rogering he'd ever done; or *had*.

Now can we get on, Faith?' Alex asked. 'I'll tell you all about it later. I promise.'

'How much later?' she asked.

'As soon as . . .' he broke off, shaking his head.

Perhaps it was stupid to have brought up the subject; he knew she was always asking awkward questions. He wished that she was already *at* the Stables, or had just returned. So much would be clearer to her; she would have no need to ask.

'The Chosen, Faith, have a . . . I don't know. It might seem a peculiar way of going on . . .'

'You're telling me,' she interrupted, making him smile, briefly.

'If a woman has upset a man, especially someone like her husband, her Master, then he can punish her for it. Some, most, do; but Rupert isn't like that. Claire felt awful for having that affair. Guilty. Rupert and Claire are a great couple and she appreciates him, she really does. She wanted him to know she felt bad about it, so she asked him to give her a strapping. In fact, she had to persuade him, *and* borrow the strap to do it with.'

'Was it . . .?' Faith began, but he quickly interrupted her question.

'I don't know any of the details. That's private, between the pair of them. Now where was I?'

'Please, Alex.' Faith looked anxiously at him. 'Make love to me. Like this, for now,' she asked.

Smiling his assent, Alex unfastened the remaining buttons of her skirt and slipped it out from beneath her, laying it on top of the other items on the chair; then he began to unclip her stockings. With a start, Faith realised that his hands on her thighs were cool to the hot flesh as he rolled first one stocking down to the ankle, then the other. Carefully, he unlocked her ankles, removed the shoes and stockings then, replacing them in the loop, locked her in again. Only the briefs remained, and these looked like being something of a problem.

But Alex was in no hurry. The back of his hand stroked up one thigh and then the other, each time ending on the straining fabric covering her moist, musky quim. She gasped as the fingers traced the lines of delicate flesh beneath the thin fabric, already damp with her fluids. Alex was kneeling between her thighs, his whole attention on the sight before him of this helpless woman with the large breasts and the inaccessible pudenda.

'Where are you going?' Faith's voice was sharp as he slipped backwards off the bed, making for the door. He made no answer until he had searched through her handbag and returned, holding up the item as he said:

'Nail scissors.'

Working at the sides, Alex soon cut a way through the thin fabric, yet left her covered for the moment while he returned the scissors. Alex was deliberately heightening her anticipation, for each time he moved, she was able to see the swaying erection which showed no signs of reducing while she lay there.

'There's a belt. Down by the side, on the right,' Alex said as he returned.

Thinking that he meant an instrument to beat her with Faith almost panicked. Alex crouched and found a broad leather band secured to one side of the bed, with a metal bar protruding from its free end, and parallel to it. It was quite thin, yet strong and about a foot wide.

'This,' he said, holding it up so that by turning her head, Faith could see it, 'fits on the opposite side.' He was still smiling at her, in no hurry. Faith's breathing became shallow and fast as her anticipation mounted. There was no apprehension, for she rightly considered that Alex would have no desire yet to inflict any pain. Perhaps later, she thought; when she had been educated more. Alex could see the worry in her eyes and smiled, thinking that, when she could see what could be achieved, she would beg for a whipping. Now, his only intention was to penetrate her.

Alex threw the strap across her body and went around the bed to the opposite side, where he found a long piece of metal, turned down into a right-angle over which the metal bar fitted. The right angle then held it secure.

Looking up, Alex found that Faith was now pinioned to the bed, unable to move even her hips, except in the most rudimentary way, for the band crossed her lower abdomen, just clear of her trimmed pubic hair. Faith had gasped silently at the touch of the cold leather, and again as it had tightened against her, thankful that she had not been too over-indulgent. But she could appreciate that she really was fastened tightly in position.

Teasing the mutilated fabric out from beneath the band took a moment, for it was extremely tight to her body, but eventually, he exposed her glistening labia to the world; the aroma of her strengthened at once, exciting him anew. He was about to reach out to touch her when she forestalled him.

'Don't, Alex, please. No foreplay. Just fuck me! That's what I'm here for; to be fucked. Fucked for as long, and as often as you want, or can manage.'

'What?' He frowned, looking at her with a puzzled expression. Faith taking a lead like that? There had been no chance yet to arouse her; but from the look of her flushed, slightly abandoned expression, stimulation would be a waste of time.

'That's right. Just get on with it, will you? Just fuck me. Ride me as hard as you like.' Yet there was pain in her voice, and he wondered whether the instruments securing her were too tight.

'Do you want me to release you?' he asked.

'No.' She smiled at him, with a slight shake of her head. 'I'm perfectly happy. Please.' She blew him a kiss.

He parted her lower lips to find her opening, listening to her gasp as the heat of his member touched her own fire; then he was inside the familiar, well-lubricated tunnel leading up inside her. Reaching up, he took her breasts in his hands, brought his mouth down to hers as his loins moved of their own volition. She lay inert, completely secured, so that it was difficult for her to move, yet her throaty cries told him that he was pleasuring her. When she tore her face away from his, it was to give vent to the pent-up pleasure within her; her cry soared across the room.

Aroused himself, Alex was taking one of her nipples in his mouth when he felt the familiar rush. He sought her mouth again, his tongue cleaving to hers as his seed sped up into her body. He could feel her strain at the contact, her upper half doing the duty of the imprisoned lower half. Her gasping cries drowned out the rushing blood in his ears as his own hairy crotch jammed against her pearl, and his member expended all it contained within her.

Alex was quite three minutes in coming round to the present, as he lay gasping across Faith's pinioned form. The effort had added a layer to his heat-induced sweat, and the warmth from Faith's body increased his discomfort. He knelt again and was about to touch her when she said, 'No, Alex. Please, no, not again. Not for a while, anyway.' She sounded more exhausted than pained.

He frowned, looking at her for a moment then said, 'I'll release your hands,' and, as he began to move up the bed to free her, an idea occurred to him. He looked at her, but her expression was unfathomable. With a sigh, Alex held his flaccid member towards her closed lips and something in the back of his mind made him ask, 'Would you open your mouth please, Faith?' There was no answer, for her eyes were wide with surprise. He reached out and pinched her cheeks together, forcing her lips apart. As soon as the end of his penis touched her lips, her teeth opened to admit him. With his member now being sucked, Alex unfastened Faith's hands one after the other; by this time he was sure he would hardly be able to walk.

'Like it?' he asked, as her tongue laved his glans, before his swelling organ slipped further within her mouth. 'Why did I have to force your mouth open? Do you prefer it like that?'

Don't risk everything now, Faith, she thought. It won't be so nice, but it will be almost perfect. Controlling her urge to shout at him, Faith relaxed back, laying her hands beside her head as if in surrender. She worked her mouth and tongue around him, feeling the organ thickening until it exploded into her throat, helpless to do anything but lie there and receive his sperm. At the last, when she could feel the quickening in his erection, and see the emotion in his face as he stiffened for the discharge, Faith relaxed back within the restraints.

When he withdrew from her, freeing her mouth, a concerned expression was in his eyes. He said, 'Tell me why you wanted that, Faith.'

'I . . .' she stopped, then swallowed convulsively again to rid her throat of the last vestiges of the salty, creamy liquid, making him breathe hard at the sight. 'I didn't do it last night, did I?' she asked. 'I thought you might want it but when you . . .' She broke off, shaking her head. 'I couldn't.'

'It was your first time.' He shrugged.

'I couldn't do it right,' she said. 'And these . . .' She looked expressively at her wrists, moving just her eyes but conveying her message. 'They made me realise that I was right. You like tying women up. You like to be the Master, don't you?'

'I am the Master,' he said quietly, willing her to accept the fact, '*your* Master.'

'And I was helpless,' she continued. 'I wanted to make up for last night, and wanted you to feel that, even with my hands free, I'd still take you in my mouth. But you had to make me, Alex. I didn't think I could do it for myself.'

'Happy that I did?' he asked, and she smiled her answer to him.

Faith watched as he released first the belly-band, then her left leg, and her right, but she lay as though still secured until her right leg was free. She continued to smile at him, swinging her legs over the side of the bed and standing up, throwing her arms around his neck.

'Thank you, Alex. Thank you very much.'

Chapter Ten

After walking back to the flat from Old Church Street, Alex asked Faith to strip to the waist; she also however removed her skirt and slip, standing in her stockings, held up purely by the tightness of the lace at the top. On being asked to sit on the bed facing away from the mirror she reluctantly complied, while he licked and sucked her left nipple until it became soft and pliable. Slipping a small gold ring into his mouth he held it between his lips and teeth, then sucked her nipple through the ring, the sharp pain making her hiss despite her bravery.

'There!' He stood back and gestured towards the mirrors. 'Take a look for yourself. You look better already.'

Swallowing uncertainly, Faith walked to stand with her breasts only inches from the mirror, looking in surprise at her reflection. The base of her nipple was surrounded by a small gold ring. As she watched, she could see it becoming a deeper pink; slowly enlarging, too. For several seconds she gazed, fascinated by the sight.

'What's happening?' she demanded. 'What have you done?'

'The blood supply enters the organ from deep within the flesh, like in a penis. But the return supply is closer to the surface. These rings are fractionally smaller than your nipples, so they constrict the blood flowing out. This makes them swell up because the tissue is elastic. You should wear them for about half an hour today, and a few minutes longer tomorrow. Wear them every day, gradually increasing the length of time, in order to get used to them. After a while, the flesh of your nipples will stay

131

distended – and Julia is right. A little bigger and your nipples will be magnificent.'

'God!' Faith gasped, looking back at her reflection and shaking her head. She felt the horror deep within her, and at the same time, she admired the way her body was responding. She was unable to come to terms with this apparent contradiction, and shook her head in silence as she looked critically at herself.

'What's the matter?' Alex asked. 'Wouldn't you like to have magnificent breasts?'

'Whether they're magnificent, or merely good . . .' Faith broke off, frowning. 'I'd like to have natural breasts.'

'Once the rings have enlarged the nipples, they will be natural,' he assured her. 'They won't retract again. All this is . . .' He stopped, sighed, waving a helpless hand to encompass her new underwear, the rings, the necklace which still lay where he had discarded it earlier. '. . . is a way of helping you achieve your potential. It's a lot less painful than some things men do to themselves.'

'Such as?' she demanded, a sneer in her voice.

'Some men have incisions made in the flesh of their penis and small stones, or ball-bearings, slipped inside; then the cuts are allowed to heal. And do you know why?' he demanded. 'Because, with a penis that's all knobbly from those inserted foreign objects, they can give their partners greater sexual satisfaction.

'It used to be just some ignorant savages that did that. In some cases, it was a tribal rite of puberty for the young men, having the women make the incision and insert the stones. The women always performed these operations, and the young men were never allowed to show how much it hurt. And why did they do it? So their wives could have that knobbly prick shoved up them!' In his annoyance, Alex was disregarding his own strictures about propriety of language, but it served to emphasise his sincerity to Faith.

'Yes! Savages!' Faith agreed with heat. 'Not in Britain.'

'If you like,' he said, going dangerously quiet and cold,

'I'll make a telephone call, invite someone round for cocktails. When he comes, I'll ask him to show you his prick. The last time I checked, he had, I think, fifteen ball-bearings in it. And from talking to women who've experienced him, they all approve. If you want to, I'll ask him if he'd let you try it.'

'You're joking, aren't you, Alex?' she asked. 'Tell me you're joking, even if you're not.'

Faith had gone quite white at the thought; her eyes were large and fixed on him. She could imagine what such a mutilated penis would look like, while trying to imagine what it would feel like, too.

'I'm sorry.' He shrugged. 'I'm not joking. Women have tassels inserted into the flesh of their mound so that they constantly stimulte their clitoris. Some have their nipples and clitoris pierced and rings put in them. One I know,' he sighed, 'had the lips of her sex pierced and thin chains put through the rings, running up to those through her nipples. Her lover merely had to tweak these chains and she was . . . well, you can guess for yourself.'

'Horrible.' Faith shuddered.

'Horrible?' he repeated, shaking his head. 'Not to the people who have these things done. They think it's right; and who are we to argue? They don't suit us, but are they wrong? If it gives them pleasure that they would otherwise forego, I don't feel I have the right either to condemn or berate them. I feel sad for them, like I feel sad for the people who can *only* obtain pleasure through pain.

'Pain and pleasure, Faith, are two sides of the same coin. They're . . . I don't know the precise connection, but I know there are many, many people out there who like either inflicting pain on others, or having it inflicted on themselves. I suppose that's the definition of a happy marriage; a sadist and a masochist. They compliment each other.'

For some seconds Faith was silent, allowing her skittering brain and pounding heart to calm, then she asked, 'Do *you* like hurting people? Me?'

'Me?' He sighed his question, shaking his head. 'No,

though I believe there's a place for pain in sex. If that's what you like, Faith, then I'm not your man. I can put you in touch with people who do though,' he added, 'but no, not me. Not as an end in itself.'

'I wouldn't want to be hurt, physically, I mean. Not badly hurt.' She was aware of the dryness in her throat. He could see that she was already thinking that, like so many of the unusual things to which he had introduced her, it was worth considering.

'Being hurt is sometimes good, Faith.' He shook his head. 'Which is why, though I don't practise it myself, I can appreciate the views of those who do.'

'How can hurting someone be good?' she asked.

'Various reasons.' He shrugged. 'Discipline. Teaching people that what they're doing is wrong. In more ways than one, too. I know that sometimes, when Max is teaching someone a particular technique, he'll make failure painful. Not cripplingly so, of course; that's counter-productive. But pain, yes. The burned child learns to fear – or respect – the fire.'

'And you think that this . . .?' She gestured to her breasts, then stopped, looking at him.

'You look beautiful, Faith,' he answered. 'Look how much you're swollen already. Your nipples should match the size of your breasts. God! You've got a 36-inch chest, Faith, with nipples that match a 34-inch chest. They'd look good on someone less well-endowed, but not on you.'

For a few moments Faith looked at herself in the mirror. Her nipple tingled, but the sensation was already working its way through her system. She glanced down at the open lips of her sex, at the deep red which, when she pressed her mound close to the glass, she could see was misting it. She turned to look at Alex's concerned features, shrugging as she accepted that he might know more about it than herself, then answered, 'I suppose I can give it a try. Put the other one on.'

'Faith.' He shook his head, though he bent his mouth towards her breast, beginning to suck the soft flesh. When he had finished and the small gold ring was in place, he stood back, turning her so that she could see herself in the mirror.

Faith could appreciate that her left nipple was now marginally larger than the right, and yes, she liked the larger size, too. But wasn't this getting just a little out of hand? Putting 'Love Balls' up into her cervix was one thing, but enlarging her nipples in this almost barbaric fashion? As though divining her thoughts from her expression, Alex said, 'What I'm trying to do is improve your appearance, Faith, your attitudes, your whole way of looking at life. As I told you before, I'm not the oracle, I don't have all the knowledge you need; I don't know anyone who does. Not even Max would make that claim; but I'll do what I can. I can only do that – as any of us can – with your co-operation. So if I ask you to wear nipple rings and fancy underwear, or a stovepipe hat,' he paused while they both sniggered at the thought, 'it's for a reason. Yes?'

'What reason?' she asked, swallowing heavily again.

'Simply to enhance your appearance, your knowledge and your ability. Nothing else. Nothing else matters, frankly.'

'You don't get anything out of it?' she asked, and smiled as he flushed.

'My darling girl,' Alex replied. 'I've already been well rewarded. If you and I never slept together again, I'd still feel everything was worthwhile.'

'By slept together, you mean fucked,' she stated.

'Why do you use that brutal term, when I'm trying to be . . . I don't know.' He sighed and shook his head.

Before she could relax, Alex picked up a small container of a light oil similar to the one he had previously used on her, and instructed her to lie down on the bed again. Nervously she obeyed, aware that already her attitude to the world was changing. Yet his expression appeared amused to her whenever their eyes met, as he gently applied the oil to the delicate flesh of her breasts.

Under her watchful eyes, Alex's fingers rubbed the oil

into her swollen nipples and, later, into the sensitive flesh between her legs. He was aware that, in doing so, he was touching her most sensitive places. Her hips stirred as he passed over the shrouded pearl at the top of her cleft, and listening to her increased breathing, he wondered how much of his interest and arousal showed.

'Now,' he said briskly from beside her, his eyes capturing hers, 'can you feel my fingers at the spot between the bottom of your vulva, where your slit ends, and your anus? That's the perineum. I'm going to tap you there, very lightly, with a finger. Like this.' And, reaching over Faith's left thigh, he struck the spot directly between her legs with the point of his middle finger.

Instantly, Faith's hips jerked and she gave a sigh of pleasure before coming to rest again.

'God,' she breathed softly, her mouth remaining open, her eyes on his, before looking up at the mirror in the ceiling again.

'Now,' he said, 'I want to show you something.' Taking his time, he did it again. There was less response but, after three or four further taps, the girl's breathing was becoming deeper; a nervous smile broke out on her face.

'I'm going to oil my fingers again,' he said and, when he had applied a little to the tips, continued, 'I'm going to run that, very lightly, around your anus, applying just a little pressure to it. Enough so that you can just feel it at first. Then, a bit firmer.'

Ten seconds later, gasping loudly, Faith's hips were straining upwards as she arched her back into the pleasure that was spreading through her body with the speed and virulence of a forest fire. Alex waited a few moments, then announced, 'I'm now going to tap your anus. Like I did your perineum.' And, as he did, the gasp rang out repeatedly from Faith's flushed face. 'Do you like that, Faith?' he asked.

'Yes, Alex! Yes!' came the breathless reply.

'Now, a little deeper pressure on the anus. A little harder on the tap. Ready?' he asked, looking her in the eye and finding no refusal there. This time there was a ragged edge to the girl's gasp, and Alex said, 'I'll stop there, I think. You'll appreciate that a bit later, when you're used to it. For now, let's move up to your honey-pot.'

She had never had a man's hand treat her vagina so delicately before, nor one able to see or appreciate it the way Alex did: the smooth dark red flesh, Faith's musky odour emanating from the opening at the base, the liquid glistening on it. Alex soaked his fingers in it, then applied them to his top lip, just beneath his nostrils.

'There, that's Faith's smell.' He smiled to himself. Faith could feel herself thrill at the gesture; she had no need to look to appreciate that his member became almost fully erect.

With a gentle smile still in place, he put his fingers in her vaginal passage, asking, 'There, Faith. What does it feel like, my dear?'

'Wonderful!' She was gasping now, her hips moving as though engaged in the sexual act, little groans coming from the base of her throat. Alex was aware that Faith was producing far more fluid than before, that his whole right hand was covered in it, the smell eating into the pleasure centres of his brain. Out of sight, his erection was pressing against the side of the bed not far from the girl's backside, for which he was thankful.

He next moved up to her clitoris, palpating it lightly within the shrouding flesh, then gently pushing back on her mons to reveal it. The little orange-pip gradually swelled as he tickled it with his tongue, rolling some of her own juices onto it with his fingers, then he licked it some more. And all the while, Faith's voice was becoming more hoarse and thick, her fists beating a gentle tattoo on his back. Her breathing was now rapid and shallow as she approached her climax, before Alex steadied her down.

He licked her sexual organs less and fondled her breasts, instead. He licked her navel, the insides of her thighs; he pushed his tongue into her vagina when he could, pressed on her anus, anything to keep her at that point of balance between extreme arousal and climax.

Faith could feel the twin agonies of pleasure and desire for release both as badly as each other. She had previously associated them together; one followed the other, usually. Now she was obtaining her pleasure without the release she desired.

When Faith finally toppled over into orgasm, Alex checked his watch, nodding and smiling. When her breathing was quieter, when her hips had ceased to gyrate and jerk, when she was lying still instead of thrashing her head from side to side, Alex said, 'right. We'll stop there. Too much of a good thing at this stage might be bad for you. Did you find that pleasant?'

'Oh,' the girl's breath sounded through her voice, 'yes, Alex. Thank you.' She was gulping air like a stranded fish.

'Don't thank me, Faith.' Alex looked at her with an affectionate expression on his face. 'Thank Max Hawes, if you must thank someone. He's the one who taught me how to do that. Another time, we'll do it and I'll mount you. You'll like that, won't you?'

'Yes, Alex,' she answered, feeling the thrills still trembling though her, yet fearful all the while.

'There's just one more thing,' he said. 'Stand up a moment.'

Standing close to, and facing the bed, Faith watched as Alex seated himself on the edge on her left, putting her left leg between his.

'Lie face down, Faith,' he said, gesturing to his naked left leg which was crooked in front of her on the covers.

The young woman laid herself down, obeying his instruction to place her hands at the back of her neck. Alex smiled when he saw her legs automatically spread apart, allowing him access to her sexual organs. He looked for a moment, just watching her, waiting for the tension to die from her back and legs, then with his left hand on the small of her back, he placed his right forefinger on the sexual opening.

Immediately, Faith's hips moved beneath him, and again as he slipped the finger slightly deeper, moving it slowly, letting Faith feel it gradually piercing her until there was a sudden exhalation as the tip of his thumb came to rest on her puckered anus; the muscles tightened up, her buttocks became hard and angular instead of soft and round.

'I'm going to press, Faith,' he said quietly, pausing while she breathed deeply, then used his strength to overcome her defensive musculature.

The young woman gasped, tightening her buttocks even more, but Alex was too strong for her. His thumb forced the ring of muscle apart, which admitted him to her rectum while his forefinger drove deeper within until the web of her perineum between them prevented further movement.

'I did something like this to you the first time we made love,' he said quietly, letting his hand rest there. 'Lillian did the same last night. Do you like it?'

'No! Yes!' Faith gasped, shaking her head into the covers, which muffled the sounds she was making. There were two pressures within her instead of one, two sources of pleasure generating waves inside her abdomen. It was a new experience, for she was unable to remember the first occasion.

'I don't believe you, Faith,' he said quietly, stroking the small of her back down to her buttocks. He paused to suppress the smile which threatened to disturb his voice as Faith's buttocks relaxed into their more usual shape.

'Why?' she asked helplessly, knowing the answer but unable to prevent her acceptance.

'Because you've not taken your hands off your neck. You've opened your legs wider,' Alex said quietly, adding, 'You've pointed your toes, even with your backside relaxed! You like this, Faith.'

'Yes,' she sobbed into the covers, surrendering herself to the delicious sensations he was producing within her, without any effort. Alex knew how to arouse her. He knew how to make love to her and was willing to teach her more.

'You're mine, Faith,' he said quietly. 'Say it.'

'I'm *yours*, Alex,' she replied without hesitation, the tension in her shoulders leaving her inert.

Deep inside her mind a sonorous bell boomed as she surrendered herself. Faith knew that Alex would be good for her, would teach her more than she could ever imagine for herself. But at what price? What would he want of her besides surrender? Whatever price she had to pay, Faith was willing to meet it; the lust rising within her would allow her no alternative.

Chapter Eleven

Alex had to be in his office early to catch the last dealings of the Nikkei index and the Hang Seng, so Faith rose with him, and they showered together. She found she liked it when he washed her, when he ran his soapy hands over her glowing skin, and especially her breasts. She had been forced to admit to him when they had gone to bed that further love-making would be wrong for her tender flesh, and had been surprised when Alex accepted it, put an arm around her, and drew her to him. Albert had usually been annoyed when she told him that, because of her period, sex was impossible. He kept a diary of her menstrual cycle and was always trying to catch her out.

But Alex had been firm about fitting the *rin no tama* into her vagina, pressing it firmly upwards, trying not to caress her and making sure that she wore the underwear and stockings Julia had brought. Faith was more used to the kitchen, managing to put together an attenuated breakfast before Alex left. He had called a cab in the King's Road the day before, to collect his car from Ennismore Gardens Mews, but had now been forced to park even further away, in Glebe Place.

Gradually Faith assembled her needs for the day, made sure that she had both the spare keys for the flat which he had given her, and his office number, whilst hoping that she would never need to use the latter. On parting, Alex had taken the bundle of notes from the pocket of his dinner jacket and handed it to her, all four hundred and fifty pounds. More money than she had held in her hands before, and all hers.

She dressed with special care in a black trouser suit, the

jacket of which reached to mid-thigh, knowing that the day was going to be a trial. A thin white blouse was obviously out of the question, for as soon as she took off her jacket, she would have every male in the office buzzing about her. It was only Albert's interest in her which had kept off the pack of circling wolves, as it was. Her outfit was completed by her black shoes and a large black leather handbag, a Christmas present to herself when Albert had refused to buy her anything.

Albert would be furious at her removing her things from his flat, but she would try to present it as a reaction to his sudden collapse at the party. She would keep Alex's existence – and location – secret for the moment in case he arrived on the doorstep. Gradually, Albert would come to realise that the change was irrevocable. She hoped the wolves would get the message, too.

The offices of Gibb McInley Gower occupied two floors of a modern block in Victoria, quite close to the station. Faith had been used either to coming to work with Albert in his Porsche, or taking the Tube and walking the few hundred yards. Now she faced a very different journey. She walked up Oakley Street – a trial in itself because of the single 'Love Ball' and waited opposite the old Chelsea Town Hall for a No. 11 bus which, she found, operated as some comedians claimed, in packs. She was about to vent her anger and frustration on the world when a passing cab, its 'For Hire' sign illuminated, halted in traffic.

Acting quickly she opened the door, gave her destination, then settled back to twenty-five minutes of social and political comment from the far-Right. She tried not answering, but it did no good. The driver, with nothing to do but look at the back of the car in front, carried on regardless. She kept her legs angled to the side, even though she knew her trousers would hide the cobweb-thin material covering her sexual organs from his voyeuristic gaze.

Faith usually arrived before most of the other office drones; she looked on it as part of her job to be first.

Coming in with Albert meant he was already giving her jobs to do as they inched their way in from West Kensington, but there were sufficient tasks left over from Friday to keep her nervously busy until the inevitable summons from the Great Man.

At ten-thirty, with what dignity she could rescue from the emotionally bruising encounter in Albert's office, Faith allowed the glass door of GMG to swing shut behind her, pausing for a moment, pale-faced.

For a few seconds she stood irresolute, collecting her breathing by force of will. Behind her in the foyer Glennys was watching her, looking for some sign of grief which could be quickly reported around the building. Faith refused to co-operate with Glennys's favourite pastime, for Glennys was 'rumour control'!

The thought of the money in her handbag returned. She damned well *would* go to Harrods as Alex had suggested! He wanted her to buy some shoes, so she would make quite a performance of it. She might look at the dresses, too, but first she had to telephone Alex to let him know that she was officially unemployed. The woman who answered the telephone number he had given her spoke in a flawless drawl which concealed a sharp mind. No, she had no idea where Mr Pellew was. He had come in earlier and had left again; would Faith like to leave a message? Faith, unwilling to tell her any more than Alex had, would. She had called, and would call again, but she was shopping in Harrods and there was no number at which he could reach her.

At twelve she telephoned again; this time the woman was more welcoming.

'Yes, Miss Small,' she responded at once, 'Mr Pellew called and asked that you meet him in Mayfair; he's talking to a client there.' The fact that Mr Pellew had given her the address to which Faith should be directed convinced his secretary that she was either a friend or a whore; both were possible. Faith heard the address and nodding, committed it to memory, refusing the woman's offer to have it repeated. What was her brain for, if not to be used?

The ornate, canopied entrance to the house in Upper Brook Street gave onto a large, chilly hallway, where the black and white marble chequered floor rang with the noise of her heels. Faith stood over six feet tall in her five-inch heels. She waited. The dumpy, elderly woman in the overalls who had answered the door knew her name, invited her in to wait, then vanished through a large heavy oak doorway set at the back of the hall. Faith liked the look of it: clean white woodwork and a beige shade for the walls, and a long leather couch under the stairs to the upper floor on the side opposite the empty marble fireplace, where there was a display of dried twigs in the tall vase. It reminded her of photographs of Harley Street waiting rooms.

'Would you come this way please, Miss?' The woman was back, her approach through the doorway silent.

Taking up her black handbag and the Harrods carrier containing her flat shoes, Faith rose from the couch to follow the woman back through the doorway into a short cross corridor from which, on the right, an open door ten feet away invited.

'Miss Small,' the woman said, entering the room; standing just inside, she allowed Faith to pass her.

The room was large by any standards. Like the hallway, the woodwork was white, though the walls – bedecked here and there with paintings, some in gilt frames – and the deep-pile carpet, were dove-grey. Off to the right was a black marble bar which curved out of the wall, enclosing a space of about ten feet. Directly ahead, four men and a slim woman were rising from the armchairs and couches which had been drawn up to the centre of the room, facing each other over a wide, low, glass coffee table. Nearest her, his jaw dropping, was Alex.

'Hello, darling!' Faith exclaimed, thinking that her appearance was the cause of his shock. 'I'm sorry I'm late. I couldn't find a taxi at Harrods.'

'Faith!' he gasped, his eyes stealing to where the others looked both surprised and grave. Behind her, the door closed as the woman left them to it.

'Alex?' She hesitated for, close to, the fire in his icy pale eyes left her in no doubt that she had committed a *faux pas* of some kind.

'Excuse me.' Alex half-turned to nod to the oldest of the three men, a short, plump figure, dressed, like Alex, in a dark suit. Without wasting a moment, Alex took her arm and turning her, frogmarched her unceremoniously to the door whilst she protested painfully, and fruitlessly, about his response.

The cold hallway was deserted as he flung her ahead of him through the doorway into the corridor, making her stumble on the shiny marble; her steel-tipped high heels skittered like the beating of her heart.

'What the hell do you think you're *doing*?' he demanded, pulling her up again and grasping both her shoulders.

Terrified by this sudden, abrupt reversal of his normal manner, Faith could only look wide-eyed at him. She had lost most of her colour; her open lips trembled in sympathy with the rest of her, and she had no strength to stand. A part of her mind admired the casual way in which he was able to support her.

'What . . .?' she managed to gasp out, before her overloaded brain stopped sending coherent signals to her mouth.

'Trousers!' he grated. 'I told you never to wear those damned things!'

'I went to the office . . .' But he was no longer even listening to her stammered explanation. Dragging her over to the couch, he seated himself quickly, then reached up beneath her jacket. Still with her handbag in one hand and the shopping bag in the other, Faith watched as he unfastened the waistband of her trousers. With a savage wrench, made worse by the matching expression on his hitherto pleasant features, he ripped the garments downwards, finding another cause for complaint.

'Tights?' He looked up at her in wonder. 'Who told you to wear tights?'

'Alex! I . . .' She would have said that she was unable to understand his anger, but the tights were being wrenched to follow the trousers, half-pulling her white panties with them. Seizing her waist Alex dragged her, face down, across his knees, holding her so firmly with his left hand that she was unable to resist as he wrenched the offending garments from her limbs, removing her new shoes in the process.

Heart beating furiously, she waited until they were off, aware of Alex's own emotion. Her hands still held the bags; she had been too surprised to release them, even to defend herself against his powerful assault. There was a pause for a few seconds when he had finished, though he still held her tightly.

'Alex! I . . .' she began, but he snapped:

'Silence, Faith!' in a tone which no sane person would ignore. He was deliberately calming himself down and wanted a few moments of quiet before he had to deal with the situation in which he found himself. Spread over his knees, her white-clothed bottom uppermost, Faith could feel his emotion dying, even as her own continued. Alex was aware of the trembling in her body and had a reasonable idea of how she must feel; but he had to treat her firmly and without emotion.

'I told you on Saturday, Faith, when we went through your wardrobe, that trousers are not acceptable items of clothing for women of the Chosen. Which, if you remember, was why we had to buy you a dress.' He swallowed and gained another notch of control as the memory returned to her. Yes! He had said that only men wore trousers, not women.

'I'm sorry, Alex; really.' She hung her head. 'I went to the office.'

'You are here, not in the office,' he said quietly, swallowing again, 'and you deserve a far greater spanking than I can give you here and now. But I'd be doing you no favours if I were to ignore . . .' He broke off, took a deep breath and with both hands, pulled her panties down to uncover her buttocks.

'What are you . . .?' Faith began, but stopped when his right hand descended quickly on the full pink buttocks, leaving a white mark which rapidly transformed itself to red.

Faith yelped in surprise, yelped again when the smack was repeated on the other buttock, yelped a third time as the hand struck just above the location of the first blow. There were tears starting in her eyes when the dozen smacks were over; her breathing came like a child's, an open-mouthed dry sobbing as he stood her upright, the stinging pain in her buttocks threatening to cause tears to dribble down her cheeks.

'I'm sorry, Faith,' he said quietly, now in complete control of himself. 'The people in there are all Chosen, and had I ignored this . . .' He shook his head as he stopped, then bent to the floor. Carefully, he held her shoes to her feet for her to put them on again, then slipped her panties back up before rising to his feet.

She watched him in silence. This was a different side to Alex from the one she knew. The sudden assault had been devastating to her, yet her mind and body were catching up now. She could think rationally, and her thoughts were a whirlpool of doubts and agonies. Faith trembled as he rose up in front of her, some of his anger still visible in his face, but there was a more tender look in his light eyes now, though he still took pains to breathe deeply to calm himself.

Albert had never spanked her! Albert had shouted at her, treated her like dirt, had kept demanding that she pay the housekeeping, that she clean his flat, that she do his bidding; but he had never spanked her. Alex had made exquisite love to her, had treated her with a care and consideration she had never previously known in a lover. Yet he had spanked her. The confusion in her mind kept coalescing as she looked into Alex's eyes, then resolved into a very simple choice. If she left Alex, where would she go?

Her things were in his flat; her future was in his hands. Albert had fired her from GMG; she was out of his flat, his life and his business. Unemployed in London, where could she go? What could she do? The only thing to do was to accept the position for the moment, and take the first exit possible.

'Leave your bags and things here.' Alex took them from her, placing them on the couch, and scooped up the offending garments to dump them in the carrier. 'We'll have to go in, now. I want to introduce you.'

'Alex!' Faith protested, 'I've got nothing on.'

'Your jacket covers your legs,' he said quietly, breaking in on her protest, 'and besides, they've all seen women's legs before. I told you, they're Chosen.'

'But I . . .' She stopped, knowing her protests were useless.

'Come on, let's try to ignore what's happened, for the moment, at least.' He turned her towards the doorway again.

The name of the rotund, oldest man was Gerald. He was about fifty, with greying hair adding to his already distinguished features. When introduced, Faith had felt his keen eyes penetrating into her skull, though he had smiled. The two younger men were his son Charles, and a nephew, Alisdair, both, like the old man, dressed in dark suits. Faith felt nervous about entering the room wearing nothing but a jacket with which to cover her lower limbs, but none of the occupants even looked anywhere but into her eyes.

'And this is Abigail.' Alex gestured to the slim woman who stood off to one side. 'This is Faith.'

Abigail was an attractive and elegant forty-year-old with a long, narrow face, neat fair hair and a reasonable figure which she concealed within a conservative day dress in cream silk. Her only decoration was a narrow black choker around her long throat. Faith smiled nervously at the older woman as they shook hands, noting how cold her hostess's fingers were.

'I expect you could do with a drink, Faith.' The

woman's voice was a familiar drawl. 'What will you have? Come and see.' She turned to walk over to the long black bar. Faith followed and, conscious of her naked legs, slipped behind the bar with the other woman, looking over to where Alex and the men had all taken their places around the coffee table again. The woman saw the look, and smiled.

'They won't be long, now. Amazing to think that they're talking about enough money to keep a bank going, isn't it?'

'Yes,' Faith agreed, swallowing. Her buttocks had been stingingly painful since the sudden assault in the hallway, but now they had settled into a warmth which was sending rivulets of thrilling sensation through her. The 'Love Ball' had been working overtime, keeping up with the constant changes in attitude as she was first dragged from the room, then upended before being placed upright. The spanking had added further layers of sensation on top of these, so that with the heat from her skin, Faith was feeling more aroused than she would have willingly admitted.

'I see he removed your trousers,' Abigail said quietly, her amused grey eyes on Faith's as the younger woman looked quickly at her. 'Was the spanking *very* bad?'

'How did you know?' Faith gulped, looking quickly away again to where the four men talked quietly. A cold hand separated the skirts of the single-breasted jacket to rest on her white-covered rump, feeling the warmth of her injured flesh thoroughly. Not wishing to add further to Alex's distress over her behaviour, Faith remained still until the hand was withdrawn. She thought it odd that she felt a sense of loss, even at that.

'I see,' the woman said after a pause. Then she asked, 'what would you like to drink?'

'Just . . .' Faith paused, not looking at this strange woman who seemed to be able to divine what went on beyond closed doors.

'I'd suggest a gin, for the heat,' Abigail said, and her intonation made Faith look round again. This woman *knew*! For a few moments Faith, inarticulate, looked at her in surprise, watching the amused expression spread until Abigail stated, 'I take it you live with Alex. Sleep with him.'

'Yes,' Faith breathed softly, trying to control her heaving bosom. The trip-hammer in her brain was fighting against her control, threatening to wreck itself and bring about a breakdown.

'He must love you very much, my dear,' Abigail said simply, leaving Faith thunderstruck as she turned away.

The shocked young woman watched the older one put the ice in the glass before pouring out a hefty gin, the tonic being added last. Handing over the fizzing drink, those cool grey eyes met her own, hesitating only for a moment before she asked. 'Hadn't you realised he loves you?'

'He's just . . .' Faith stopped, open-mouthed as Abigail reached for the gin bottle again, interjecting with:

'He's spanked you, yes; I know,' adding, 'You richly deserved it, too.'

'What?' Faith gulped down some of the cool liquid as Abigail continued.

'As I understand it, Faith, you're being put forward for membership. Chosen women don't wear trousers, *ever*. That's why Alex gave you a spanking, and you deserve a more thorough one, too. If I'd done as you had, my husband would have taken a strap to me.'

'I forgot.' Faith's tight expression betrayed her guilt. He had told her, and she had ignored him, thinking that as she was going to the office, it was of no account.

'You mustn't forget,' Abigail said quietly, sipping her straight gin. 'If you were just someone casual, someone he cared little about, then things would have been different. You would have come in as you did, had a drink as you are, and that would have been the end of it. Even knowing that you were living with him, we would all have known that you were no one special. But that didn't happen. He immediately took you outside, stripped off those trousers – charming though they may have been –

and spanked your backside. That shows that you mean a great deal to him.'

'If I meant a great deal to him, he wouldn't *do* that!' Faith's resentment broke through her surprise.

'Don't be silly, Faith.' The woman shook her head, her scorn like a douche of cold water on Faith's grave intensity. 'If he were to allow you to get away with a gaffe like that, pretty soon you'd be unable to be admitted to the Chosen. You're not disciplined enough, you see. Coming here in trousers proves that.'

'I didn't know I was coming here,' she answered in her own defence.

'That's rather like saying you were only speeding because you didn't think the policeman was watching. If you only adopt such things when you know you're on display . . .' She shrugged, taking another sip. 'Still, I expect you'll learn, in time. We all do. Are you coming to the Club with us, later?'

'The Club? What Club?' Faith frowned.

'Ah!' Abigail nodded thoughtfully, her eyes clouding at Faith's ignorance.

Business concluded, the men rose to their feet, smiles replacing the frowns of concentration. Alex went to the far end of the room where large windows overlooked greenery, though from the bar, Faith could only see the vague shapes beyond. Smiling, Gerald approached the bar, flanked by his son and nephew, neither of whom were much taller than he, though both much slimmer.

'Faith,' he smiled, 'I expect you're glad all that business is over, eh? You can have Alex all to yourself again.'

'Is Alex coming to the Club?' Abigail asked before the younger woman could answer. 'And if he is, will it be all right for Faith to come along?'

'Of course it would!' Her husband seemed surprised at Abigail's comment. 'Has Alex told you about the Club?'

'Apparently not,' Abigail broke in, removing some of the smile from the older man's face, though it seemed to amuse both of the younger ones.

Abigail poured drinks for the three men without asking

their preference, a pale Scotch, a brand Faith had never seen before. There was a fourth drink left on the bar, which Alex collected when he returned.

'All done,' he sighed, sipping some of the drink, his smile back in place. 'That's going through right now, so we might get a better price ahead of the rush.'

'Do you want Faith to come with us to the Club?' Gerald asked. The two younger men, both about Alex's age, had been looking speculatively at her smooth bare legs, so that she was glad he returned when he did.

There was a pause for a moment while Alex looked at Gerald, then at Faith, before answering, 'Yes, why not?' He shrugged. 'Lunch.'

'That's what I thought!' The old man nodded, his smile slipping as he looked as his watch. 'Now I have to rush off, but I'll try to meet up with you in time for lunch. Yes. If you'll excuse me, then?' He retreated from the room, followed by Abigail.

In the hiatus before the woman returned, the three men talked business; the price of some shares which seemed set to fall another few shillings. Once back with them, Abigail's presence appeared to inhibit simple business considerations. Faith stood quietly behind the bar watching them, their faces animated as they talked about mergers and 'staging', terms she had heard but never understood.

Twenty minutes later, Faith was seated in the back of a taxi with Alex, being driven to an address not far from St James's Square.

'What's this club, Alex?' Faith asked. Her behind was hardly less hot than before, and standing about had done little to alleviate her need for release.

'What Gerald said,' he answered in a short tone. 'A club. We're to have lunch there.'

'Abigail knows you spanked me,' she said quietly, as much to prevent the driver hearing as a result of her own nervousness.

'Of course Abigail *knows*,' he sighed, turning on her. There was a vestige of the same anger within him, yet tempered by some other quality into a measure of irritation. For some seconds he looked into her eyes, then slowly let out his pent-up breath. In a more reasonable tone, he said, 'They're Chosen, Faith. They knew as soon as we walked out of the room that I'd have to do something like that. Spanking you was only one option; the least of them, in fact. When you came back without those damned trousers – ' He paused. 'They knew I'd hauled your knickers down and spanked you.'

'Are you going to spank me again?' she gulped, feeling conflicting emotions rising within her.

'Yes, why? Going to report me to some passing policeman, are you?' There was some amusement in his voice, but she flushed a little.

'No, of course not,' she answered, shrugging. 'I just wanted to know, that's all.' She felt the sudden lurch within her. Alex was going to spank her again, and her backside still stung from the last time.

They were silent on the remainder of the journey, and Alex reflected that it could have been a whole lot worse. The best deal he'd done in weeks, almost ruined because Faith had arrived in trousers. Had he not acted, Gerald would have been polite and charming as usual, but there would have been no sale, and no profitable purchase, either. He had reacted without thinking, outraged at Faith's *faux pas* and yet, it seemed to have been just the thing. Faith's shock was much less than he had supposed; she had said nothing at the time. He thought that she would be berating him now for spanking her like that, but something seemed to have changed her mind.

The Club had no imposing entrance such as others had, but then, the membership was more restricted. There were only fifty or so Members, with about the same number of Associates given access to the facilities once each month. Entering the hallway, where Rankin the porter was already checking the memberships of Charles and Alisdair, they stepped into another world.

It was a world of scarlet plush, with heavy mahogany woodwork straight out of a Victorian setting. In fact, the originals of much of the decoration and furniture had come from Victorian theatres which had been demolished. Reproduction workshops had been busy creating an ambience a late Victorian would have found comfortable.

'Are you playing, sir?' Rankin, a small man with a clipped, military manner, asked. He was missing part of one arm, caused when he had ventured too close to an exploding mine.

'No, thank you, Rankin. Nor is my guest,' Alex gestured to Faith, who wondered where the gaming tables could be. She left both her carrier and handbag with him, assured by both men that taking them into the dining room was not permitted.

The hallway was about the same size as that of the house in which she had just been, with three doors leading off at ground level, and thickly carpeted stairs which led up into darkness. All the curtains, carpeting and soft furnishings were in the same shade of scarlet, yet without a trace of a monogram. No brass plate proclaimed the name of the place to the outside world, no cleverly-worked device on Rankin's uniform hinted at it, yet something stilled Faith's enquiring mind. Normally, she would have asked, but if such pains had been taken to conceal the name, then Alex might jib at telling her, especially in front of someone.

Alex tucked her right hand in the crook of his left elbow as he led the way through the right-hand door at the back of the hallway, which gave directly onto a long, narrow yet well-lit dining room. A row of tables ran down each side of the room, with two across each end, leaving the central space free. By the curtained doorway through which they entered, a dumb-waiter disgorged dishes from the kitchen in the nether regions of the basement.

At the far end, at a table for six, Abigail and the two men were already being seated; a waiter hovering with menus looked round as Alisdair gestured towards them. Faith found herself seated with her back to the wall, from where she could see the rest of the dining room. Quite a few tables were taken, prompting Abigail to comment to no one in particular, 'Looks as though there may be a good game of forfeits, later,' to which the three younger men nodded their agreement.

A glinting light attracted Faith's attention off to one side, where a middle-aged man was lunching with an attractive woman in her early forties. She had black hair which was carefully coiffeured, an expensive yellow silk suit and black shoes. It took a few moments for Faith to realise that the man was feeding her. They were talking quietly, yet every few moments he would hold up a laden fork for her to eat, then take some for himself.

'Something wrong, Faith?' Abigail asked from her left. Alex sat on Faith's right, next to Alisdair and then Charles; the seat between the two women was empty in expectation of Gerald's arrival.

'That man's feeding . . .' Faith began, then stopped as the reason for the flashing light jumped into focus. The woman's wrists were encased in shiny handcuffs behind her, yet neither the staff nor the other diners seemed at all put out by it.

'Yes.' Abigail looked back with a nod. 'He's feeding her, isn't he? Do you want Alex to feed you?'

'No!' Faith exclaimed at once, looking in a startled manner at the amused grey eyes, then looking down at the menu before her, feeling her blush rising. Out of the corner of her eye she could see Charles's mouth twitch into a smirk, but the subject was dropped.

When it came to ordering, neither Abigail nor Faith were asked what they wanted; the waiter dealt exclusively with the men, asking them, 'And for Madame?' solicitously.

Charles ordered duck for Abigail whilst Alex stuck to lemon sole for the two of them. Both during the meal and whilst waiting for the food to arrive, Faith noticed that the woman in yellow was not unique. There were three or four women being fed by their partners, one of them in a mixed party. None seemed to resent this humiliation, and Faith was surprised at a burst of laughter from the large party half-way down the room, and at seeing the young woman concerned rocking backwards and forwards with every sign of enjoying herself.

By two-thirty, most of the other diners had already left the room, exiting via a door which took them close to where the party were seated for coffee. Faith was struck by the elegance and grace of most of those who walked past, their erect, graceful posture. Most wore black ribbons at their throats, broad or narrow – the woman in yellow silk had a narrow one tied in a bow at the front while others wore cameo brooches or medallions on broad ones – and all looked elegant. Watching them, Faith was reminded of Claire's sinuous locomotion. The waiters had been rushing around like dervishes during those last few minutes, getting coffee to all the tables and, a few minutes before a small silver bell chimed once, they vanished from the room.

'Shall we go through?' Abigail asked. 'Take the coffee?'

'Why not?' Charles asked. 'Father will have to meet us there,' shrugging his acceptance of the situation.

As they rose, Alex said, 'Faith and I should leave now; there's lots still to do today.'

'Of course.' Alisdair smiled his thanks to the tall man, whilst the fair-haired woman looked at Faith with an encouraging smile before preceding the two young men from the almost-deserted dining room.

In the taxi heading for Chelsea, Faith listened while Alex gave her a brief explanation of what he had been doing. Gerald had been unhappy with some investments, so Alex had found both a buyer, and another investment. Both had been profitable.

'How much will you make then, when it's completed?'

'Not much; under a mil, but it keeps the wolf from the ancestral door for another day or two. What about you?'

'Alex!' She suddenly remembered. 'I've been fired!'

'Really?' he shrugged. 'Forget it. They're not worth worrying about.'

'But I don't have a job.' She stopped as he shook his head at her.

'You don't *need* a job. You won't have time.'

'Julia has a job,' she protested.

'Julia has a hobby,' he emphasised, 'not a proper job. Unless you want to be a model or something, of course.' He mused in silence.

For the rest of the journey back to the flat, Faith thought about this. In quiet moments since the party, she had considered Alex and Claire's comments about the Chosen. She had almost rejected them outright, but was attracted all the same, both by the people and the sex. Especially, perhaps, the sex. For someone who had scorned sexual attraction for so long and who had received so little stimulation from Albert, she knew that she was breaking out. But this was an opportunity too good to miss.

Nothing was said about their difference earlier in the day and at seven-thirty, Alex announced, 'I tell you what. To save messing about, why don't we dine out? Nothing fancy; spaghetti in the King's Road would do. Just so long as we don't have the trouble of cooking.'

'Whatever.' Faith glowed at the thought of going out to dinner.

'Good. Actually – ' he paused. 'There's a chap I have to see there; I hope he's got what I asked for. I'll just make a call. You could be getting ready, if you like; this won't take long.'

They ate in a Chinese restaurant in the King's Road, hardly bigger than a coffee stall from the outside, but which was surprisingly roomy within. Once finished, they strolled towards Sloane Avenue, but turned into Markham Square and, while Faith waited, Alex went into a house for a few minutes, re-emerging with two large, long and weighty boxes. They were white cardboard, three feet long and fifteen inches wide. All identifying markings had been concealed by thick, brown, plastic adhesive tape. Faith was hardly surprised when Alex hailed a cab. Even had they carried one each it would have been difficult, for the boxes seemed to be weighted at one end.

Once in the flat, Faith was ready to relax, but Alex,

still carrying the boxes, insisted that she go with him into the bedroom, where he placed the boxes on the bed as he asked, 'Well? What do you think these are?' From his delighted, boyish expression, Faith guessed that they contained something for her, but shrugged.

'I give up; you're too good for me, Sherlock Holmes.' And, putting her wrists side by side, the backs of her hands uppermost, she said, 'Clap the derbies on me and we'll be away to the nick!'

For a moment he paused, looking at her seriously, his mouth half-open as though in shock. Briefly, Faith thought she had said the wrong thing, but he recovered himself to reply in a declamatory style, 'You see, Lestrade, what you failed to take into account was the aroma of leather arising from these items. Long. Lop-sided weight. Leather. What does that suggest to you?'

'The horse I backed in the Derby last year,' she answered, provoking a guffaw which suffused his face bright scarlet until he managed to control himself again.

'Then you'd best open them,' he replied, 'but first, take off your skirt and blouse.'

'What?' Faith's jaw dropped.

'Just do as I say, Faith,' Alex urged quietly. 'Take off your skirt and blouse first.'

'Okay.' She held out her hands, fingers extended towards him, keeping them at waist level and pressing down on an imaginary surface. 'Take off my skirt and blouse. To hear is to obey.'

'I wonder,' he mused thoughtfully.

Standing in her underwear, she searched for and eventually found the opening at the end of the first box. She prised it open with the metal comb from the dressing table, becoming almost like a child at Christmas, frantic to rip the wrappings off; then her mouth hung open again as she gasped. 'Boots, Alex?'

'Boots,' he agreed. 'Black, high-heeled, zip-up boots, size seven and a half. When you're used to them, I'll take you along to my bootmaker and we'll get them made specially, but this, I'm afraid, will have to do for now. Try them on. See how you like them.'

'Boots are out of fashion,' Faith protested, selecting the least emotive term she could find. He looked at her evenly for a moment, his expression neutral.

'Try them on,' he repeated, his face serious.

'Try them on.' Faith nodded, sighing, then sat on the bed to feed her left foot into the boot. Before she could begin to zip up the long fastener, Alex was kneeling in front of her, fitting the other one to her right foot and, as she stood still, he began to zip them up. Being waited on like that, especially in her underwear, made her feel even more decadent.

Faith discovered that the boots were more than either fashion appendages, or warm footwear. They fitted snugly to her legs, reaching up to within an inch of the lace top of her stockings, which were a bare inch again from her crotch.

'I can't wear these, Alex,' she protested, uncertain of how to tell him when he had gone to so much trouble to find and purchase them. 'Honestly, I can't.'

'Why not?' he asked in a reasonable tone.

'Because . . . because I can't bend my knees. I need to bend them to walk.'

'Try walking without bending your knees,' he suggested, indicating the open space between the side of the bed and the door into the hallway.

'It's impossible,' she protested again, 'I'll never manage.'

'These are to improve you, Faith.' His face looked sad as he shook his head. 'They'll make you walk a little more slowly, it's true, but you'll have a more stately gait. And you know, it's amazing what you can do with willpower, and practice.'

'I *have* bought high heels, Alex,' she answered. 'You saw them.'

'Good.' He smiled pleasantly. 'Now, try walking to the door, turn around, and come back. That's not so difficult, is it? He looked at her with the expression of a sad, lonely child. Faith had been around men long enough to know that expressions like that were the last warning before they erupted into rage.

Alex sat on the bed, silently watching while she began her first faltering steps in the black thigh boots, finding herself wobbling more than she had believed possible. Her tight, round, plump buttocks showed through the gauze of her knickers as though she were naked, yet the long, strong muscles of her thighs were encased and circumscribed. He found the bare inch of white lace at the top of the boot highly erotic, which so neatly framed her dark triangle of hair. When she walked away from him, the soft flesh of her buttocks jiggled deliciously.

When Faith returned, her expression bordering on the rebellious, Alex was ready.

'There; you didn't go so badly, did you? Practice and willpower. That's all.'

'Alex – ' Faith shook her head – 'I know it's sweet of you but this will never work. It's not the season for boots. The middle of May is next week. Spring.'

'Walk.' He gestured towards the door and, taking a deep breath, Faith turned and began to walk again.

Gradually, she started to get the hang of it. After quarter of an hour – during which time she went from the bedroom all the way to the front door and back without so much as a wobble, her buttocks moving in a highly controlled manner – she looked pleased.

'Yes,' Alex said, 'there is some movement, you see? The leather is very thin and fine, but cut close. They had to look through God knows how many pairs to get them for you. Your thigh measurements, you see?'

'Those measurements you took on Saturday?' Faith asked.

'Yes. Just as Julia made your underwear, someone looked out these boots. They'll make you walk with a more upright, languid gait, Faith; more like Claire. At the moment you're too round-shouldered. You slouch. But soon, you'll walk like those women you saw today at the club, the ones you pointed out as being so stately. You'll learn, Faith. You'll learn.'

'What about the other box? Another pair?'

'Yes,' he agreed. 'They had two pairs, so I took them while I had the chance.'

'When will I ever wear them, Alex? Honestly?' she asked, indulging him.

'Come here, Faith.' He held out a hand to her and, when she stepped close, wrapped it around her silk-encased buttocks, drawing her, teetering, towards him. When she was alongside him, with the front of the boots touching his right thigh, he raised his hand to her back and pressed, bending her over his knees so that her head and shoulders were resting the bed to his left.

'Part your legs please, Faith,' he said quietly and, without a thought, Faith did as she was told, though her legs were not parted as wide as he would have liked.

Gently he inserted his four stiff fingers between her leather-clad thighs, then gently pressed to his left, the side of his forefinger coming into contact with her heat. He smiled when he felt it, though it was much cooler than the day before. He began to saw his fingers up and down, just touching the silk on the other side of which were Faith's sex lips. After a few moments of silent sawing, Faith gulped, and he looked round to see her wetting her lips. Her thighs were beginning to tremble as she tried to hold them still.

'Good.' He nodded. 'When you feel your pleasure, lick your lips or just stick your tongue out a little. I'll know then how you're feeling.'

'Alex,' Faith's voice held a quaver but he shushed her, saying:

'You're a lovely young woman, Faith. You could be a beautiful one; a *really* beautiful one. Everyone who has met you agreed; but you really must trust me. We know what we're doing.'

'Who is "we"? The Chosen?' Faith asked anxiously, her legs closing momentarily. As the fingers ceased their sawing motion, however, she opened them again, feeling the tiny tendrils of that terrible wanting rising within her. Was this a prelude to him mounting her? If so, she was more than willing.

'The Chosen believe you have a great future, Faith. And, having the promise of a great future, we want to see you achieve it. So we're helping. I know it doesn't feel like helping when I ask you to totter around the old place on stilts like that; but believe me, it is.' His fingers were stroking the soft flesh at the top of her inner thighs, possibly the most delicate flesh of all. He ran the pad of one finger down the crease between thigh and buttock, making Faith's flesh tingle.

He could feel her breathing deepen as her legs inched wider apart, and he turned his hand to allow the backs of two fingers to caress the double curve of her sex. Faith's breathing caught; she pushed her rump up into the air, and reached down with the toes of her outspread boots to support herself, legs spread as wide as he would have liked. He regarded it as a victory to have brought her this far. She no longer lay on his lap, but was supported by her toes and her hands, pressed flat on the bedcover. Faith was in a position to be mounted, whenever he chose to remove her underwear, a position which she had taken of her own volition.

Alex found the silk wet. Smiling, he slipped his left hand beneath her to imprison her left breast, his fingers finding the protruding nipple.

'What I suggest is: you stand up, I fit your nipple rings, and we take a little more time to practise walking in those boots. Mmm?'

'Later?' she breathed, turning her anguished face towards him.

'Later, when you've improved in both areas, I'll take you to bed. Would you like that?'

'Yes.' Her reply was almost a sigh of contentment.

While Faith was pacing up and down the hallway, going from room to room, working on a circuit to determine whether she was doing well or ill, another part of her mind thought about this mysterious Chosen. They comprised the people at the Brooks's party, but there were more. She was fairly certain the muscular frame of Max figured in it, but he had claimed to have been a 'technical adviser', not a participant. Gerald and his family too, of course.

The Chosen, of course, could include anyone; but why were they so interested in her? Lillian was astonishingly beautiful and an expert in the erotic arts, too. Her poise, her charm, her obvious wealth, made her a much more suitable subject, yet why had Alex told her of these things if they were untrue? It was so unusual that it had to be true.

At ten, Alex called a halt. He removed the rings from her breasts, helped her to divest herself of the boots, then saw to it that she slipped straight into bed wearing only the proverbial dab of perfume. He was busy with a few telephone calls in the hallway for about ten minutes, but he talked in a low voice so she was unable to hear what was said.

When he came to bed, Alex drew back the covers, and looked her in the eye.

'Get out, Faith,' he said quietly. 'It's time I completed your spanking.'

Shocked by the calm on his face, Faith found herself standing by the bed, swallowing convulsively as he seated himself on the edge, his left leg crooked in front of her.

'Discipline, Faith. The lack of it is your besetting sin. You're like an eager, willing young pup who's ready for anything and everything. You bound around, heedless of help or instructions, expecting everything to go as you want it. So far, it has; but a time will come when, if you haven't curbed your impetuous nature beforehand, you'll *have* to learn discipline. And the longer that's left, the harder it is to learn. Some never learn it at all, of course. And the hardest is also the best; self-discipline. With a self-disciplined person, anything can be done.'

'I know.' She could feel the whine rising in her voice as she looked up at the ghostly figures overhead.

'You almost ruined a deal for me today by disobeying

what I told you about wearing trousers. No! Don't interrupt.' He quelled her at once. 'Hold out your hands.'

Faith held her hands out, inhaling sharply when he produced a pair of shiny handcuffs similar to those she had seen earlier in the Club. Without haste, he put them on her wrists as she held them out in front of her, then helped her to raise her hands until they were behind her head. Finally, he fastened a black silk scarf around her throat, holding the cold swivel in place on her spine.

'Bend over my knee!' His voice was sharp, but she would have obeyed anyway. She could feel the churning deep inside her suddenly working at her vitals, and knew that soon she would be calling to him for release from that sweet, familiar ache in her loins. She expected him to begin at once, but he inserted the second 'Love Ball' before repeating his previous examination of both her openings. Holding his digits within her while she strained her legs apart, he saw her revelling in both her position and the sensations which were being produced until, after five minutes, he said quietly, 'I'm going to begin now,' removing his fingers and wiping them.

Alex smacked her plump, yielding buttocks at a very quick rate to start with; his hands covered the skin with the blows, summoning the blood to the capillaries. Once her behind had been reddened, he slowed, watching her unclench her muscles before delivering another smack. These later smacks were a good deal harder than the earlier ones.

Faith had gritted her teeth at the initial onslaught, though tears rolled down both cheeks, but at the later, harder smacks she began to sob into the covers, trying to muffle the noise she was making, her shoulders shaking with the effort. When it was over, Alex slipped out from beneath her and rested his left hand on her behind for a moment, before bringing the tip of his erection up to her vulva.

The young woman lay quiet after the smacking stopped and Alex rose from the bed. She hardly noticed that he was gone, for her whole attention was focused internally.

He had inserted another 'Love Ball' and then followed up with his intimate penetration of her, both of which had worked against her.

As the smacking had become harder, so the pressure on her had increased. Towards the end, Faith was biting the covers as she fought to conceal the fact that she was experiencing an orgasm just from the spanking. She understood Alex was experienced enough to know what was happening to her; he had probably planned for this very thing.

When his erection touched her, Faith's head and upper body jerked as she cried out in a long, wavering wail of pleasure and presented her behind for him to mount her. As he did so, very slowly, her gasping voice reached him.

'Alex, darling! Fuck me, please! Hard! Hard!' She gasped as his hands found her breasts. He showed no mercy to the injured flesh against which he was thrusting himself; that was part of the performance. Faith had been spanked and then pleasured, the contact with his flesh heightened by the sensitivity of her own battered behind.

Though she had experienced two orgasms during the spanking, Faith's body was wracked with another; the pleasure gave her no peace, even though it provided momentary release from the ache. She continued to move beneath him, begging him to continue, pleading with him for the same again. Anything, anything he wanted, she would do. She would walk naked down the King's Road during rush hour if he wanted, but he *had* to satisfy her need.

When she was quiet, Alex loosened the scarf at her throat though leaving it in place, then removed the handcuffs. Faith lay on her back, her arms reaching up to grip the rail at the bedhead, and asked, 'Would you fasten me to this, Alex? Please?'

'Another time,' he agreed.

'Why did you do that, Alex? Why did you spank me and then . . .'

'You know why,' he answered. 'You had to learn that

pain can be used. You deserved the spanking, but you could learn the lesson, too.'

'I deserved the spanking, yes,' she admitted. 'Why did you give me the lesson?'

'Because you're willing to try,' he said. 'Now go to sleep, or you'll get another in the morning.'

'Promise?' She smiled, then snuggled up to him like a warm, contented cat.

In the darkness of the room Alex relaxed, a happy man. Not only had he managed to save the deal, he had been successful in introducing Faith to the next stage in her development. She had accepted bondage, and he would bind her closer to him in the coming days until she would never be released. Would never want to be, either. Faith was to be his own Pleasure Slave; he would possess her mind and, through that, her body. He would be her Master!

Chapter Twelve

Before he left the following morning, Alex looked gravely at Faith across the tiny kitchen.

'I want you to go to see Lillian this morning,' he said quietly, 'she's expecting you. Take everything with you as you are, the rings, balls and so on. And wear that black scarf on your throat. It makes you look delightful.'

'I don't know where she lives, Alex,' Faith replied, frowning. What was going on?

'She's got a place in Royal Avenue.' He nodded. 'I've looked out the address and left it on the bureau. Be there between nine and half past. Take a taxi if you're not sure how to get there.' His expression gave nothing away.

At nine, Lillian telephoned to remind her to bring the boots when she came. Faith was too surprised to ask how she knew about them. Perhaps that was the content of the mysterious telephone calls Alex had made before coming to bed the previous night.

Sitting in the taxi on the way to Royal Avenue on a bright Tuesday morning, the boots and a handbag her only accessories, Faith thought pleasurably about the meeting ahead. Her ambition – for Faith had her own – was to have her own flat in Chelsea. Near Alex, if possible, for she liked him and enjoyed his company. There was something about him she found more attractive each time she thought about him.

The house in Royal Avenue was quite old but had been properly maintained and, unlike many, was not divided up into flats. Ringing the bell, Faith waited until the door opened to reveal Lillian in a floor-length, *eau de nil* silk dressing-gown, the frilled collar and sleeves making her appear even more feminine than she already was, with her nipples pressing through the fabric. She was kissed decorously crossing the doorstep, then the woman led the way down the passage and up the wide stairs, commenting that it was a good climb.

Lillian guided her into an almost bare room, with stark white walls and only one kitchen chair. On the floor was a low, narrow couch, hardly six inches high.

'Undress, Faith,' Lillian said quietly, opening a cupboard built into a wall, within which were bottles and jars. When Lillian turned back, Faith remained in the same position.

'Faith!' She spoke sharply. 'I told you to undress.'

'Why, Lillian?' Faith asked, swallowing at the prospect, for the woman held a black jar in each hand.

'Because I'm going to massage you. Didn't Alex tell you? Until next weekend, you'll come here every day. Come on, get your things off. That scarf, too.'

Unwillingly, Faith removed her loose white shift and, under Lillian's frown, stripped off Julia's brassière, knickers and stockings. Naked, she lay face down on the padded leather couch, her hands up by her head in what she would later realise was a submissive gesture.

'Good,' Lillian commented, a tiny thrill of pleasure in her voice at the sight, 'but you have to spread your legs wide, Faith. How am I going to reach your bottom with your legs like that? I'd have to have fingers like a gnat.'

'My bottom?' Faith half-rolled to look up as Lillian divested herself of her dressing-gown. As Faith had expected, Lillian was naked beneath it.

'Lie down! I've put my finger in your bottom before.' Lillian was already dipping those fingers into one of the pots and, before Faith could object, she began applying the oil to Faith's shoulder. 'Did you dislike it?'

'No,' she answered, 'it's not that . . .'

'What is it then?' Lillian asked. 'Worried that there's only the two of us? I can't take your virginity, so what are you worried about?'

Faith had no answer, for her fears seemed trivial when

Lillian was working on her, kneeling beside the couch. She had surprisingly strong fingers which, combined with the sparing use of oil, seemed to tone up her skin as she worked.

'You could get someone more expert than me at a health club, Faith,' Lillian explained after a silence. 'But they wouldn't use what I'm using. Or do what I'm doing. When you turn over, I'll trim your bush.'

'What?' Faith stiffened. She knew that her legs had widened slightly since she had lain down and now she brought them closer, making Lillian chuckle.

'You're applying to join the Chosen,' the older woman said, 'and, in case you didn't notice on Saturday, most of us do without a lot of pubic hair. It's up to our individual Master, of course, but even Julia has hers trimmed. Much nicer if you keep it like that.'

'How much?' Faith asked, worried. 'I mean, how short?'

Since leaving school, Faith had trimmed hers to about a centimetre long, a neat triangle, but was that short enough? From the look of Lillian, there was hardly any hair left.

'Hardly any on the mound – enough to protect the clitoris, but not much more – a few at the sides and none on the lips,' she replied. 'I have everything to hand, don't worry. Do you want to see mine properly?'

'Oh!' Faith gasped, licking her lips in doubt.

Lillian's fingers were down around the base of her spine. As Alex had done, Lillian allowed some oil to trickle down the 'natal notch', following it with her fingers, massaging the coccyx before pushing down towards the small pink anus.

As her questing finger touched it, Lillian asked, 'No one has entered you here, Faith, have they?'

'No,' she answered, tensing for the pressure to come.

The woman paused and removed her finger while Faith waited, wondering what she would do if Lillian made any advances. Then something cold touched her anus, making her close her legs further, provoking a fierce hiss from

Lillian. The cold item was withdrawn as Lillian snapped, 'Open your legs, Faith! I'm trying to insert a dildo into your bottom, and you're not helping.'

'What?' Faith half-rolled to look at Lillian in complete surprise.

The woman was serious-faced and waiting, a small black cylinder in her right hand, as she stared at the younger woman in silence. Then, when Faith's defiant gaze finally dropped, she explained, 'Alex asked that I oil your bottom and insert a small phallus. He wants it oiled to keep it pliable and sensitive. I agree with that. I thought he would have told you. Do you want to speak to him about it? I have his office number.'

Lillian had a clear choice. She could either snap at the girl and terrify her into compliance, or she could act as though it were all perfectly normal. On balance, the rigours of the Stables were inappropriate here, she thought, so she remained quite firm and calm. The serious expression convinced Faith that the woman was telling the truth, but Alex had said nothing about this to her before he had left that morning.

'Why?' she asked. 'Why does he want to do that?'

'Apart from keeping you pliable, you mean?' Lillian asked. 'The oil I'm using has a mild aphrodisiac in it, and his instructions to me were that I put something stronger on the phallus. He wants you sexually aroused for when he comes home. Probably wants to give you a good rogering, that's all.'

'All?' Faith gasped, not knowing whether to smile or not, but the thought of Alex . . .

'You partly belong to the Chosen, Faith,' Lillian said, appearing to mollify a little, 'so I suppose I can tell you. Normally, we don't talk much about ourselves. We all want you to join us, Faith. Really. You're young, clever, attractive; just what we need. You're undisciplined, but that will come in time, with training. We'd like you to enjoy us. I don't suppose Alex has told you, but there's another party this weekend, here, in fact. Don't worry,' she said quickly, allaying her concern, 'you won't be the centrepiece, this time.' Her assurance evoked a smile from her audience. 'But Alex thinks you would be better prepared if you were aroused beforehand. It would help at home, too.

'We have strange ways, Faith, but there is one overriding principle: no one is harmed. You can be hurt – some of our people like other pleasures – but as soon as it appears to be harming you, they stop. I've known someone get a little mark after a party and everyone was worried for weeks. Most of us concentrate on sex, not spanking. Nothing worse, anyway.

'I know that Alex spanked you yesterday; I heard about it. In case you don't know, you deserved more than a spanking. With a different Master, you'd have received a sound thrashing.' She paused to rub in some more oil. 'I also know that Alex has tied you up and fucked you, so you see, you're beginning to learn how enjoyable bondage can be. What Alex has arranged is this: you'll come here every morning and I'll massage you like this. We'll do some shopping – Alex has given me his blessing to buy things for you – and I'll try to steer you away from the more obvious charlatans in the King's Road. You'll go back to Alex each night feeling like sucking him dry. Have you got your balls in?'

'No,' Faith answered, surprised at the question.

'Faith!' Lillian grimaced in irritation. 'Those are meant to help. Where are they?'

'In my handbag,' the younger woman answered, a little frightened by Lillian's annoyance.

'We'll insert them later,' Lillian said.

Again the cold item was brought to her anus, this time being pushed directly into the ring of puckered muscle, making her jerk as she felt the tip being inserted.

'It's only a short one; and thin, too. If Alex wants to sodomise you, he'll prepare you first with larger dildos. Otherwise, it might hurt your bottom, and that would never do.' Lillian smiled at Faith's back. The girl did not realise that this was exactly what she was doing. Lillian was beginning the preparation which would result in Alex taking 'the Master's right'. And when she experienced that, she would not only be completing her entrance examination into the Chosen, she would be grateful to him for doing it.

'Roll over, and keep your legs wide; as wide as if you were offering yourself to me.'

Faith did as she was told. While trying not to tense her buttocks against Lillian's caress, she thought about the stiff rod in her rectum, and the suggestion the woman had made; that she offer herself to Lillian. Was that what she wanted? Was Lillian telling her, indirectly, that she should make the offer?

Obedient to Lillian's instruction, Faith placed her legs wide apart as though about to welcome a lover, whilst Lillian quickly knelt between them. Carefully she used first an electric razor than a cut-throat to remove most of Faith's pubic hair from her mons, then from the sides and lips of her vulva, impersonally rubbing oil in afterwards as the younger woman lay tensed up. Faith could see Lillian's own trimmed state, the fair hair only serving to draw attention to her cleft and clitoris.

Once done, Lillian began to apply the oil to Faith's shoulder. She looked her in the eye as she worked, keeping her smile in place as she moved down her breasts, being especially attentive to the nipples. When Lillian had finished, Faith lay legs spread, hands submissively by her head, her skin tingling all over. Then Lillian placed her own hands on either side of Faith's head, covering her wrists, and lowered herself carefully onto her.

'There!' She kissed Faith's parched lips, moving her hips gently. Faith flushed as her own hips moved in response.

'What's the matter?' Lillian asked. 'Put your tongue out if you feel pleasure, Faith; that's the rule. And you *do* feel pleasure, darling, I know.'

'I . . . I . . .' Faith tried to speak, but Lillian's hip movements distracted her, making her gasp quietly.

'What's the matter?' Lillian asked. 'Worried because

you're rubbing your clit on mine, darling? Or are you worried because you enjoy it?'

'Both.' Faith's quick, breathless answer made the older woman smile.

'You're an honest strumpet, anyway,' she chuckled. 'Do you think I'm a lesbian? Does it worry you?'

'Yes!' Faith's face was showing her fears, prompting Lillian to raise herself on all fours above her.

'I like women,' Lillian answered, 'I won't deny it. They can make love for hours, *far* longer than any man. But believe me, Faith.' She paused, her eyes locking with those in the pale face beneath her. 'There is no feeling in the world like that of having a hot, stiff erection in your cunny. And when it comes, well!' She stopped. 'But you know that for yourself. You had your fill of come on Saturday.

'In the Chosen, there are no exceptions in our choice of lovers. You must be able – and willing – to make love to Harry or Julia. Well, perhaps not Julia, but Claire. Or me. We don't often use vibrators or phalluses, though there are times when we might. But being like this, just the two of us, is something you'd best accept. You're here to be taught and I can teach you, in ways that Max would find difficult. Why do you think Alex sent you to me, mmm? Because he knew I would introduce you to this side of things. You see? He wants you to join us. As I said, we *all* do.'

For some moments Faith lay quiet, looking up into those blue eyes, aware that Lillian was slowly moving her body from side to side, letting her nipples brush against her own. She could feel herself becoming aroused; was that the oil, or Lillian?

'It's just so different,' she protested.

'How old are you, Faith? Twenty-three? Four?' Lillian asked, her expression retaining its amusement.

'Twenty-two, why?'

'Twenty-two,' the woman smiled. 'Of course it's all new to you, and different. You've never slept with a female before, have you? Fucked would be a better way of putting it, actually. Have you ever fucked or been fucked by a woman?'

'Saturday . . .'

'Saturday, nothing,' Lillian snapped. 'Saturday, I roused you, and after the Masters had their way, Claire and I enjoyed you, too. But you've never actually had a woman on your own, have you? It's all right! I'm not going to suggest we go down to my bed and fornicate.' She smiled at Faith's relief. 'But perhaps later, when you're accepted, you might like to think about it.'

'Perhaps,' Faith agreed.

She doubted whether she would ever consider doing such a thing. Lillian's expression indicated that she knew it was only an excuse, but she accepted it. Once again, Lillian lowered her hips until their sexual organs touched. Carefully, her breasts descended onto Faith's and, as their lips were almost meeting, Faith suddenly sobbed, feeling her hips jerk upwards into Lillian. A soft look came into Lillian's eyes as she looked at the blushing young woman.

'Darling,' she said, just before their lips met, 'I'm going to make you come for that.' Faith groaned as Lillian began to move.

After a time, Lillian asked, 'Do you know the best way to arouse a woman, Faith? Really arouse her?'

'By touching her, of course,' she answered. Faith was surprised to find that she was less upset than she had been when first introduced to the concept. She had seen the others writhing in pleasure, not agony, and she had suffered no harm.

'Where, though?' Lillian asked. 'Anywhere? Or somewhere special?'

As she looked at Lillian's impish expression, a feeling of foreboding came over her. This woman knew her too well, she thought. Lillian could rouse her by pressing the right buttons, as Max had said. And she knew all the buttons. Faith could vouch for that.

'Would you like me to stroke you with this, though?' Lillian asked, smiling, handing her a strange item.

It was a large loose glove which, she realised, was made

of sheer silk. Faith could feel the cold, slippery softness and her imagination ran riot with thoughts of the sensations this would provoke within her. Putting this on her hand, Lillian said, 'I'm going to touch your breasts quite lightly with it, darling. And fondle you as I would a lover.'

'No!' The girl breathed sharply, licking her lips as she lay on the low couch. It was as though she had been tied in place, as Alex had tied her, unable to move, whilst Lillian hovered above her with this strange, fearful object.

'Well may you protest, darling; it's extremely arousing. Just your breasts, though. You have lovely breasts, haven't you? Such delicious nipples.' Her voice lowered to a soft, sensuous tone, almost a hoarse whisper. 'I'm going to bring my hand over your left breast,' she went on, still smiling, but her voice and the words she used were full of menace.

'No, please . . . aaaah!' the girl gasped, as Lillian's hand stroked lightly across the delicate flesh.

She could feel the nervous reaction of gooseflesh on her skin, but knew also that she was straining into her touch. Lillian smiled her approval, showing her teeth as she moved on to the other breast, then Faith's jaw, before returning to her breasts. She could see the conflict being set up within the young woman, and could appreciate the dilemma. Faith had never been pleasured this intimately before, not by a woman, in the seclusion of a room like this. This was where Faith would have to learn to obey, to hold still while Lillian fondled and caressed her. If she could do this, then she should be suitable for the Stables; but if she rose, or protested more than a minimum, then it looked as though Alex might be doomed to disappointment.

Down to Faith's stomach Lillian slid the glove, then back again, gently caressing the skin with her soft, slippery, almost oily touch. Lifting clear, she brought the glove of sheer silk down on the almost-naked mound just above her clitoris, letting her feel it for a moment, heavy with the threat that soon, she would be allowing the now-warm fabric to caress even more sensitive flesh; the pink folds of her sex.

'Aaah! Aaah! Aaah!' Faith cried, lifting her hips as the overpowering smell of musky young woman rose from her. Lillian's eyes closed in relief at the sight and sound, and she blessed the girl.

She was young, yes, but she was in full possession of her faculties and would train well. Alex had been right on Friday; he had judged rightly as soon as he saw her. Smiling and exultant now, Lillian opened her eyes to look down at the expressive wantonness in Faith's own, half-closed, before taking some of the liquid seeping from her hot sex and placing it on her upper lip beneath her nose, rubbing it in well so there would be no chance of wiping it away. Then she reached between her own thighs to her gaping sex, removing some of the liquid from the walls of her vagina and did the same to Faith, letting her smell her outpourings.

'There my darling,' Lillian cooed, 'that's me. Next time, you can take it from me yourself, with your tongue. Would you like that? Your tongue's out. Tell me. Would you like to lick my cunny? Say so. Say you'd like to.'

'I'd like . . .' Faith broke off, sweating, chest heaving. 'I'd *love* to lick your cunt.' Faith blushed with the shame that this arousal wrought in her, but she meant it. Lillian had brought about another wonderful feeling deep within her and, despite her shame and humiliation, she knew that she would do just what this woman wanted.

'Would you take Alex's prick in your bottom, darling?' Lillian asked.

'Yes, anything. Anything,' Faith answered, hardly knowing what she was saying.

It was later, in a quieter moment that Faith's memory of the words returned. Had Lillian been serious? Was she seriously suggesting that Alex would want to . . .? Yes. She recalled Harry and Julia. And Rupert. He had, yes! He had taken Julia from behind, too. Was that how Julia preferred to have sex? Was that why Lillian was doing as Alex wanted? Massaging oil into her anus so that it would be pliable enough for him to sodomise her? The full horror of the suggestion struck her when she realised that, if Alex proposed this, she would comply. She would quite deliberately spread her legs to allow him to force his way past the restrictive muscles of her anus.

Enchanted with this reaction, Lillian brought the glove around to her vulva in a long, light, sweeping movement; then down to her anus, back to her breasts, and then her stomach again. Up the inside of her arms she travelled, finding each erogenous spot, caressing her with the silk. The thoroughly aroused young woman was soon gasping, almost screaming with savage joy. When Lillian was satisfied she could provoke this response from Faith at will, she removed the glove and said, 'I'm going to touch your anus. You remember earlier I inserted a small dildo?' She tapped a finger on the end of the item in the small, puckered opening, making Faith's muscles contract automatically. Lillian smiled at her, thinking that Alex would be pleased with this reaction. 'I'm going to remove it now, right? Any objections? Do you want to keep it in a bit longer?'

'Yes. No. Please. Take it. Take it out.' Faith's worried face looked relieved, until Lillian went on:

'Then I'm going to test it before I insert another. We have to prepare you for the Chosen.'

'No,' the girl breathed, but by now, Lillian was hardly paying her much attention.

This time Faith's reaction was greater, a long, lingering groan of pleasure, repeated several times as, having removed the short dildo, Lillian pressed and tapped the small, pliable opening. She went to a small table behind the door of the room and returned with a smooth, black plastic cylinder about six inches long and an inch in diameter. One end was rounded whilst at the other, the cylinder tapered sharply to about a quarter of an inch thick and the same again long. There was a round flange at right angles to the cylinder. This would have been a base, but the thinner section continued for three inches beyond it, a kind of handle.

Lillian dipped the rounded end of the cylinder in the bowl of oil which had been left from the massage session; then, holding it upright, she said, 'I'm going to insert this, now. Slowly, but firmly.'

'No. Please, Lillian. *No!*' the girl pleaded, stopping her in her tracks.

'Why don't you want it, Faith?' Lillian asked, looking her in the eye. 'Don't you like it?'

'Yes,' she answered, licking her lips.

'Is it perhaps too nice?' Lillian asked.

'Yes,' the girl answered, then, '*Yes!*' in a loud yell as the tip touched the fissured surface of her anus.

Lillian pressed a little, admitting the tip into her behind, then pressed it deeper as Faith's hips bucked and jumped. She added a few drops of oil to the dildo to assist it.

'It has a narrow band at the end to keep it lodged inside,' Lillian said. 'The baffle prevents it being sucked in any further. We use them equally for anal and vaginal penetration.' She was completely matter-of-fact about it, stopping when the girl's anal muscles slipped tightly around the narrowed part, securing it within her.

Once she realised the pressure had been released, Faith became quiet again until Lillian said in a low tone, 'Come on, Faith, grip it with your muscles. Grip it tight! You're not using those lovely muscles, Faith. Show me how you can grasp with them. See?' She smiled as Faith desperately tightened up her sphincter on the dildo. 'If those were my fingers, I might have difficulty in releasing them. You've got wonderful muscle control there.'

Lillian reflected in silence for a few moments, thinking that even Angela, possibly the most passionate of the Chosen she had known, had never once been half as aroused as Faith had been. Perhaps Max was right. He usually *was* about sex.

'It seems so brutal,' Faith protested, her expression fearful as she relaxed the pressure. 'I mean, it's different.'

'Brutal?' Lillian asked, a half-smile on her face. 'That's what we're trying to avoid. I started by tapping you, Faith, arousing you very gently. Tomorrow, I might be able to show you how a clitoral ring fits. And if you want to be aroused, you will be, all right. You'll be begging me, screaming at me, either to fuck you as hard as I can, or to find someone who will. You'll be hanging onto the fiercest climax of your life, probably unable to do anything about it.

'But don't worry; that's part of the training. You have to learn that, you see? You have to learn what it feels like, how to handle it. How to control that ache. You may find tomorrow more brutal.'

'Why do you do it, if it does that to me?' she asked, her eyes wide, more afraid than ever.

'Because you're a dear girl, and I love you very much,' Lillian answered simply. 'You need this actually, Faith, which is why you were sent to me. I'm preparing you for the Chosen and, more importantly, for your Master.'

'I don't understand.' The young woman breathed anxiously, now able to move a little, though still feeling the rod deep within her.

'I wish I'd known you longer, Faith. But both Alex and I realise that, if you're going to make a successful marriage, if you're going to obtain full sexual value and *remain* at full sexual value, you have to be taught. Which is where I come in. I'm teaching you, though this is only one stage in it; there are others.

'After a week or so, you'll go on to learn other things, you'll move onto more advanced subjects, until you can really enjoy sex. In the Chosen, you'll be available to anyone who asks and to anyone whom your Master permits to fuck you. You have to be able to derive the maximum amount of pleasure from being mounted, for only in that way will you give the maximum amount of pleasure.

'I know! Whores give pleasure without getting much themselves, but I said "maximum". Faith, and I meant it. If you're busy roaring your head off in an orgasm, the chances are that your cunt will be squeezing someone's prick. And your hands will be grabbing their balls, too. It's not something that always comes naturally, if you'll pardon the pun, so we teach it. I teach it, in fact.'

After a few minutes' silence, Faith asked in a quiet voice 'How did you know? About Alex and . . .? Did he tell you?' And when Lillian frowned, 'About the spanking and about when he tied me up?'

'Tell me?' Lillian asked. 'No! You wore a black scarf. Did Alex tell you to do that? I've got a nice black ribbon for you instead. It'll go with more things. It's what we use to indicate someone's preferences and accomplishments. Black means you've been mounted while restrained. Did he tie your hands?'

'Something like that,' Faith answered, the cold seeping from her brain to her spine so that she shivered.

'I know he spanked you and then made love to you,' the woman said. 'He called me this morning. He meant to just spank you at first, anyway. But he said you looked so lovely, so vulnerable, that he wanted you badly.'

'So he had me,' Faith said.

'Of *course* he had you!' Lillian grated in sudden annoyance. 'He can have you whenever he wants! You're *his*! You've surrendered to him, told him! What do you expect him to do? Ignore you?'

Faith looked up at the concerned face above her, and her eyes dropped in acquiescence. Lillian saw the further bond forging in the young woman's mind; the acceptance that Alex was her Master, and she would do what she was told. Perhaps it might be as well to reinforce the lessons, soon, and explain some more, otherwise this intelligent addition to their ranks was going to be unhappy. And that would never do.

After Lillian had sucked her nipples through the rings, Faith practised walking up and down in her boots – including mounting and descending stairs – finding it strange to walk about the house naked in the long, black leather boots. Lillian also insisted she walk with her wrists behind her, resting on her rump, as an aid to posture, though Faith found it irksome to be so upright.

'Come back here, Faith,' Lillian said from the drawing room as the young woman exited into the hall. She returned and stood facing the window, making an effort to hold herself upright and to put her hands behind her. Before she could protest, almost before she realised what was happening in fact, Lillian had slipped the familiar cold metal cuffs on her wrists.

'There,' she said quietly, 'that should help a little. You should get used to that, Faith.'

'Why?' Faith asked, looking at her hostess in troubled surprise.

'You've been to the Club, haven't you? You've seen the members' ladies there. If Alex wants to take you there for lunch, what are you going to do? Embarrass him by screaming the place down when he cuffs you? Don't be silly. Now walk.'

The firmness in Lillian's voice and features gave Faith no hope of early release. Until twelve thirty she walked up and down Lillian's house, naked but for the boots, her racing mind gradually coming to terms with her restrained wrists.

After removing the dildo and handcuffs, then dressing, they window-shopped their way to lunch somewhere smart, where Lillian was well-known. Late in the afternoon, Faith was packed into a taxi for the return to Cheyne Walk to await Alex.

This set the pattern for the week. Each morning, Faith would take a cab to Lillian's house where, in the bare attic room, Lillian would rub oil into her skin, insert a slightly larger dildo into her anus and then they would caress for half an hour. Faith was less frightened on subsequent occasions, especially when she told Alex what had happened; she was surprised to find him encouraging, instead of angry or jealous.

In the evenings after dinner, Alex would often put her through her paces in her boots, following Lillian's example of handcuffing her wrists behind her and frequently allowing her to suck the glass *harigata* up within her, noting the speed with which her hot, hungry flesh took it from his palm. She was beginning to have slight control of her orgasms, too; something about which he was particularly pleased. Usually he took her straight afterwards, often from behind, moving gently within her until they climaxed.

Faith's orgasm always erupted long before Alex was ready to release, which humiliated her, for she was trying to stave off her pleasure, but he smiled and assured her that he had a lot more experience than she had. Though occasionally tempted, Alex made no attempt to discipline her. He would have liked to have spread her over his knee and spanked her naked buttocks, or caned them while she stood, fastened to the bedframe. But that would come, in time. Faith was being trained.

Chapter Thirteen

That first Saturday, they attended rather a wild party at Lillian's house. The same crowd as before was in attendance; Rupert and Claire, Colin and Prudence, Julia and Harry and Lillian with Simon, who seemd to be the front-runner with Lillian at the moment. As no other guests were there, they shed their clothes from the moment they arrived, though Faith was nervous about joining in the activities as she had so little experience. Whilst sympathetic, they all insisted she be included for, to most if not all of them, Faith was becoming part of the furniture.

After Lillian and Simon got the party under way by Simon bringing Lillian to a climax with his nose, Faith knelt beside Julia and watched the petite woman give a 'master class' with her expert fellation of Rupert. The young woman was fascinated to watch Julia running her tongue up and down the underside of his erection, loosening and then tightening her grip on his scrotum, sometimes even pinching his shaft at the base as he gasped and groaned above her. When his climax was finally allowed, Julia took it all calmly in her mouth.

Then it was Faith's turn with Alex. This was the first time she had voluntarily brought a male member anywhere near her mouth, but Faith was firm in her resolve. She remembered the effect it had had on him when she was secured to the bed in Old Church Street, which was justification enough. Pulling back the foreskin, she caressed the glans with her tongue as she had seen Julia do, slowly running the tip delicately around the soft flesh beneath the rim. Still holding the purpling head exposed, she continued on down the length of the shaft beneath, nipping him gently here and there with her sharp front teeth.

Alex's breathing was beginning to sound harsh in her ears as Faith, with Lillian on one side and Julia on the other to advise and encourage her, took both testicles, one after the other, into her mouth. He was gulping air when her soft lips closed lightly around the purple plum at the top of his shaft, running slowly up and down, back and forth. When the tip of his glans touched the soft palate at the back of her throat, Faith pulled away again, her tongue still rolling around the shaft.

Gradually Alex's breathing was quickening, his chest making little heaving sounds which grew louder and faster with each caress until finally, he was relieved of his seed. Faith, in her haste and nervousness, removed her mouth at the wrong time, so that Alex's semen cascaded over her face, temporarily blinding her, and setting her back on her heels. Lillian and Julia were instantly at work.

They began to smear the fluid into her skin, rubbing it gently but firmly into her nipples, down over her clitoris and, more than anywhere, applying it to her 'natal notch', where an inordinate amount was worked into her anus. These attentions had the effect not only of relieving any unpleasantness, but also of stimulating her again. They made sure that Faith licked some of the semen from around her mouth, checking that it was on her tongue before making her swallow it. Faith felt hesitant at first, but allowed them to persuade her, finding that the salty, creamy fluid was not unpleasant.

Later, Harry drew her arms behind her, holding her tightly just above the elbows in a grip which, though not painful, made it impossible for her to move her upper torso. Alex and Rupert sat on either side of her and spread her feet widely whilst they crooked one knee around her ankles so there was no possibility of movement. Finally, Lillian, who knelt in front of her, using only her fingertips and tongue, caressed her lightly on her open sex, holding off her orgasm for almost forty minutes. When she was finally released from the terrifying inner pressure, her legs trembling with the extended tension in the long muscles of her thighs. Faith threw her head back and screamed her release to the ceiling, whilst her body shook like a rag-doll being thrown down the stairs.

The following morning, still a little jaded from the late-night party, Alex was standing at the open window looking out across the Thames when Faith arrived alongside him. For a few moments they remained in the comparative, companionable silence of the the bright morning until Alex said, 'We're going out on the river, later. Harry's boat.'

'That should be nice,' Faith replied, wondering why Alex's expression was less than cheerful.

'Harry and Julia, Max, Lillian, and us.' He looked round at her. 'It's time you learned a bit more,' he finished enigmatically. Faith asked what he meant, but he ignored her, returning to his contemplation of the vista before them.

At ten-thirty, Alex and Faith set off, walking along past Chelsea Old Church to the Chelsea Marina, on the far side of Battersea Bridge. Beyond lay the pocket-handkerchief of Cremorne Gardens, with Chelsea Wharf, Chelsea Creek and the new, soaring heights of Chelsea Harbour behind. But boats of all shapes and sizes were drawn up between the bridge and Cremorne Gardens and, on a large catamaran, they found Harry and Julia.

The small woman with the almost flat, white scarf across her chest and the short, dark blue flared skirt, looked elated, her face devoid of make-up appearing absurdly young, but suffused with excitement as she watched them board. While Harry and Alex went into an immediate huddle, she took Faith into the large cabin placed centrally between the hulls.

It looked like a film set, with pastel colours and a deep, fleecy carpet on the floor. Around the cabin benches were fitted, padded with thick cushions whose patterns matched the decor, whilst in the centre of the cabin, a table on four stout legs occupied the space. Yet there was still room to pass between the table and the benches, though eating at it might be difficult.

'Where are we going?' Faith asked. 'Up river, or down?'

'I don't know,' Julia answered. 'I leave all that to Harry and the other men. Lillian shouldn't be too long, then we can get away.'

Lillian and Max arrived together within minutes, leaving their taxi at the entrance and walking side by side, without speaking, towards the vessel, making Faith think that there had been some disagreement. Julia welcomed the serious couple as they stepped aboard, Max immediately going to help Alex cast off while the two women came down to the saloon, where Lillian's face brightened at the sight of Faith.

'I didn't know . . .' She broke off, shaking her head. 'Of *course* you'd be here, if Alex was coming.' Like Julia, she wore no cosmetics, her long, loose dress apparently her only adornment. Faith, in a white jumper and narrow skirt, felt over-dressed in comparison.

No sooner were the ropes cast off than Harry, up on the bridge, powered up the engines from idle to reverse them out of the berth, before making the slow turn towards the main reach of water.

'Like to see what it's like from up there?' Alex asked, coming into the saloon from the small doorway opposite the one Faith had used. Behind him she could see steps and the hairy legs of a seated man: Harry.

'Yes!' Faith was interested at once. 'Could I?' As she moved after him, the two women began to pull the curtains over the wide windows which gave such excellent views of Battersea Bridge, under which they were passing. Harry was steering down-river.

Alex slipped into the seat which Harry had vacated, gesturing to Faith to take the other one, whilst the owner walked aft down the side of the boat and out of sight. It felt good to be up there in the bright air, with the catamaran moving slowly downstream. Alex even allowed Faith to steer for a short while, but took control when the wake of the river bus sent them wallowing gently. There were several boats about on the Thames, large and small, all pleasure craft; being Sunday, the commercial traffic was reduced. She saw the small, low shape of the Police launch, the dark flag at the stern hanging limp, hovering near the Battersea shore as they cruised towards Chelsea Bridge.

A noise behind her made Faith turn, and there was Harry, looking red-faced but smiling, climbing up the steps.

'I'll take her, Alex,' he said briefly, slipping into the seat at once, for Alex had anticipated him. Julia, looking a little pale but with a thin smile on her face followed, displacing Faith from the soft padded seat. Faith slid back the door, stepped out into the open, then like Alex, walked back down the hull past the curtained windows. It was only when she had reached the doorway that she realised that Julia only wore the scarf around her breasts; her dark blue skirt had vanished.

Alex was already at the doorway waiting for her, an intent expression alerting her even as she passed him and entered the cabin already containing Lillian and Max. They seemed to be expecting her, their faces turning hopefully towards Alex as he closed the door behind him. Then his voice said in crisp, clear tones, 'Max is going to strip you, Lillian!'

'Yes, I rather thought he might,' she said at once, her eyes flickering to the younger, taller woman.

Alex's hands rested lightly on Faith's shoulders, an unspoken restraint, as Max unfastened the bodice of Lillian's loose dress, peeling it from her shoulders. As usual, she wore nothing beneath.

'Bend over the table, Lillian,' Alex said firmly. 'I'm going to spank you. I think you know why.'

'Yes, Alex.' Lillian's expression changed from firm to contrite, her head lowering in submission as she turned, stepping out of the dress at her feet.

Faith's mouth dropped open as the woman laid her

torso flat across the table, her wrists crossing behind her back, her forehead down on the surface.

'Go to her, Faith,' Max said quietly as Alex stepped past her, 'Kiss her. Just hold her head if you would. She needs you.' The woman looked uncomprehendingly at him, so Max moved Faith by the elbows, as on Alex's command, Lillian spread her legs wide apart.

Max placed her directly in front of Lillian as Alex laid his left hand on the small of her back, then brought his upraised right hand down, very smartly, on her naked, exposed posterior. Lillian gave a yell which she tried to suppress, her face contorting in agony, and she jerked off the table where her forehead had rested not a foot from Faith.

As the last strains of the bitten-off cry ended, there was the sharp crack of Alex's hand striking Lillian's flesh again. Again Lillian yelped, unable to control herself. Impulsively, Faith bent forward to fasten her mouth on Lillian's dry, swollen lips, finding that the woman responded greedily, her tongue piercing through into Faith's mouth. The third smack produced an explosive grunt from the older woman, who began sucking Faith's tongue fervently.

'Hold her!' Max snapped. 'Hold her breasts!' And without thinking, Faith obeyed, slipping her hands beneath Lillian when next she jerked off the table as Alex's hand landed.

By the sixth slap, tears were standing in Lillian's eyes, her breathing was difficult and, for a moment, Faith released her, thinking she needed air. But the wailing plea Lillian voiced brought her back again, to kiss away the hurt. And all the while her mind whirled, knowing that Alex was spanking Lillian *very* hard, making her cry, for the tears were running down her cheeks to wet Faith's skin and dribble saltily into the corners of their mouths.

Why was Alex spanking Lillian? Why had she stood stock still while Max removed her clothes? Why had she lowered her head meekly and accepted this? It was a side of Alex that Faith had rarely more than glimpsed, but even as she squeezed Lillian's breasts and kissed her, she was aware of a terrible truth. Lillian was becoming excited, sexually excited!

It was in the sounds of her throat: the groans were no longer of pain but of pleasure. Was it true, then, that even without 'Love Balls' there was pleasure to be had in being spanked? A moment's thought convinced her that this must be the case, for Lillian was presenting her rear to Alex for more.

When Alex stopped spanking, he was ready for the next phase. He quickly doffed his clothes and naked, he stepped forward to insert his erection directly into her hot opening. Savagely, Lillian freed her mouth from Faith's, groaning as she did so, her wrists still crossed and resting on her rump.

'Alex! Alex, darling!' she cried. 'Fuck me! Fuck me as hard as you can!'

Surprised, Faith looked up at Alex's intent expression as he thrust himself against the hot, abused flesh in front of him, his erection fully within the submissive woman. Each time his loins clashed with Lillian the woman grimaced and gasped, but there was an expression of demented lust on her face. She made no complaint, bucking her hips in time with the man who was mounting her so strongly and with such obvious determination.

Faith's unease was compounded by Max's solemn gaze as he stood on her left, arms folded, watching impassively as Lillian was first punished, and then ridden to a weeping, exulting climax, her face distorted with the agonies of her pain and lust. At last, almost exhausted, she lay quiet on the table. In the sudden silence, broken only by the chug and vibration of the engines and the hissing slap of the water outside, the aroma of love-making filled their nostrils.

Releasing Lillian's breasts, her hands feeling softer than ever, Faith watched as the two men bent over the slumped woman with every show of tenderness, as she slowly recovered. As soon as she was able to rise stiffly from the table, she embraced Alex, sobbing drily into his neck as she laid her nudity against his long body. Lillian obviously bore him no ill-will.

When the woman retrieved her dress and was about to move away, Alex said in a curt tone, 'Under the table, Lillian. You haven't finished, yet.'

'Of course not,' she said, dull-eyed still, but dropping to her knees, she moved between the metal legs supporting the pillory. Alex looked at Faith, whose blood ran cold; her heart began to beat faster, knowing that he was about to pronounce her fate.

'Do you love me, Faith?' he asked quietly.

'Of course I do, Alex,' she returned, surprised at the question. 'You know I do.'

'We'll see, shall we? I want you to remove all your clothes and bend over, as Lillian bent over. I'm going to put handcuffs on your wrists and spank you, too.'

'What have I done?' Faith asked. 'Why?' She swallowed as she tried to control her rising fear.

'Why?' he repeated quietly. 'Because you love me. What have you done? Nothing. Simply because I ask you to.'

For a stunned moment Faith looked into his calm features, hardly aware of the other two people watching. She was torn between her feelings for this wonderful lover, and the agony she had seen Lillian suffer; then she recalled Lillian's arousal. It had been the first time she had really seen her turned on and, despite herself, Faith found the prospect of having her wrists secured before being entered thrilling.

Deep within her, her muscles were responding, moving the 'Love Balls' in the familiar deliciously lubricious ways she was coming to know. With trembling lips and little sobs which she thought were fear, but which the others recognised as excitement, Faith removed first her jumper, then her skirt, followed by her brassière and knickers.

Facing the table, she put her hands behind her, feeling the sudden chill as Alex slipped the handcuffs over her wrists, the sound of the ratchet's teeth echoing loudly within her. Without waiting to be told, Faith bent forward to lay herself on the still-warm surface of the table, splaying out her legs, resting her forehead as Lillian had done. Her breathing was still a thrilling sob which rattled up from deep within her chest, a tremor which threatened her composure until she felt the familiar, moist warmth of Lillian's mouth on her sexual organs.

Lillian seperated Faith's labia with her fingers and thrust her tongue deep into the entrance to her vagina, before removing it to remark, 'She's soaking already.' Then she replaced her tongue and proceeded to slip that organ up towards Faith's aching button. Max stood in front of her, his large hands sliding beneath her to seize her breasts, her nipples painfully locked in the crook of his fingers.

The first slap struck just as Lillian's tongue reached her hot, excited button, the spasmodic jerk away from Lillian coinciding with the equally spasmodic jerk away from the slap. Pinned between them, and with Max sending further messages of sweet delight from her nipples, Faith's gasp was more pleasure than pain. The 'Love Balls' moved, her breasts and buttocks moved, her clitoris moved, the boat moved. Faith, by the third slap was gasping so loudly in her lust that she thought people on the Embankment must be able to hear her.

So did Max, for he roughly thrust a gag between her teeth while Alex slapped on, driving all thought of a pleasant Sunday trip on the river far from Faith's mind. All she could concentrate upon were the lewd sensations she felt coursing through her, emanating from between her thighs and navel, and threatening to overwhelm her senses. The actual pain of the spanking soon dulled into an ache which awoke more desire than it quelled, for as Alex spanked, her hips moved, presenting her behind for his hand. He was very accurate in general, keeping each buttock separately warmed, but occasionally he would miss slightly and, if it were a blow to the sensitive flesh where the buttock and thigh met, the stinging stroke would strike the edges of her labia, sending rivers of molten fire through her.

When the spanking stopped, Faith was aware of the tears which filled her eyes for the first time; she was also aware of another great truth however: they were tears of happiness! She was ready to be mounted, and in such a state of agitation that it could have been anyone.

Movement around her impinged on her consciousness and there was Alex in front of her as a hot, hard erection pressed gently against her opening. With a groaning cry of release, Faith pressed herself backwards against it as Max had intended, surrendering herself to him. He knew her condition, that she wanted only to be mounted, and that it was important that she see Alex. As he pressed himself slowly forward, feeling her muscles tighten and release until he was firmly lodged within her, he nodded to the tall man who now stood in front of Faith.

'This is the hand that spanked you, Faith,' Alex said quietly, holding it out for her inspection. As the shaft in her began to move, Faith reached forward and, opening her mouth, fastened her lips wetly and lasciviously around his fingers. And all the while, Lillian knelt beneath the table, keeping up her stimulation of Faith's sex, driving her to distraction so that, all too soon, with a high, keening scream, she climaxed. Arching her back and lifting her body from the table, she lost Alex's hand in the ecstasy of her orgasm, before passing out.

When Faith's senses returned, she was lying on one of the bunks by the drawn curtains, with a cold cloth being wiped over her overheated body. As her eyes opened, through a slight gap in the curtains, she could see Westminster Bridge and the Houses of Parliament, its tall tower shrouded in scaffolding, pass by on the way back up-river.

'Are you all right, darling?' The familiar voice of Lillian sounded anxiously close as Faith opened her eyes.

The fair woman had the cold cloth in her hand and beyond her stood Julia, hands on hips, still only wearing the scarf. Both had concerned expressions.

'Are you all right, Faith?' Lillian repeated.

'Yes, thank you,' Faith managed to mutter through parched lips. Immediately she licked them, a cold drink was held up to her mouth, cooling the hot dryness of her throat.

'What happened?' Faith asked, unable to believe her memory; it was so bizarre. Lillian and then herself had been spanked and then . . . She refused to think about it.

'Julia and I got what we deserved,' Lillian said. 'Less than we deserved, really. And you had your education advanced.'

'What you deserved?' Faith frowned, looking at the steady blue eyes.

'I burnt a soufflé, my dear – ' Julia's quiet voice held no sullen remorse – 'so of course I had to be punished. Look.' Turning, she showed her naked buttocks.

The pallid skin of Julia's behind was now marked by long red weals about half an inch across, on a background of dull red. It looked hot from where Faith lay, six feet away.

'What . . .?' she began, but Julia was already speaking.

'A whip, of course! Harry was very kind about it. I had to be punished so, instead of just spanking me and leaving me – which would have hurt terribly – he used the whip and made love to me afterwards.'

'I got beastly drunk, earlier this week, darling,' Lillian said. 'Thursday, when we lunched in that little *trattoria*, remember? I had Chianti till it came out of my ears, and then a couple of cocktails after you'd gone. Then I dined in a restaurant and made a complete fool of myself! Alex had no choice but to spank me. I was lucky that's all he did.'

'Alex?' Faith frowned. 'Why should Alex spank *you*?'

There was a sudden pause as Julia inhaled sharply, her eyes looking to Lillian as though wondering what her answer would be.

'Because he's my Master, of course,' the woman said.

'Your what?'

'My Master. I've been given to him,' Lillian replied.

'You gave yourself, Lillian,' Julia warned, 'as I did to Harry. And you did, Faith, to Alex.'

'Me?' Faith gasped. 'But this is slavery,' she protested. 'They can't do that.'

'If I choose to have a Master,' Lillian said, 'then that's my business. Alex is responsible for me – and enough people saw me – so he had to punish me. I'm lucky; he fucked me, too. That made it not so bad.'

'It's still slavery!'

'We're Slaves of Pleasure,' Julia answered, 'just as Claire and Prudence are. Our Masters give and receive pleasure, as do we.'

'As do you, Faith,' Lillian said, her eyes never leaving the young woman's gaze, locked in a trial of strength.

'Me?' Faith's question was barely audible.

'Tell me you didn't have one of the most wonderful experiences ever Faith, and I'll believe you're not devoted to Alex. It was Alex who ordered you to undress, to take the spanking for no reason, and Alex who gave it. And while Max filled your cunt, you *sucked* Alex's fingers as if they were his dick!' There was a strength in her voice as she saw the gradual acceptance revealed by Faith's face. It was slowly dawning on the trembling girl that Lillian was right.

Alex had been leading her to this position for some time now. Old Church Street, being handcuffed in the bedroom, being spanked in Brook Street, the women in the club. They had all been pointers to what was happening. Slowly and surely, he had been seducing her into becoming dependent on him, into loving him. And, as she sobbed quietly and openly, her features distorted, there came the realisation that she loved him for it. It was true: she *was* his slave. If he wanted her to bend over the table again now, he would not need the handcuffs to quell her. Faith knew she would accept the punishment from his own hands.

'Are you all right, darling?' Lillian asked solicitously, stroking her hair from her eyes.

'How can we . . .? How can I . . .?' Faith broke off, shaking her head.

'How can you get away?' Lillian looked round to Julia, whose nod confirmed that Faith was accepting the situation. No longer was she denying her servitude; she acknowledged it and sought an escape. It was easier to deal with like that.

'Yes.' The sobs were quieter.

'Walk away if you want, darling,' Lillian answered. 'The men are up on the bridge, leaving us to talk to you. You can dive off into the Thames if you like; they won't stop you. Or, when we get back to the Marina, you can come with me, to my place. I'll get your things from Alex and you can stay as long as you like. I won't mind and nor will he. It's not really slavery, you see. Not the way you think.'

'But he . . .' She stopped.

'He spanked me, yes, and fucked me. He spanked you and let Max fuck you,' Lillian said, 'because he couldn't have both of us in such a short time, and Max hadn't fucked you before. I think he did a good job. You certainly seemed to enjoy it.'

'And you . . .'

'And I sucked your clit and played with your slit until Max took over,' Lillian admitted, 'and you passed out from sheer sexual ecstasy. Max was impressed.'

'If you don't go with Lillian, dear,' Julia said, 'would you like to stay with us? It would be no trouble.'

'Why are you helping me to escape?' Faith asked, gulping.

'We're not,' Lillian said. 'We're helping you come to terms with it. You can leave if you want. I think you know you'll regret it if you do. Think about it. Anyway, we've got to get this place tidied up and both of us changed. I've washed your quim as best I can, but you might like to do it yourself before you dress.' The woman, her voice businesslike, stood up.

* * *

After mooring again at the Marina, the three couples walked in a group to Alex's flat; the other five chattered like magpies, while Faith walked with her head down, thinking. Her behind was still warm from the spanking, but she could feel the surge of lust coiling within her again. It was as though one mounting was insufficient to cool her ardour.

Upstairs in the flat, she and Alex set about getting drinks for everyone and, as it was almost two, Faith set about preparing a few light snacks. She was busy in the small kitchen when her attention was drawn to the doorway, where with a start she saw Alex, lounging against the opening, arms folded behind him, watching her. How long he had been there was a mystery to Faith, but his expression was amused rather than cross or impatient.

'Alex?' she asked uncertainly.

'I love you, Faith,' he said simply.

'Do you?' Her fear was growing and yet, the higher the apprehension rose, the tighter was her grip on the 'Love Balls', with the appropriate results. Slowly her insides were liquidising again.

'Yes,' he almost whispered, 'very much.'

'I . . .' She broke off, unable to continue, and turned away.

'Who is your Master, Faith?' He spoke in the same, soft half-whisper which seemed to penetrate her mind directly without passing through the logic centres of her brain.

'You.' She looked round and up at him, an agonised flash of self-discovery on her pleasant face.

'Who is my slave?' he asked in the same measured tone.

'Me.' Her head dropped as her chest heaved.

'Turn around Faith,' he said quietly, 'away from me.'

Faith did as she was told, listening to the rustle of clothing as he moved, and the all-but-silent clink of metal. Something cold touched her mind as he closed with her. Slowly and gently he removed all but her stockings while she remained motionless, not turning, looking out of the window at the grey concrete of Battersea across the river.

There was a touch of cold metal on her back as the clinking sounds were repeated, then something icy was placed about her neck with a snicking sound which sent shudders down her back, slowly changing to gooseflesh. She could feel the cold, sharp metal at the small of her back as Alex raised first one arm and then the other behind her back, fastening them into broad metal cuffs attached to the chain which was suspended from the back of the metal collar around her throat.

'Turn around,' he said quietly and, when she did so, he looked directly into her eyes.

'Who are you, Faith?' he asked.

'Your slave, Master,' she answered.

'Then come and show yourself to the others,' he said, concealing his relief that she had taken it all so calmly.

Following in his wake, Faith walked with bowed head from the kitchen, down the passage and into the silent drawing room, where the four guests had been waiting apprehensively. When Alex had left them, after telling them what he was going to do, Harry and Lillian had expressed doubts about whether Faith was ready. It had only been a week and she was undisciplined, so putting her into a collar this soon could ruin everything. Although he nodded his understanding of their reasoning, Max had hoped they were wrong. Faith had been an intelligent and willing young woman; he liked her and probably his prejudices in her favour made him hope Alex would succeed.

When Alex stood aside to reveal the chained and almost naked Faith, clad only in stainless steel and white stockings, her head bowed in submission, there was a collective sigh of relief. One after the other they rose to kiss Faith and then to greet Alex, whose own relief was patently obvious to them. Faith waited, wondering what she should do. Did she just stand there with bowed head until one of them wanted to have sex with her, or spank her, or what?

'Here,' Alex began unfastening the cuffs first, and then

the collar from her neck, 'I'll take . . . no! Don't turn around. Not yet, anyway,' he said, moving away from Faith, leaving her facing Harry, who smiled at her. Within seconds something else cold was being pressed around her neck, heavier than before, and thicker. It too snapped into place with a final snicking sound which sent the same shivers through her.

'That's your collar, Faith. It needs a key to remove it, and you don't have one. Who is your Master?'

'You are, Alex,' she answered, without thinking.

'And what are you?'

'A slave.'

'*My* slave,' he emphasised, 'my Pleasure Slave.'

'Your Pleasure Slave,' Faith corrected herself, lowering her head. The collar felt bulky as well as heavy.

'Go into the bedroom and change into something more appropriate, slave,' he said, though there was more than a trace of humour in his voice. Blushing, Faith required no second telling. She fled, bursting into the bedroom in a flurry of wobbling bosom and flailing limbs only to stop short.

The mirrors all around revealed her all at once, and at wildly different angles. Trembling, Faith walked up to a wall-mirror and looked at herself. Her breasts were jutting out, her nipples thick rubbery cylinders while from her sex came the musk of an aroused woman. But the collar! It was the collar which took her eye.

It was gold, about one and a half inches high and thick enough to be genuine. With a band of jet about quarter of an inch wide running around the centre of it, there was a loop at the front and, feeling, she found another at the back, at the bottom edge. But it was the sight of the plain gold ornament that took her breath away and she was still there when Julia came in some minutes later, her expression anxious.

'Are you all right, my dear? What's the matter?'

'It's this,' Faith replied in a dreamy voice. 'Isn't it beautiful?'

'Your Slave Collar, yes,' Julia nodded. 'You'll have to wear it, my dear. Out in the street, too.'

'I don't care.' Faith turned, her exclamation of joy making the small woman blink. 'I'm *his*!' She threw her head back and, flinging her arms in the air, stood with her eyes closed until Julia began to fuss around her, helping to dress the young woman who felt as though it were her bridal day.

The others left at five. Max and Lillian had been invited for cocktails, so Harry and Julia went too. As they were about to close the doors of the lift, Lillian asked, 'Faith! Do you want to come with us?'

'No, thank you.' The younger woman shook her head, standing at the door of the flat next to Alex. 'I'll stay with my Master.' He put a hand on her shoulder as the doors closed and, as they sank from sight, he felt his heart lighten. One way and another, it had been quite a day.

That night, Alex supervised Faith as she practised walking in just her boots, this time with a chain leading from her collar, her hands secured behind her. There seemed to be a new confidence about her, for she made no complaint at this treatment. He was her Master, responsible for her and if this was what he wanted, then this was what she would do.

When they went to bed, Alex fastened her wrists and ankles to the brass frame before slowly mounting her, bringing her to a climax with his tongue before delving with deliberate speed into her. Faith lay, groaning softly, feeling that every thrust deep within her might tear her apart with its sweet and gentle strength.

Chapter Fourteen

Before he went to work on Tuesday morning, Alex told Faith that he would meet her for lunch that day at the Club. On her arrival at Lillian's house, when she mentioned it, she found the woman already knew.

'I'm coming with you, darling,' Lillian said quietly. 'I couldn't let you do that on your own. Gerald and Abigail will be there, too.'

'I don't know what you mean,' Faith said, hissing slightly as Lillian worked another phallus into her anus. Lillian never said and Faith never asked, but she was certain that these were larger than before.

'Alex is going to feed you in public.' Lillian's tone was resigned, prompting Faith to ask:

'Lillian? Is everything all right? I mean, between you and Alex?'

For a few moments there was silence, then the woman answered, 'He's going to give me away in a few weeks.'

'Give you away?' Faith felt herself go rigid. It was impossible! Alex was Lillian's Master, and if he could give her away, what future did Faith have?

'Yes,' Lillian said. 'I was looking forward to it at one time, but now I'm having second thoughts.'

'How can he?' Faith asked.

'Easily.' The woman added oil to the polished surface and began to turn it. 'Unlike Julia and yourself, I was *given* to Alex. His family and mine were, if not founders of the Chosen, then in at the beginning. They thought it would be a good idea if Alex and I were married. So they gave me to him, when I first came back from the Stables.

'Like a lot of good ideas, it didn't work out like that in

practice. We've known for some time that we'd never be a pair, and your coming on the scene only made that more obvious.'

'I'm sorry. I didn't know,' Faith said quietly. 'Do you know who . . .?' She found it difficult to ask.

'Oh, yes.' She cheered up at once. 'He's giving me to Max. It's a wonderful idea. At least, I thought so, at first. Now, I'm beginning to wonder.'

'You mentioned the Stables. What stables are these?'

'It's a place down in the country.' Lillian decided that if Alex had kept the truth from her, then it would be as well to divert her attention. 'Sort of a college for the Chosen.'

The two women were decanted from the taxi outside the anonymous address in St James's. The front door opened as they approached. Rankin asked their names, allowing them into the hallway as they were both on his list, and indicated a long, buttoned-leather couch against the wall just in front of the stairs where they could sit until collected. After leaving their handbags with the porter, both sat upright, Faith with her gold choker, Lillian with a broad velvet band around her neck.

Gerald and Abigail arrived within a few minutes and stood chatting until, on the stroke of one, Alex and Rupert arrived to claim them. The greetings over, Alex said quietly to Faith, 'I'm going to secure your wrists now, Faith. Put them behind you.' From his tone, Lillian knew that he was nervous about this, for if Faith objected strongly, it was about as public as could be imagined. The young woman looked at him, smiling as she lowered her head and turned, placing her hands behind her. Standing at the foot of the stairs, with Gerald looking on approvingly, Faith's wrists were secured with a simple chain with a snap at each end which hooked into one of the links.

'Your girl's come on no end in the last week, Alex,' Gerald observed as they drifted after the others towards the dining room.

'Yes, she has,' Alex said.

'Difficult, was it?'

'No! She's very intelligent,' her lover replied. It took Faith a few moments to realise that they were talking about her.

Throughout lunch, the three women remained quiet unless spoken to, listening to the men discussing various business ventures and the state of some negotiations in which Gerald and Rupert had an interest. Abigail and Lillian were free to eat, but Alex was a most attentive host, feeding Faith in preference to himself. Being tall, Faith knew she attracted attention from other tables, especially as she sat bolt upright. Lillian had told her that it was expected of her. Dressed in a light blue outfit which Lillian had pressed her to buy, she ignored the eyes which roved over her from time to time.

As the meal wore on, one or two of the people at other tables stopped for a few words, nodding to her when introduced. They seemed to have sharp eyes which missed very little, and the older men were usually quite abrupt in their manner. Most asked if Alex was playing, but he refused. Faith thought that the lure of the gaming tables was either so strong that he had to avoid them altogether, or else held no interest at all. Rupert and Lillian went through the doorway with Gerald and Abigail at the end of the meal, while Alex took Faith out into the hallway, where her wrists were speedily released.

In the car on the way back to Chelsea, she asked, 'Don't you gamble, Alex? Or is it just at lunch that you don't play?'

'Play? No,' he snorted, shaking his head. 'It's not that.' He paused, thinking, then shrugged. 'Most afternoons there's a game of forfeits in the part we call the Theatre. People get called up and are given forfeits; it can get quite ribald, at times.'

'And you don't play?' she frowned.

'Not at the moment. Not until you're better educated, darling.'

'Educated in what?'

'In our ways. After all, it's under a fortnight since you moved in, and you're still learning.'

'You said I was intelligent,' Faith said quietly.

'All right. I didn't want you going up on the stage and having to suck somebody off you'd never seen before!' he answered sharply. 'It seems that trying to be gentle with you doesn't work.'

'I'm sorry,' Faith said at once, 'I don't know these things, and if I put my foot in it, it's because you don't tell me.'

'Yes, I know. It will soon be over, though,' he nodded.

On Thursday night, Alex took Faith to one of the better restaurants just off the Sloane Square end of the King's Road. He was known there; the table was secluded and the service all Faith could have desired. She wore the dress Lillian had persuaded her to buy that afternoon; she had felt tense when Alex had looked at her; he meanwhile was stunned and unable to speak for some moments; she had never looked lovelier. For a mad instant he considered cancelling all the arrangements he had so carefully made during the previous fortnight, abandoning the plans he had discussed with Max and Lillian, forgetting all about his family. Yet common-sense prevailed. He would exercise 'the Master's right' at the proper time; he would have Faith accepted, and then she would be taken to the Stables to begin her training in discipline.

Lingering over dessert, Faith eventually asked, 'What will happen tomorrow, Alex? What's this place called? You never said.'

'Marigold's place?' he mused. 'It's part of the old Garland Estate, the biggest part, as it happens. Marigold married Peter Garland. But I was forgetting. You don't know the Garlands. Why do you ask?'

'It's important, isn't it? Tomorrow?' She let her dark eyes rest on his, willing him to answer. The tension she had felt on Sunday had increased if anything, but he was trying hard to be the same, loving man she had come to know. His worries must be business, she thought.

'Yes, slightly.' He nodded, which made it only slightly less important than National Security.

'What will happen?' Faith repeated. 'I'd like to know.'

'You mean, what form will your initiation take? That's what it is, Faith, an initiation into the Chosen. The first main hurdle.'

'If I knew what to expect . . .'

'You can back out if you want,' he said at once, but her hand crossed the table to cover his in an instinctive gesture of affection.

'Don't be silly. I wouldn't do that. Tell me.'

'I can't, Faith, honestly.' He grimaced. 'You're not Chosen; not yet,' he said. 'You *will* be on Sunday evening. And by then, the whole question will be as redundant as a sedan chair.'

'That's when we come back, is it? Sunday evening?'

'Only if you fail, my darling. If you pass – and I'm sure you will – you'll go to the Stables; but forget I said that,' he added quickly. 'I can't tell you about that, either. Not until Sunday, at least.'

'I don't understand,' she complained quietly.

'You will. Tomorrow.' He squeezed her hand.

He halted the car at the open gateway, switching off the engine and letting the sound die away in the late afternoon sun. Faith turned her worried eyes on him. Alex had been silent as he drove the large car from London, keeping his speed down, steering automatically. When he was ready, he looked across at her, fixing her eyes for a few moments, then explained. 'This is your last chance to back out, Faith.' He sighed. 'So, I'll tell you what will happen once we drive in.

'The others will arrive for dinner soon and afterwards, we'll hold your "trial". You've applied to become a member, so they have to be sure they want you. Anyone can ask a question, or just state their opinion. If they've made up their minds, they vote; if they're undecided or they ask questions, you can persuade them. I can't do anything for you except amplify things. I mean, if what you've said needs to be explained, I can do that, but I can't put up your defence. You understand? Not because I don't want to; I just can't. It's not allowed. You have to succeed on your own merits.'

'I see,' Faith said. It sounded fairly straightforward, at least.

'After that's over, they come to a decision. It can be either Acceptance, Refusal or Penance. Refusal or Acceptance are obvious. Penance means they're not sure; they want to think more about it. That's what worries me, actually.'

'Lillian said she thought it would be all right.' Faith tried to sound hopeful.

'Lillian's a friend,' he said. 'And she'll probably speak up for you.' He shook his head. 'But she doesn't know what the others are thinking. Frankly, I wouldn't like to put money on it. Not a penny.'

'What?' Faith gasped at his serious expression, 'But they're, they've . . .'

'I know,' he said, trying to calm her. 'They're nice people and you've enjoyed them all, and they, you. But this is the Chosen, Faith. This isn't some *fan-club*, where by turning up, you can join. This is serious. This is for life, too. I think the best we can hope for is Penance.'

'Penance?' Faith asked. 'That sounds horrible.'

'It's not so bad.' He shrugged. 'The trouble is that you're neither fish nor fowl. You're in a sort of limbo, you see? You mustn't leave the estate, otherwise you forfeit everything.' He sounded unhappy. 'None of us can help you; you're on your own until they come to a decision.'

'What would they do?' Faith could feel the trembling in her lips begin as he sighed.

'They can't harm you, Faith. They may hurt you: slap your backside or something like that. But they mustn't draw blood or leave a permanent mark because, if you're accepted, that would mean the person who did it would have to leave. You might get a spanking, or be made to have sex. The best thing is to avoid people.'

'How long for?' Faith began to feel the apprehension rising within her like an acrid cloud in her stomach.

'Until they've decided.' Alex replied. 'We're here until Monday; all of us. It could mean a couple of nights laying low. Think you could manage that?'

'I don't know.' Faith found herself becoming more and more nervous about something she had taken to be a formality. From the sound of it, some of the people she took to be friends were hardly that.

'Does everyone have to? Did you?' she asked, changing her question.

'It's mostly an overnight thing for women,' he said. 'The men get worse. It lasts a lot longer; they're rougher, too,' he said, with a weary, reminiscent smile.

'Claire? Lillian?'

'Everyone. Julia, too. They've all been in your position and survived. They'll all be there to sit in judgement on your application. They're the Chosen, so they decide who'll join us. This isn't peculiar to them, Faith. There are various Lodges, or Chapters I suppose you could call them, all over the country. Each of them admits members in the same way. You have to undergo a "trial" in order to prove your worth to the Chosen, and *how* you endure that trial is as important as surviving it.'

'You'll be there, won't you?' She sounded concerned.

'Yes, but as I said, I can't take part. I have to stay on the sidelines. What I can do is help a little if you do get a Penance.'

'How?' Faith asked. 'I don't like this. I'm afraid.'

'If it is a Penance, you've every right to be afraid, darling,' he agreed. 'But it's only one weekend. You have the rest of your life to consider. I remember how Claire sobbed with relief when she was accepted.'

'If Claire can do it, so can I,' she answered, her chin tilting at the thought of the former model. Alex smiled as he realised how simple it was to stiffen her courage. It was just the unknown that Faith was worried about, but it had been pushed back again by the thought of Claire. If she got any worse, he would have to 'dare' her; she wouldn't be able to refuse that.

'That's my darling Faith,' Alex grinned at her, and started the engine.

Marigold Garland was in her early forties, a medium-sized woman with short, dark hair and an attractive figure which her close-fitting bottle green hacking jacket and white jodhpurs enhanced. She looked as though she had just come in from the stable as she received them in the drawing room, with a crop in one hand, her bright scarlet lipstick a stark contrast to her pale features. She had a small, round face with a sharp chin and high, prominent cheekbones which looked like swelling carbuncles. The crop looked too large for her small hands to hold, yet it looked right between her fingers.

'Alex.' Her smile was almost a simper, which exposed small, glittering teeth as she extended her left hand to him. Alex took it, holding it up to his lips almost a foot above her own; their eyes locked for a moment, then she turned. 'And *this* is the young lady you hope to "run"? Hmm. Attractive. You're to be congratulated, Alex. Where did you find such a beauty?'

'Faith Small. Marigold Garland.' Alex kept his features straight.

'Faith,' the woman said, allowing the name to trickle from her mouth as though tasting it.

Faith found the gleam in her eye rather disturbing, for she seemed to be appraising the tall woman as she would a horse. Good withers, plenty of power in the hips, deep chest, good coat, alert ears. Any moment, she thought, she will open my mouth to take a look at my teeth.

'Mrs Garland,' Faith answered politely as she approached. The woman flashed Alex a brief smile.

'Very *good*, Alex,' she complimented him. 'You *have* trained her well, haven't you?' She walked around Faith, whose surprised expression caught Alex's admonitory one. 'Lovely breasts, too.' The woman stroked the shaft of the crop across the outswell of Faith's left breast. 'Just right for a crop. You must allow me to use her, Alex.'

She smiled up at Faith's astonished gape. 'I'm sure I could bring her to a new understanding of her status. You could profitably watch, dear heart; you'd learn a lot about how to discipline young women.'

'I'm sure I would, Marigold,' he agreed, 'but while the light lasts before dinner, do you mind if I show Faith the estate? She's never seen one like it before.'

'You naughty boy,' the woman reproved him, lightly tapping his forearm with her crop. 'If you want to fuck, why don't you just go to your room? Or is it the open air that attracts you? I suppose that's it. All right.'

The Garland Estate consisted of the house, a modern, two storey construction with wings which seemed to go on forever, surrounded by a wide, flagged patio on which a variety of plants in tubs provided decoration and some shade. Several outbuildings stood near the house: stables, some storage sheds, a small gymnasium and an indoor swimming pool which had been emptied, its blue tiles looking deceptively dull. Encircling all this was a park in which isolated trees stood at intervals. There were woods, but at a greater distance from the house, and separated by open ground, where anyone moving would be seen at once.

Out in the open, walking through the woods which bordered the drive on the way back to the house, Alex asked, 'What do you think of Marigold, Faith?'

'She's serious, isn't she?' Faith asked, aware of her trembling limbs. Marigold Garland had frightened her. The intent, glittering smile and fixed, almost drooling expression, coupled with the constant tapping and swishing of the crop all added up to a picture of a woman intent on subjecting Faith to abuse.

'Yes, of course she is,' he admitted. 'She's always been more interested in flagellation. If she had her way, she'd have the skin off both our backs, just for the fun of it.' He grinned. 'Still; you can out-run her. If you have a choice of being caught by Marigold or someone else, choose someone else. Claire or Lillian, for example. Or

Rupert: he won't hurt you. He might fuck you, but he won't hurt. Simon or Harry . . .' He shrugged.

'Can I run? I mean, it's allowed, is it?'

'Yes, of course,' he grinned, 'unless they all specifically want you confined. It's up to them, really. But if they allow you your freedom, then they have to catch you. It's just a bit of fun, really. If you break away, then they have to recapture you. Colin's the one to watch. He's fast on his feet.'

The others had arrived from London for dinner while Faith and Alex had been tramping around the estate in the evening light; all of them were flushed and eager like children. Max Hawes had arrived from abroad, still feeling jet-lagged but without any explanation of where he had been, his pleasant smiling features a welcome change from Marigold's fixity. Lillian had greeted her with a warm kiss, her hand around her waist as they turned towards Simon. It was a comfort to know that the blonde woman was there, for during the previous fortnight Faith had come to respect her advice.

When Simon went off, Lillian said in a low voice, 'What's the matter, Faith? You look like this is your funeral rather than the happiest day of your life.'

'Marigold, for one thing. She frightens me,' Faith answered, trying not to put too much dislike into her voice, in case she was a particular friend of Lillian.

'She frightens a lot of people,' Lillian said quietly, not looking at her. 'Anything in particular?'

'That whip of hers. Does she use it?'

'Not on the Chosen,' Lillian said. 'At least, not as hard as she does on other people. It marks, you see? And for all practical purposes, you're Chosen, my darling.' Lillian squeezed her waist.

'Alex doesn't think so,' Faith said. 'He thinks it isn't . . . What's wrong with me, Lillian? I've tried. You know I have.'

'Sometimes, trying isn't enough, Faith.' Lillian said quietly. 'Some don't try hard enough. Some try too hard. Trying isn't the same as succeeding, you see.'

'You thought that I was ready.'

'Yes,' Lillian said, 'I know. But I've been talking to people, and what they say is true. I've told you this myself, so it should come as no surprise. You need discipline. Badly.'

'Don't you think I'm getting better, though?' Faith asked. 'It takes time. Time and practice.'

'Time is something you haven't got.' Lillian shook her head, looking at her shoes, then up to Faith's frightened face. 'You have this weekend to persuade people you're fit to be Chosen. I'm sorry if I misled you about how easy it would be; I thought I was right. I didn't appreciate how . . .' She shrugged. '. . . tight people had become.'

Dinner was very pleasant. The Château d'Yquem proved to be the highlight of the meal, with Max and Rupert both 'nosing' carefully, their praises ringing around the table to Marigold's delight. Marigold normally had four or five people working on the estate, but they had all been given the evening off after dinner had been prepared. They knew of Mrs Garland's parties, and would return to work on Monday, when any evidence of 'goings-on' would have been discreetly removed.

There seemed no haste about the meal, though it ran to several courses, or about clearing up afterwards. Each of the women there, all wearing a black band of some kind around their throats, helped to carry the dishes through to the large, well-appointed kitchen where everything was put in the huge dish-washer. Marigold professed not to know how it worked, but Julia had it going in seconds, her expression revealing to Faith that she thought the woman pretentious.

As they left the kitchen, the expressions on the women's faces began to alter; the pleasant atmosphere dissolving into rigid indifference, as though with every step, Faith was being cut off from them. They walked back to the drawing room, where Alex waited for her outside the door with a welcoming smile; yet he looked worried. Whilst the others passed without speaking, he held her to him, feeling her trembling limbs, quieting her.

'You can't back out, now,' he whispred softly. 'Well, you could, I suppose. You could tell them to go to hell and that would be the end of it. No one could make you "run", no one would try. But you would forfeit any chance of becoming Chosen and I wouldn't like that, Faith.' His facial expression was bleak as he brought her to a stop by the door.

'Would it disgrace you?' she asked. 'Would I?'

'Never mind that.' He shrugged expressively. 'You and I could never . . . well. I'd . . . we'd . . .' His pallor showed the depth of his concern.

The thought that Faith could totally reject the Chosen at this stage was a very real worry to Alex. The build-up had been deliberate, letting her realise just how serious this step was, the make-or-break which would decide her future, and whether she would have a part in his. She knew he was a proud man; it was one of the traits she admired in him. The thought of shaming him before some of his closest friends stiffened her resolve.

'I won't disgrace you, Alex,' she said quietly, 'not even if Marigold *does* catch me. She'll have to be pretty fast on her feet, too.'

'Good girl.' He gave a version of a grim, pale smile. 'Ready?'

'Just watch.' Faith moved closer to him for comfort.

'Then let's go in to the others.' He kissed her lightly on the forehead.

Chapter Fifteen

The men had altered the seating arrangements around the room while Alex and Faith had stood outside. The couches and armchairs which had occupied a more central position, placed as for sociable conversation, had been moved and turned to face in one direction. In the middle of the open space, a single, plain chair had been brought from Marigold's study. Though comfortably padded, it was more upright than the others, which Faith found encouraging. She would have to keep her wits about her; had they provided an easy chair, her guard could have relaxed.

There were ten of them in the drawing room, their slightly flushed, impatient faces looking up at Faith as she preceded Alex into the room, all anxiously scanning her expression for some hint as to her state of mind. Though they had to judge her acceptance, none of them were so cruel as to wilfully tear down her self-confidence; it would be better if they were just to reject her outright than to do that. Stopping by the solitary chair, Alex looked around the group with Faith at his side, his alert expression running over their faces, asking, 'Well. Shall we start?'

While Alex retired to the sidelines, literally taking an easy chair which stood against the wall to Faith's right, the young woman took a deep breath, spread her long skirts sideways, and sank onto the rather high seat, her back upright against the support. Two couches had been drawn up alongside each other to face her, with a comfortable chair at each end and slightly in front, while two chairs were placed behind all of these. Rupert took the chair at the front to her left, with Claire beside him on the couch, next to Simon. Lillian was next, then Max, Prudence, Julia and Harry, who had the chair opposite Rupert. Marigold sat between and behind Simon and Lillian, whilst Colin's thin frame showed above Prudence's head. No one was smiling.

It was Max who appeared to be in charge of the proceedings; he waited a few moments until they had all finished moving, before asking, 'Anyone made up their minds already? Rupert? I think you mentioned something earlier?'

'Yes,' the man said, transferring his attention to the face of the young woman in front of him. 'I'm sorry, Faith.' He shook his head. 'You're a dear child, but that's what you are; a child. This isn't for children. I'd say that no one should be admitted to the Chosen until they were three or four years older than yourself. You've just come down from Oxford; you know very little of the world.' He paused, shrugging, his expression one of regret in refusal. 'I'm sorry.'

Faith knew that she was blushing, yet resentfully felt that her age, which she could do nothing about, was being held against her. If Rupert felt that way, why had he been so keen to mount her? Or was that a stupid question to ask? Yes, probably. He had been given a chance to fornicate with someone different, and he would have been stupid to refuse it. He could enjoy the benefits of enjoying her and then rejecting her all in the one process. Colin was speaking now, his eyes boring into her from over Prudence's shoulder.

'Not just that, Rupert,' he paused, 'though I agree with you in some ways. The Chosen need a degree of maturity which Faith, I'm sorry to say, just hasn't got. She walked out on a perfectly good job. I know that, if we admit her, she won't need to work, but really! It shows immaturity, doesn't it? Lillian? You know her better than any of us.'

The angry protest died in Faith's throat as her eyes switched to Lillian's concerned expression. Here, she thought, was someone who would speak up for her, someone who knew how important this loomed in her life. Yet Lillian hesitated, her eyes on Faith's in the chill silence which had filled the room so insidiously that Faith wondered when it had begun. She willed Lillian to speak, her anxious expression transmitting her fear to all of them. As the seconds ticked away, Faith's apprehension mounted as Lillian dropped her eyes, not wishing to meet Faith's anxious, almost tearful gaze.

'I have to say,' Lillian began in a low voice, 'I have doubts about Faith. I really do.'

A sheet of ice smothered Faith's spine, shocking her into dull half-awareness as she fought to maintain her position; she gasped and gulped for air, her pride trying to conceal her anguish from all of them; probably most of all from Lillian. This was the woman she had thought to be her friend, her closest ally in the Chosen, the one who, more than any other, would speak up for her. On the sidelines, Alex watched her carefully. He had expected a protest at Colin's accusation, and had been pleasantly surprised when she had made no comment. Faith was more mature than he had thought. Now Lillian was applying the 'killer' and it was certainly having an effect. It looked as though Faith might collapse at any moment.

Barely able to remain on the chair, Faith kept her features impassive as she listened to Lillian, who continued, 'I don't doubt her commitment to the Chosen; not at all. If admitted, Faith would be everything we would want. But I have to question her discipline, her *self-discipline*. As some of you know, Alex wants her to wear nipple rings to enlarge her nipples, and thigh boots to improve her gait and posture. I've had to insist – on several occasions – that she comply. It seems she forgets easily. We know we have to do things we dislike; Faith doesn't, not yet, anyway.' She gave a quick smile. 'I also have to say that I love her very much. She's a delightful girl and, if rejected, I shall still try to be friends, and help her. But,' and here Lillian's gaze dropped at last, 'I have doubts about her suitability for the Chosen.'

The shock of Lillian's qualified support drove away the

little blood which remained in Faith's face. Her eyes swam in her head, and Alex quickly signalled to the others to keep quiet. Rupert brought a glass of thick, syrupy wine which Alex managed to make her drink, slowly moistening her lips so she could lick it off, then moistening them again, until she was sufficiently recovered to sip it. Gradually, order was restored; everyone returned to their seats as Faith sat upright again, her chin tilted high, defying them all. They were glad to see that sign; Faith was hardly about to surrender at the first instance of adversity.

When Julia was asked her opinion, the petite woman smiled for a moment at Faith before answering, 'In part, I have to agree with Lillian. Faith does need discipline, but she's young. Twenty-two. God! What were any of us like then? Lillian is right: Faith has to be more disciplined, but that problem isn't insuperable. I think she's more disciplined than some of us were, *years* later. I'm glad I didn't apply for admission at her age.'

'Harry?' Max asked quietly, looking past the smiling face of Julia to his frowning one.

'Julia's got a point,' he answered, nodding. 'Faith's young. Perhaps Rupert's right, too; perhaps she's too young. But we should give her the benefit of the doubt.'

'You have doubts?' Prudence asked. 'I know I have.'

'Anyone else?' Max asked. 'Anyone in favour of Faith?'

'Yes,' Claire answered quietly, looking at Faith directly. 'To my mind, we're being beastly to the poor girl. I can quite see how she would react to you all. We've thrown her into the middle of an adult game of musical beds. It's taken us years to become accustomed to our lifestyle, yet you expect her to adjust in what, a fortnight? It's unrealistic. And what's more, you know that, yet none of you suggested to Alex when he proposed Faith that he reconsider. No one – not even my husband – thought to advise Alex that Faith wasn't ready. No; you were all quite happy for Faith to be examined. So now you can accept her.'

Faith returned a grateful expression to Claire's encouraging smile as Max broke the silence by asking, 'Marigold? You don't know Faith very well, but do you have a view?'

'She wants a good whipping.' The woman's voice sounded cloying as she spoke, slowly and with relish. 'I'd be happy to oblige. I have all the facilities.'

'Well.' Max raised his eyebrows to Simon, who shrugged, but said nothing. 'So it looks as if we're divided. Faith had better do Penance until we can decide.' Max sighed, looking perturbedly in the direction of Alex, who was already on his feet, his face anxious.

'Am I allowed to say anything for myself?' Faith asked, as Colin and Rupert rose from their seats.

'Don't, darling,' Alex's voice whispered in her ear, his mouth an inch away, 'you might make things worse.'

'Have you anything to say?' Max asked, frowning at her.

'I just wondered, that's all,' she amended quickly.

'Then I think, Alex,' Max sighed, 'we'd better remove Faith until we know what we're going to do with her.'

There was a pause, the slightest hesitation, then Marigold's voice piped up in a syrupy tone, 'I have something upstairs that would serve, if you want to use it. A cage. Very useful.'

'A cage?' Max looked at her, his expression curious.

'Yes. As you know, I *do* have other interests, dear man.' She smiled astutely at him, gauging his response accurately.

'A cage?' Max breathed, looking to where both Rupert and Colin were nodding their agreement. Faith's heart began to pound as Julia and Lillian's heads nodded too; and Rupert's! If Claire and Harry were on her side, they were outnumbered. She could feel the trembling beginning all over again in her limbs.

'But I'm not having her in that dress.' Marigold gestured with her ever-present crop at Faith's skirts. 'And she should be secured, too.'

'Have you any . . .? Yes.' Max nodded. 'You'd have restraints about the place, wouldn't you?'

'Max!' Alex protested. 'Is this really necessary? I mean, restraints.'

'She's an undisciplined child, Alex.' Marigold's voice was pure sugar. 'You heard everyone agree on that. Who knows what she'll do until a decision is reached?'

'It's agreed, Alex,' Max said quietly, then, as though to placate him, 'I'll go with Faith, don't worry. She'll come to no harm, I promise you.'

'God!' Alex turned the young woman towards him, holding her shaking body, feeling more than just a muscular spasm there.

Faith had listened to this discussion with mounting trepidation, unable to protest or even to make a noise. Her larynx felt as though it had been gripped: no sound emerged, though her mouth opened and closed.

'Darling,' Alex breathed in her ear, 'I'm sorry. There's nothing I can do. Most of them agree and we're democratic in the Chosen.' He sounded as though he disagreed with it, too.

'Alex.' Her voice was close to breaking. Feeling the tears rise to the surface, he held her.

'Faith! Faith!' he admonished in an urgent whisper. 'No, my darling, no tears. Face them, Faith. Spit in their eye. You must be brave.' And, dropping his voice even lower; 'I'll try to sneak up later, when they're not looking.'

Unwillingly, Faith allowed herself to be turned towards Max, whose grave face was an indication of the seriousness of her position.

'Come along, Faith,' he said. 'The sooner we get this done, the better.'

'This way.' Marigold's expression was triumphant, as she turned towards the door, her intentions obvious. Faith looked at the others before she left. Lillian was whitefaced with shock, her mouth hanging open as though amazed at the turn of events. Julia and Prudence looked grim; and Claire was staring at Rupert, who looked sheepish. Colin and Harry were glaring at each other, with apparently mutual dislike shining from their eyes.

Marigold led Faith and Max upstairs and along the carpeted corridor which twisted right and left a few times. Faith kept her face pointing downwards, not interested in where she was going. Max had a strong hand on her arm; she knew there was no possibility of escaping that grip other than pleading with him to release her so that she might flee the Chosen; that was the only thing which would put an end to this nightmare in which she now found herself. Eventually she arrived at a stout door where a key stood in the lock. Turning it, Marigold entered ahead of them, snapping on the light, and smirking as Faith gasped at the sight within. This was indeed a cage.

The room was roughly twenty-five feet square. The walls were plaster, painted a dark shade of grey and devoid of any other colour or decoration, thus giving the room a gloomy aspect. A double-glazed window in the far wall had been largely painted over so that only a small aperture remained, which was now blacker than the room itself. Despite herself, Faith shivered, for against a far wall was a long bench. Even from the doorway Faith could see that there was a variety of implements on it, including several whips of various kinds.

In the corner behind the doorway, set high on the wall, were two metal bracelets attached by stout chains. The open clasps of the bracelets were an invitation to put someone within them. Faith had little doubt that Marigold had already measured her up for them. At floor level beneath them, several feet apart were two more, shorter, but equally effective. Anyone held there would be stretched taut, yet their legs would be wide apart, their sexual organs vulnerable.

But the cage dominated the room. It was ten feet square, occupying the centre of the floor, made from flat pieces of metal two inches across. These metal strips were woven together, then welded, bent over to form the floor and ceiling also. The cage stood about seven feet high, with dangling chains both secured to the sides and to the ceiling.

'Shall we flog her first?' Marigold asked, gesturing towards the manacles behind the door, and tapping her crop into the palm of her hand, her eyes alive again.

'No, Marigold.' Max shook his head. 'Faith is just waiting to hear her fate.'

'She can be strung up in the cage, though, can't she?' Marigold asked. 'I'll show you how.'

'No, Marigold,' Max answered, looking anxious. 'I agree about restraining Faith, but really.'

'You've lost your sense of fun, Max,' the woman replied in a sour tone.

'Faith. Remove your dress, please,' he began, but Marigold was too fast for him.

'Strip, girl!' she snapped, bringing the crop up sharply beneath Faith's right breast. The blow startled her more than it hurt, shocking Faith into action. Reaching behind her for the zip, Faith moved towards Max as though seeking his protection. With fumbling fingers, she managed to find and lower the zip, as Marigold pushed the fabric off her shoulders.

As Max gathered up the dress from which Faith stepped nervously, Marigold's expression changed to one of lust. She stroked the crop across the underside of Faith's breasts, then down her stomach, licking her lips.

'She'll have to be prepared,' Marigold said quietly.

'Yes,' he said. 'Your wrist please, Faith,' he said and, taking her left wrist, he led her to the far side of the cage where a plain bench stood. Above it was a pair of manacles fixed to the bars, about five feet apart. Without another word he closed one around her wrist as Faith faced the ironwork. Marigold took hold of the other wrist and pulled it into place, with Faith leaning over the bench in an uncomfortable position, aware of the vulnerability of her behind.

'Get your feet up on the bench, Faith,' Max said in a curt tone and Faith complied gladly, even as Marigold flicked the end of the crop against her right buttock, making her hiss at the stinging caress.

Faith was now crouched over, for her wrists were now

at waist level, and it was Max who brought her feet out sideways so that she crouched, legs wide, facing the bars. If anything, she was more exposed than ever.

'I've got everything, Max,' Marigold said silkily. 'Why not leave it to me?'

'Yes, all right.' He nodded. 'Goodnight Faith. I'll see you later.'

Pride stopped Faith pleading with him to remain; she looked straight ahead at the metal which imprisoned her, listening to the thud as the door closed behind him.

'Now, Faith,' Marigold's voice sharpened, 'let's see how sensitive you are, my dear.' She ran her fingers over the protruding globes in front of her. With a sudden gasp, Faith felt the woman's fingers probe both her entrances, pushing deeply within as Alex had, and with the same result. Within her, the 'Love Balls' moved and the pressure began in waves around her clitoris. Then she felt further pressure on that sensitive organ as Marigold began to stroke the folded leather of the tip of her crop against it, listening to the gasping desire which came from the young woman.

'You like this, Faith.' Marigold made it sound like an accusation. The prisoner made no answer, earning a nod of respect from her tormentor. The pressure went on, building up within her until, withdrawing her fingers suddenly, the woman said, 'Has this little bottom ever had a man in it? Or perhaps she prefers something harder?'

'No man,' Faith answered, swallowing as she wondered what was about to happen.

'Then we'll have to make you comfortable, won't we?' Marigold asked, leaving the cage.

Faith tried to look round to see what the woman was doing, but it was impossible. However, when she returned, Faith found out soon enough.

'Is this big enough for you?' she asked, and with a firm stroke, pushed a greased phallus into Faith's oiled, pliable bottom hole, making her gasp. This was no smooth dildo, this was a carved soapstone phallus, a faithful replica of an erect penis which was being inserted firmly up to the glans within her behind. Then, to Faith's shame, her muscles began to suck on it, pulling it inside her until the testicles prevented further movement as the girl almost hung, sobbing, on her restraints.

'You like being buggered, then, Faith?' Marigold asked. 'I'll cure you of *that*.'

Faith cried out as a strap was brought sharply against her exposed buttocks, and then another. The searing pain of her first strapping felt like the end of the world. She was piniomed against the bars, unable to defend herself; having been buggered with an outsize phallus, now here was Marigold subjecting her to yet more degradation.

But the worst feeling of all, beyond the immediate pain of the phallus in her rectum and the strap on her buttocks, was the pleasure that these two sensations were producing. It was as though they were the fuel which was stoking the fires within her, and the more Marigold struck, the higher her desire built up.

Marigold Garland knew how to wield a strap; no two strokes overlapped and they were sufficiently spread out to inflict maximum effect with minimum physical harm. As arranged, she had put an aphrodisiac on the phallus; this would be absorbed by Faith during the night and the strapping would add to her desire. When she rode the 'Three Horned God', Faith would be ready.

Eventually, as Faith's tears were fading into dry sobs which wrenched in her chest, Marigold unfastened her from the manacles, secured her wrists behind her with handcuffs and quit the cage, locking it behind her.

'There's a bed there,' she said heavily, 'and in case you're thinking of escaping, I'd like to see you get through that door. There's two inches of oak.'

Faith perched on the edge of the hard bed in the darkness, shivering as the cold began to eat into her flesh, and wishing she had thought to ask about lavatory facilities. She was naked, still trembling from the arousal Marigold had wrought within her, and she thought that pretty soon she would need to pee. What had she let herself in for? She had thought that joining the Chosen would be so simple. Alex was popular, wasn't he? They all liked her, at least, they had all been pleasant. Not that she could trust any of them; not now. Did she really *want* to be Chosen after this?

As she asked herself this question however, she realised that if she refused, Alex could hardly be the same loving partner he had shown himself to be. A few weeks before, when still living with Albert, she would have tossed her head at the thought of aligning herself with any man the way she had with Alex, subordinating her opinions and manners to his, subjecting herself to the shame and delightful licentiousness of his ways. Albert was a convenience, she thought: useful for as long as she needed him. She could see now how she had been growing away from him for weeks, taking exception to his moods, to his obsessive need to be praised. At least Alex had never needed that.

Now she was facing the fact that Alex had altered more than the shape of her calves with those high-heeled boots. He had changed the way she thought about things, but not just men, though he had done that, too. He was the first man to have cared enough about her to take the time and trouble, and yes, who had the money to improve her. But it was getting colder. She had thought there was double-glazing. Had the woman left a refrigerator open, leading into the room?

It seemed like hours passed before Alex sneaked in without putting on the light, bending close to where she lay on the hard bed and kissing her. He brought a couple of thin blankets which he laid over her. There was a tone of defeat in his voice which prevented her asking about the decision; the decision both to consider her application, and to imprison her in the cage seemed to have taken some of the fight from him, yet she could detect a steely note there, as though he were willing her to maintain her courage.

When he returned to the faint sounds of music and laughter coming from below, Faith allowed the tears to fall, burying her face in the rough fabric of the mattress, her shoulders shaking while she unburdened all the hurt welling up within her. Lillian had been right. This was supposed to have been the happiest day of her life, the day she had been looking forward to for a fortnight. And there she was. While the others had fun, possibly indulging in one of their orgies, Faith was naked, her wrists secured behind her, locked in a cage, hungry, cold and alone. And the only prospect was that of Marigold coming upstairs to beat her with that riding crop, or another strap. At least it would warm her backside!

Chapter Sixteen

The night was colder than the early evening had been and Faith, despite the blankets, shivered in the cage. The cold metal around her seemed to take all the warmth from the air. She had cried herself to sleep and, waking a couple of times in the night, had cried again. She knew that she looked dreadful; her face was probably streaked with the shiny tracks of the tears, and her hair was a mess. It would take quite some time to restore her to something approaching a human being again. Lying flat, her face turned from the doorway to stop her giving vent to her longing, Faith tried to avoid counting the hours.

It was mid-morning when she heard her name being called by a familiar voice. Standing up, Faith found Julia coming towards her, carrying a tray with a steaming bowl of something and a plate of white sandwiches alongside. The day was dull; a cold, grey light filled the room, making even the food look dismal.

'You poor thing.' The woman made her lie down again. 'I've brought you some soup and a few sandwiches. Not much like breakfast, is it? But I expect you'll appreciate the warmth. It's terribly cold in here.'

'Thanks.' Faith managed a weary smile. 'But is there any chance of using the lavatory? I'm getting a bit desperate here.'

'Of course. Come on; you look frozen.' The older woman tutted. 'Alex would have brought warmer blankets, but they came off *his* bed, and there are few enough for any of us.' There was a wealth of meaning in her voice as she opened the door to usher Faith out to the lavatory just across the hallway, unfastening her wrists before closing the door.

When she came out, Faith went back into the cage without any urging. She sat on the bed with the food, her wary eyes on Julia. Whilst the older woman watched her, an anxious expression in her eyes, Faith ate in silence, glad of the warmth of the soup but more worried than ever about her fate. At last she asked, 'How . . . how is Alex?' changing the question at the last moment. She had wanted to ask if any decision had been reached, but was afraid of the reply.

'Alex?' She smiled. 'He'll survive. Didn't have a good night; probably thinking of you. He's not used to sleeping alone, now. I know I miss Harry terribly if he has to be away overnight. I'm used to him being there, you see?'

'Thanks for speaking up for me last night,' Faith said. 'I appreciate it.'

'I told the truth, dear. You *are* young; perhaps Rupert is right; perhaps you're *too* young. But Claire had a point, too. No one went to Alex to suggest you withdrew. You could have been put forward another time, and I think that you agreed with some of the remarks. You want discipline.' She gave a sudden smile. 'But it's nothing that can't be cured, you know? It's not the end of the world.'

'Yes, but . . .' Faith shuddered again, hitching the blanket around her.

'Anyway, I'll get back,' Julia said. 'I'd better secure you or Marigold will have a fit.'

'I'll manage, thanks,' Faith said.

'Faith.' Julia's expression became more serious, her eyes growing round. 'I know you don't know what's happening. You might think calling the whole thing off is an attractive idea, but it's not. You'd confirm to Colin how immature you are. One more night, Faith. We have to decide by tomorrow, and Alex is *desperately* worried in case you give up. He can't come here. The others stopped him last night when he came out, said he was cheating, bringing you those blankets. He had to promise not to return. Otherwise, I think, he'd have camped here with you.'

'Yes,' Faith agreed, 'probably.'

But hot soup and sandwiches, no matter how warming, were insufficient to stave off the pangs of hunger and the rigours of her shivers. Faith was using up energy just by remaining still. The light had all but gone from the sky, the sandwiches just a memory of crumbs when she heard the sound of someone unlocking the door, someone she had no way of identifying but, by that time, Faith's resolve was gone.

She was chilled to the bone in the cold, unheated room, hungry, deadly tired and ready to give up. It had been a nice idea; she would have loved to have been Chosen, to have lived in Chelsea, to have worn nice clothes without having to work too hard. To have lived with Alex, perhaps. That would have been the best of all; living with Alex and making love so deliciously. But the price was too high. Faith knew that if she spent another night, naked, in the room, she would probably become ill. Taking up what vestige of courage was left her, she scrambled awkwardly to her feet in the darkness as she heard the door open, her wrists still fastened behind her. She blinked as the light came on, blinding her.

'Faith,' Lillian's voice sounded out as the woman approached the cold bars of the cage.

Something warm was put around her shoulders, and she leaned into Lillian.

'You poor darling. You're chilled to the bone!'

'I'm giving up, Lillian,' Faith mumbled. 'I want to go home. I've had enough of this.'

'Oh, darling!' Lillian's arm reached around her shoulders, supporting her. 'Would you like something to drink? I know it's beastly here, but it'll warm you up. I tried to get brandy, but all I could sneak was this wine. Here. No glass, I'm afraid. Get it inside you.' Her wilful, cheerful refusal to listen to her infuriated the young woman.

'I'm giving up, Lillian!' Faith said loudly. 'I want to go home. I want to get out of here.'

'Of course you'll go home, darling,' Lillian agreed, tilting Faith's face to put the mouth of the bottle to her lips.

The wine was sour but Faith drank, spilling it from the sides of her mouth as Lillian misjudged the angle, coating her face and breasts with the sticky red fluid. Faith drank eagerly, for the soup had been salty and there had been nothing to quench the thirst which had been bothering her for some time. Her lips were parched and dry; she felt they were cracking.

'I'm giving . . .' she began again, but Lillian took her shoulders and, turning her, looked her in the eye, a fierce expression lurking in the blue.

'No! You're *not* giving up; I won't allow it! You've not come this far to give Marigold the satisfaction.'

'I'm cold, and I'm shaking, and I'm . . .'

'I'm taking you back downstairs,' Lillian broke in. 'At least you'll be a little warmer. Come on, or I'll use a strap on your behind.' She brandished a foot-long length of pale beige leather in her hand.

By dint of Lillian's encouragement, which consisted of her occasionally giving Faith a stinging slap across the rump with the slipper-like strap to keep her moving, she forced herself to come out of the cage, her joints stiff both from lack of use and the low temperature, and moved slowly towards the door. Only when they reached the corridor did Faith see that Lillian had put her own wool coat around her shaking form. Faith had other things on her mind however; chief among was getting some warmth into her. Even the corridor was less cold, and she felt as though she were shuffling across a beach covered with soft sand, the pleasant sunshine on her.

Someone must have been keeping a watch, for most of the party were there when Lillian helped her across the threshold into the drawing room.

'Just a moment, Lillian,' Max said quietly. 'Has Faith given up, or what?' His expression was strained.

'No. I think she had better get a little warmth, Max, otherwise we might damage her health.' Lillian looked at him as though willing him to agree. Faith frowned at the exchange for, to the best of her knowledge, Lillian and Max were good friends. Yet she saw nothing untoward in this, particularly since her brain refused to function properly.

'What are you going to do with her?' Rupert asked as he emerged from a well-lit doorway. 'As if I didn't know.'

'Why don't we all have a drink?' Prudence asked. 'No point in standing about is there? Lillian? Scotch? Brandy?'

'Yes, thank you,' Lillian answered, as a hot hand was applied to Faith's back between her shoulder-blades.

'She's freezing!' Colin's voice was surprised. 'I say, is she all right, Lillian? She's like ice.'

'All right.' Max sighed, shaking his head in apparent disbelief. 'Let Faith stay for a while to get warmed up a bit.'

In the drawing room, Faith was seated on a couch next to Lillian, who, although she had freed her wrists, refused to release the hold she had on the younger woman's arm. Julia was already pouring drinks when they arrived, and wordlessly handed Faith a glass as she went past. Like the wine Lillian had brought, it tasted sour, but Faith knew nothing of wine, so remained silent. When she had warmed herself a little – and finished the glass – Julia poured some more. Around her the conversation moved on as though it were taking place before somebody else, and somewhere else, too. Voices came and went as though someone was playing with the volume control of a radio, turning it up and then down again, so that at some points the loud boom was almost painful, whilst at others she could hardly hear a word; nor make sense of most of it.

Faith supposed that she was beginning to feel the effects of the sleepless night, for her eyes were becoming heavy and, for minutes at a time, they closed. She awoke two or three times to find Lillian or Julia helping her to more wine, tilting back her head. They seemed to want her drunk and yet, though her perceptions were dulled, this was only part of the story.

She could feel an itch in her crotch, the beginning of that familiar ache she had recently come to know. The 'Love Balls' of course! Alex had made sure she wore them when they left Cheyne Walk, and they were still in place. The sensation seemed to be getting worse, too, so much so that she dropped a hand into her lap to rub herself a little.

'What are you doing, Faith?' Rupert's voice came to her from a distance.

As if by magic – though Faith realised she had probably lost consciousness – she found herself lying on her back on the couch, with Lillian's worried face beside her. Hands were holding her knees apart, and her arms were raised above her head. Something was tickling her itch. As she realised this, her hips jerked forward, provoking a sigh from some of the people about her. She thought she recognised them – they looked like faces she had once known – people whose names were familiar, yet she seemed unable to focus on them. Lillian was the only one she knew, yet there was something about the woman she found unpleasant, though she could hardly remember what it was.

A broad-built man was crouching over her with something soft in his hand, but she was unable to identify it. Again the tickling sensation came, and she jerked her hips into it. Yes! Someone was tickling her clitoris, her open sex. Something stiff filled her bottom, like one of the dildos Lillian had inserted. It felt enormous. With a feeling of rising panic she bucked her hips as the pleasure began to come more strongly; her tongue poked out from her mouth, and was immediately captured by Lillian, whose mouth descended on her own.

As if that were a signal, two digits were sunk into the inner part of her thigh; her pleasure died almost instantly, but the tickling went on. Not increased, not intensified, it just went on, rousing her again within a minute as the wave of liquid pleasure surged through her. Her breasts felt on fire, her nipples positively ached. Even with the nipple rings she had never known such agony and yet, it was a peculiar kind of pain. The quality was different; the flesh of her breasts felt as though it had been slapped, hard, and often. Her whole skin seemed as though on fire.

As her tongue reached out again the digits were pressed into her thigh, digging deep into the muscle, just on the pressure point. Yet it had only a limited effect, for her hips continued to thrash. She felt the hands which reached over and began slapping the undersides of her breasts, working around to the sides and gradually, her tongue was stuck out again. Her eyes opened, and there was someone who reminded her of a woman called Claire, both of her small hands working on her breasts, carefully slapping them in a measured manner, her expression as impersonal as though she were utilising a tin opener.

Faith tried to rise, but there were hands holding her down, hands possessed of a strength too powerful for her weakened state to challenge successfully. Her breathing was difficult; her chest ached with the heaving of it. She felt as though this had been going on for quite some time, yet how could it have been? Had she been unconscious? Had these strange people been trying to rouse her all this time? Had they been hurting her to prevent her climaxing? Why?

Voices seemed to come from very far away. One voice dominated the others, evoking a picture in her mind, unbidden, of a woman with a whip, a woman whose dark, intent eyes seemed to be focused on Faith. Straining, concentrating hard, Faith tried to make out what was being said through the wine-induced fog.

'I know where she can stay: the pool! It's empty, and I have facilities there.'

'Facilities?' A familiar voice sounded, a voice which made the lust in her loins spring up again. Alex? She tried to open her eyes to see him, to call out to him, but as soon as her mouth opened her tongue shot out and Lillian took control of it.

'She can be secured until we need her in the morning,' the female voice spoke again. 'Bring her.'

Hands grabbed Faith, raised her to her feet and propelled her, stumbling, sagging and slipping from the room. It seemed she was walking through a nightmare where half-familiar faces loomed close, where a doorway would be followed by a room, and another doorway and a corridor, and another doorway, and another, and another until she was no longer walking on carpet on loose, rubbery legs but on tile. A smooth, polished tile. A pretty blue tile which stretched out in all directions; but mostly downwards. It was chilly there, and shady; the dark was better for her eyes, but it sucked the warmth from her. Yes; warmth. She had felt hot in that room, and now she felt cold again. The odd lighting made recognising people less, rather than more likely, yet her brain was refusing to co-operate.

'Here! I've got the chains,' the female voice said as Faith was forced to her knees and held in place, strong hands on her shoulders.

She could feel the dull movement of something cold around her ankles and a dull pressure on her skin before she was laid down flat on her stomach beside a shiny strip of something, with her wrists drawn up behind her. The same dull feeling was at her wrists as she was half-rolled to one side and some fabric was placed beneath her. Then she was half-rolled the other way and the fabric was smoothed out, partial insulation against the deadly cold of the tile.

'Lillian!' the female voice called, 'What are you doing?'

From quite close came an answer: 'Just a minute. I don't want these chains to chafe her skin.'

'Lillian?' Faith gasped quietly, and then felt a warmth at her shoulder, the warmth of human flesh.

'Faith! It's me, Lillian. Can you hear me?' A soft hand trickled down her abdomen to her labia, provoking the

231

wanting again. She groaned in that terribly familiar manner, before she found her voice.

'What? Lillian. What's happening?' Faith whispered, as her hips jerked at the touch.

'Marigold has insisted you spend the night in the empty swimming pool, darling. It was the best I could do. I didn't want you back in the cage. Do you feel anything?' The anxiety was back again. She remembered a white-faced woman, mouth open in shock. Was that Lillian? Was that the same Lillian who had said some nasty things about her? Impossible.

'I want Alex,' Faith admitted, her hips surging again.

'Look.' Lillian paused. 'Marigold has had you chained to a steel bar here, though what she wants with one at the bottom of her pool, God alone knows. They've been pumping aphrodisiacs into you since I brought you down from the cage. There's some up your bottom, and in the wine, too. They wanted you to put on a show, but you're too far gone. Give us a few minutes, Faith, and then you can rub yourself on the bar. I've made sure you can turn. Your hands are chained behind you so you can't use those, but you can get *some* relief. All right, darling? I'm sorry. It's the best I can do.'

'Please, Lillian. Let me go home.'

'You'll go home in triumph, my darling.' Lillian's mouth closed briefly on hers, and then she was gone, the sound of bare feet on ceramic tiles Faith's last memory of her.

Faith waited as her pleasure rose, the skin of her abdomen growing hard again. Faith began to move slowly, each tiny effort a result of the sum total of her concentration as she rolled to where the shiny bar stood out several inches from the ceramic tiles which made up the bottom of the pool. Two round stainless steel flanges bolted the bar to the tiles, preventing anything from moving as Faith's weight suddenly fell against it. She had difficulty in slipping her leg up to the bar, and then over it, inching her way until she half-lay across it. With one breast on either side, her gaping sex inched ever desperately closer as the pleasure mounted, begging for release.

She must have passed out again for her next memory was of waking with a start, her body moving in that familiar parody of lovemaking. Her open sex was gripping the smooth bar, her clitoris pressed hard against it. She expected the metal to be cold but instead it was quite warm; how long had she been doing this? Hardly any time, for there seemed to be no end to the ache within her. And the sound. Those very familiar sounds. Sounds which took time to analyse.

There was her harsh, frantic breathing, and the high, desperate keening from within her, the deep-torn whimperings of her lust demanding release; and something else. A variety of sounds. A varied cacophony across the register, high and low, musical and flat, accompanied by a jeering!

Abruptly the sounds snapped into focus in her mind. Laughter. Human laughter. She turned her head to the left, peering through the curtain of her hair, up towards the source of light and, yes: there were people there in a line, just shapes for the most part, but shapes of people she thought she knew and recognised, people with glasses in their hands. All laughing at her working her sex organs on the steel bar.

Faith lowered her face, allowing her hair to cover her humiliation, trying to fight the climax which was approaching with the speed of a train. A hoarse cry of delighted release broke from her throat as the pleasure came, flooding her body with warmth, oiling the bar beneath her, racking her body with the sobbing echoes of love. She was an abandoned young woman. Her lusts were fully equal to those of the Chosen, yet she was not to join them. Alex was not for her. She had given way to her weakness.

Chapter Seventeen

Faith awoke to the sound of feet approaching, slapping on the cold, smooth tiles. Beneath her was the old rug which had at least kept the full ceramic chill from her body during the night, though she was still desperately cold. The light was little better, but she knew she had slept for at least a few minutes. She also knew that she had worked her passion off on the bar several times, to the amusement of those watching. They had fallen silent after a time, so much so that Faith had to peer upwards every so often to see if they were there; she had finally been convinced they had gone when the lights were switched off, leaving her alone in the cold darkness for a second successive night.

She felt drained of emotion as she listened to the sound of the feet nearing; she did not even both to raise her head to see who it was.

'Faith?' Alex's familiar voice said softly as a warm hand touched her shoulder. 'God! She's chilled through! Have you got the water running? We're going to need it.'

'Poor darling,' Lillian's voice sounded. Then strong hands lifted her, whilst behind her she could hear the metallic rattling of the chains. Things seemed much more clear this morning, even though her eyes were giving her problems and she had a sharp headache, concentrated in the centre of her forehead.

'Alex?' she mumbled. Her eyes screwed up as her wrists were freed and he turned her onto her back.

Before she could speak again, his lips met hers in a soft kiss which took her breath away. Lillian freed her ankles. Then Lillian's lips met hers, more strongly, though for much less time, as Alex said, 'We've come for you, Faith. We'll get you warm.'

'Warm,' Faith repeated as though such concepts were unknown to her. His strong arms picked her up as though she were a child, holding her against his warm, naked chest. Lillian put Faith's hands around his neck and, after they fell the second or third time, interlaced her fingers behind his head.

He carried her with apparent ease up the slope of the pool, stepped up onto the surround, then walked carefully through a doorway into a warmer atmosphere. Steam rose gently from a shallow bath into which he carefully laid her, keeping his right elbow under her neck as though she were a baby; meanwhile, other hands took her ankles, slipping her down until Alex released Faith's head to rest it on the side of the bath. Instants later, an inflatable plastic cushion was slipped beneath her head and she was pushed further into the warm water until it reached her breasts.

Taps gushed hot water into the shallow bath, raising the temperature and the level until it came up just short of her chin. Faith lay in the warmth, her eyes closed, feeling the heat gradually seep through her chilled flesh and bones. Several times Alex had spoken but she had remained silent until, at last, she felt she could make sense and opened her eyes, much to the relief of the two people bending over her anxiously.

Perched on either side of the bath, as naked as she was, Alex and Lillian looked apprehensively at her pale, drawn face.

'Hello,' she whispered, trying to smile, but finding she had little enough to be cheerful about. 'I'm sorry, darling.' A tear sprang from her eye. 'I tried, I really did. I just couldn't stay there any more.'

'What are you talking about?' he asked, his expression immediately cheering as she spoke.

'I gave up, Alex, I couldn't take it. I'm sorry.'

'Not what I heard,' he smiled. 'You're Chosen, my darling.'

'No.' She shook her head in a slow, weary movement which spoke volumes for her physical as well as her mental state. 'I can't lie to you. I gave up; Lillian will tell you. I told her when she got me out of the cage. I gave up.'

'Lillian?' He smiled across to the woman, then turned as a figure darkened the doorway.

'Congratulations, Faith. Welcome.' Prudence, as naked as any of them bent over, kissed her lips and passed on. Faith was about to protest when:

'Hello Faith, darling. We knew you could make it. Well done.' Julia kissed her, then left.

One by one they came, congratulated and kissed her, then passed on into another room, leaving the trio alone. When she had recovered from the initial shock she looked up at Alex and Lillian with wide-eyed curiosity, then with an effort of will, she managed to ask, 'Alex. What happened? Why are they . . .?'

'You're accepted,' he said with a quiet shrug.

'Tell the truth, Alex,' Lillian said quietly. 'She deserves the truth.'

'You filled me with . . . something,' Faith said. 'I remember that. Wine. And aphrodisiacs.'

'Not really,' Alex said. 'A sedative: a mild aphrodisiac. The rest was suggestion and Max arousing you, denying you release. That's all it took, darling.'

'But why?' she asked. It seemed too cruel.

'Later, Faith,' Lillian said. 'Are you feeling warmer? Come in for a plunge.'

'Yes,' Alex was already reaching for her, putting his hands beneath her arms, lifting her straight out of the water.

Her legs were better now; she was able to walk with a little assistance through a doorway into a noisy room which, as she entered, fell silent as though a switch had been operated. A sunken bath occupied the centre of the room, the only item in it, around which nine people were up to their necks in warm water. Willing hands helped her in, taking her weight, directing her to a seat between

Lillian and Alex, whose shoulders touched her on either side, holding her upright.

Faith leaned back against the warm, smooth side, letting herself go, feeling drowsy again. She could hear the voices talking around her, but like the previous night, they made little sense. She felt the warmth of the water and of their acceptance, marvelling at both. Their acceptance. It hardly seemed possible. She had been ready to give up, she *had* given up, but Lillian had refused to accept it. Or acknowledge that she had surrendered. Why? What was going on? Alex and Lillian helped her from the deep tub when they were alone again – where had everyone gone? – drying her and walking her up to the bedroom, where she was slipped between the rumpled sheets. Her last memory was of soft lips kissing her before she dozed again.

The insistent shaking roused her, hungry and alert, almost at once. She felt that, unlike her dream, where she had slept in an empty swimming pool, then warmed herself with a plunge, this was reality. Lillian, wearing little more than a large silk scarf sat on her bed, a look of patient interest on her face. She brightened when she saw the clarity of Faith's eye. Faith was not to know that the woman had been flitting in and out of the room for some half an hour, watching the restlessness of the sleeping young woman approach the point where she might awake naturally.

'Good afternoon, darling.' She leant forward, kissing Faith's mouth. Startled, Faith froze as the realisation set in; it was no dream. She *had* been Chosen!

Lillian initially had difficulty in keeping Faith in bed, controlling her excitement, and ignoring the torrent of questions which poured from her. Whilst Lillian maintained her expression of amused detachment, Faith gradually wound down until she lay back on the pillows, just looking at the older woman.

'Happy?' she asked then, but before she could answer, said, 'You shouldn't be.'

'Why not?' Faith asked. 'Where's Alex? What has he been doing?'

'Making arrangements for you,' Lillian answered, her expression slipping into a grim cast.

'What arrangements?' Faith asked.

'You're to go to the Stables, darling,' Lillian said. 'Tomorrow. Alex will take you.'

'What's at the Stables? Why should I go there? Oh! The college you mentioned.'

'You're to learn discipline,' Lillian said, then smiled, 'but knowing you, you'll knuckle down there and be out in no time.'

'Discipline?' Faith echoed, then sagged a little. 'You said I needed it.' Her manner was reproachfully accusing.

'I told the truth, Faith; so did the others. We all noticed things about you and we were right. Whether you knew it before or not, we told you the truth. Everyone agrees you need discipline. You need to learn to obey.'

'I do obey,' Faith retorted, but without heat.

'Not as well as you should; and you'll learn, there. But that's tomorrow!' Lillian brightened. 'We have the rest of today to get through, though it's more than half over. Come on. Shower.'

'What should I wear?' Faith asked as she pushed the covers back.

'You won't need very much,' Lillian smiled.

Lillian's 'won't need very much' meant a dab of perfume but, when she came out of the shower, Faith had a far greater problem.

'My nipples are huge, Lillian. Look!'

'Yes, darling.' The woman nodded. 'We put you in rings yesterday. Three different sizes, one after the other. They kept on swelling. They'll go down, don't worry, though they might stay a bit enlarged. You're going to have to work on those.'

'What happened, Lillian. I'm all confused. When did they . . . ? When did *you* decide?'

'The first time we saw you, darling.' The woman handed

Faith the perfume. 'At Rupert and Claire's party. You were virtually Chosen that night.'

'Then why was I . . .?'

'Because unless you pay for something, it's not worth having. The more you pay, the more you value it. You paid by being cold and alone, sexually humiliated. You were aroused in front of everyone, and then had your pleasure denied. I was supposed to jeer when you were fucking that bar.' Lillian's eyes lowered. 'But I turned away and cried instead. I remember when I did something like that for *my* initiation.'

'Then, I don't understand.' Faith stopped, her expression close to tears.

She recalled the hours of cold misery in the cage, waiting for the time when she would be warm again. An anger was flaring within her, an anger at all of them, Alex included.

'You're lovely. Without trying, you could have any man in London, but you've got Alex. Alex is Chosen and he knew what an asset you'd be to us, so he organised an introduction, which we approved. When you went home that night, we had all agreed: you were Chosen. But you still need training, my darling. Discipline, for one thing. If you're to be a Pleasure Slave, you *must* be trained.'

'A what? A Pleasure Slave?' Faith demanded. 'Oh! Yes.' Her memory of the catamaran returned.

'There are two kinds of Chosen: men and women. "Masters", and "Pleasure Slaves". We're supposed to minister to the Masters' every wish.' Lillian chuckled. 'More like the other way round. But you have to be disciplined, Faith. You're too flighty. You haven't got that poise, yet; that basic obedience. If you had, you'd have been wearing those boots Alex bought you. And you haven't learned nearly enough about sex and pleasure. You have to be trained for that, too.'

'Trained for sex?' Faith tried to suppress a nervous laugh without success. 'It's easer than I thought.' Lillian's expression grew a trifle more stern.

'It's serious, Faith. I've had an extensive training, from

239

the best! And I'm still learning. You'll have to be trained in sex, too. Some of it at the Stables, though they're mainly concerned with discipline. The rest you learn later, when you come back.'

Lillian went with Faith down to the modern kitchen where she prepared a light breakfast whilst explaining the events of the rest of the day.

'It's just a party, in some ways,' she said as Faith perched on the stool. 'We all have a good time. We usually take turns to entertain the others; now, it's Claire's turn. After that, you'll finish your initiation by riding the "Three-Horned God".'

'The what? The "Three-Horned God"? What's that?' Faith asked. She was intrigued by Lillian's scarf which floated about her as she moved, erratically revealing and concealing her fine figure.

'You'll find out at the time. Don't worry, I'll be there, holding your hand, helping you. You'll enjoy it. I promise.'

'You're making me nervous. Why can't you tell me?'

'You should know the answer to that, Faith,' Lillian sighed, turning her head from the toaster. 'Surprise is part of the fun, for you, too.' Lillian would not be drawn.

By seven, members of the group were slowly drifting into the games room, but one like Faith had never seen before. The floor, ceiling and walls were covered in champagne-coloured, long-haired sheepskin, making the interior both warm and womb-like. The furniture was sparse; a few raised sections in a semi-circle, all similarly covered, padded beneath with a firm yet yielding fabric, so that walking on them felt as though walking on a live animal. The lighting was subdued and subtly indirect, ensuring illumination without glare. There was a panel which controlled the stereo system, which Rupert immediately commandeered.

Faith half-lay on Alex; his hands gently fondled her breasts as he talked quietly to Harry about some financial arrangement. Her breathing was soft as she allowed her body to be caressed so intimately, and she licked her lips at the sensations which were emanating from behind her nipples. The music changed abruptly to a brassy, strident piece as the door was opened wide, to reveal Claire in a dramatic pose, standing with her hands against both sides of the frame.

She wore a long evening-gown in dark blue silk, with a V-neckline reaching almost to her bosom. The music sounded familiar and when Faith asked what it was, Alex replied, 'Sounds like "Finlandia",' but his eyes were on the fair-haired woman who strode into the room, her hands on her hips as the string section took over the theme. Rupert laid himself down on one of the long, padded benches which were slightly raised off the floor. For a few moments Claire stood looking down at him, then she began to twirl a black tag dangling from her waist as the percussion section trembled its punctuation.

Slowly, Claire began to move about, not so much dancing as striding until, as the full orchestra took up the familiar music, with the violins building up to a crescendo, Claire slipped back to her husband's side, slapping his chest with the tag. It was attached to her waist in a way that Faith was unable to determine. The tag was of leather. The sounds it made on Rupert's chest were loud enough to be heard above the music, though Claire ensured that their rhythm coincided with the tune. There were marks on his smooth skin, too: pink weals which rose immediately.

Rupert waited for another dramatic moment, when the strings were sawing away, and timed his strike to take the tag just as Claire brought it down. Immediately it was in his hand, Claire whirled round, waltzing away from him, leaving her skirt behind. Faith watched wide-eyed as Claire stopped dead, looking back at Rupert who was bundling up the skirt and laying it alongside him, still watching her all the while.

Claire's outfit looked more like a skating skirt now, though she wore long, dark blue stockings supported by a suspender belt of the same colour. Dark blue high-heeled shoes completed the picture. As the music went on, Claire began to move more freely, her skirt no longer encumbering her legs. She had obviously had dance lessons for she moved well, raising her legs in large circles, showing everyone that her briefs were of the same colour.

Approaching Harry, she turned her back to him, swaying from side to side in time to the music, and inviting him to collect the dark tag at the top of her back. Game for anything, Harry took hold of it as Claire bent forward, running her hands over her bare thighs, whilst coaxing his other hand down between her legs where she ensured he rubbed the soft silk of her briefs, before starting to move away from him. As Claire's zip pulled down slowly, Harry retained the tag; her shoulders wriggled to release the restraint, and the garment slipped down her legs.

Her slip reached to her hips; just. Like the remainder of the outfit, it was of dark blue silk. The music changed then, to Offenbach's famous overture to 'Orpheus in the Underworld'. As the orchestra began the lively piece, Claire began to dance again, her legs spreading wide as, with unrestrained abandon, she thrust herself at everyone.

It was to Lillian that she offered the tag to her brassière, moving herself voluptuously against her as the willing helper unfastened it, lowering the straps over her elbows. Claire was still moving sinuously, making no attempt to leave Lillian's side, thus provoking her into putting both hands within the arm-space of her slip and holding Claire's breasts. The dancing woman's body stopped moving; her head rolled back as she breathed deeply at this caress.

They were facing Faith and Alex as the brassière slipped almost unnoticed down the inside of the slip, making Faith's breath catch. She knew that she was being aroused by the sight of this, knew too that she was not alone. Alex's erection was pressing against one of her buttocks, so she moved slightly on his lap to allow it to slip between them. His hands covered her breasts as Claire's were covered; but the dance was moving on.

Claire sped away from Lillian, laughing with her as she escaped and turning to blow her a kiss; then after a few steps, she moved towards Rupert again. Her husband lay smiling up at her, his eyes alight with anticipation. For a few moments Claire moved languorously in front of him, then carefully placed her left high-heel beside his head, bending her knee to pull her crotch closer to his face. Rupert had lain back as her leg came over his chest so that supine, he looked up at his wife's pudenda encased in the thin, dark blue silk.

Not a word was spoken, but Rupert unfastened the suspenders on Claire's left leg, rolled the stocking down to her ankle beside his head, then removed the shoe and stocking while looking straight up at her. Her mound was only six inches from his face, and it came closer as Claire knelt on her left knee before placing her right on the other side of Rupert's head.

With her silk-covered sex less than two inches from his face, Rupert unfastened the suspender on Claire's right leg, repeating the process of removing her stocking and shoe whilst his wife moved her hips slightly, bringing her soft flesh ever nearer to him. Claire had judged it properly for, when he had finished, he was able to move his nose slightly to touch her swelling sex.

Even Faith and Alex, on the far side of the group, were able to see that Claire's briefs were moist, delineating the labial lips. As she knelt over him, Rupert's hands moved again, slipping the suspenders out of her briefs at the sides. Rupert had moved down a fraction so that, with Claire's knees spread wide on either side of his head, his mouth was able to reach the hot, aromatic sex she presented to him.

Almost in slow-motion, Rupert's hands reached over Claire's thighs to slip the suspenders into the front of her briefs and out from the top. All the while, his hands stayed within her garment. Faith could see that he was stroking her mound, moving ever lower as she pushed her sex forward. His mouth fastened around her clitoris through the silk, making Claire gasp again; throwing back her head, she whimpered her desire. His fingers separated her sex-lips, withdrawing again to leave the silk trapped between them. So thin was the fabric that her blood-filled lips were perfectly defined.

Rupert withdrew his hands from her briefs, running them upwards over her abdomen beneath her slip and around her back to the catch which held the suspender belt on her body. He released it and cast the garment aside. Claire's hips were moving slowly and steadily about Rupert's mouth; her breathing was ragged with lust as she fought to control her climax.

His hands moved back again to the sides of her hips as the music changed to Sibelius, the 'Karelia Suite' with the fast, thundering brass. One side of her briefs came apart as he unfastened the popper there, exposing half her mound which still rested on his mouth. Then the other side gave way, the fabric falling over Rupert's face, though he seemed not to notice. They could see that he was still mouthing her sex through the fabric which, very slowly, Claire began to draw between her legs from behind.

As his mouth met her bare sex for the first time she gasped, pushing down with her body to anchor herself to him, rocking her sex back and forth with a desperate look of abandon on her face. Her musk diffused among the spell-bound onlookers as Rupert's hands rose within her slip to cup her breasts, his fingers setting off tremors within her which made her moan.

Claire crossed her hands across her body, grasped the hem of the slip then, as she rocked more violently above him, began to draw the fabric slowly upwards. But her passion was too urgent for that. What had begun as a slow movement ended – as the 'Karelia' approached the orgiastic climax – in a frenzied removal of the dark blue slip. With her hands poised above her, Claire threw back her head; her hoarse, harsh cry of ecstatic release, delivered with closed eyes and her tongue poking defiantly out of her mouth, rent the air.

Faith found herself breathing almost as raggedly as Claire, the emotion of watching the woman seduce her husband filling her with a similar lust. Yet it was tinged with shame too; a shame at sharing such an emotional and private moment. She had watched Rupert penetrate Claire before – had seen her take three or four men within her – in fact. But there was something so very intimate about that; something Faith could hardly begin to understand. She knew that they had put it on as an entertainment; had been entertained by it, too. Yet to Faith's mind, that hardly detracted from the notion that it was, essentially, a private moment. To have shared it made her feel like an interloper.

When the tension of the moment of climax died away, Faith looked at some of the others, finding that Harry had moved to Julia, who was bent over, obviously with his erection wedged in her bottom. Julia's flushed expression of lust was sufficient to convince the younger woman that she was being satisfied in an acceptable manner. Lillian was stretched out on her back, Simon's lips at her breasts and his hand between her thighs whilst her chest heaved and her tongue poked out. Prudence was kneeling before Colin, his member in her mouth, her head moving back and forth slowly as her hands grasped the hairy base by his scrotum. Colin's eyes were closed, an expression of bliss on his face. Marigold was bending forward while Max held her breasts, but there was no other evidence of sexual activity.

Alex's erection felt enormous between her buttocks, and the aroma of her own musk was rising from her hot, wet sex, yet he had made no attempt to adjust his position to penetrate her, which she found slightly worrying. Had he lost interest in her? Was he intending to fill Claire's honey-pot when Rupert was finished with her?

Chapter Eighteen

Faith had hardly had time to recover when Lillian, having spread a thin sheet of clear plastic on the floor, called her forward to the central open space.

'Come along, darling. Time to ride the "Three-Horned God". Kneel down now.'

'But . . .!' Faith was about to protest when Alex whispered in her ear:

'Darling, it's very important. This is your final acceptance.'

'Well . . .,' Faith shrugged, rising from Alex's lap, looking back as she heard a ragged cheer. His erection was standing straight up, making her blush even as she knelt in front of Lillian, though facing directly away from Alex. If anyone was to see her sex, it should be him, she thought.

Lillian nodded to Simon, who placed a wide-necked jar of oil just next to Faith's right hand. The older woman wasted no time in starting; scooping up some oil, she knelt in front of Faith, running her hands down to the younger woman's swinging breasts. She kept her own knees apart so Faith could see the tip of her clitoris and her breasts. Then Lillian circled Faith's breasts with her oiled fingers, squeezing them concentrically towards the nipples. Though Lillian's touch was light, the pressure on her tingling nipples was too much for the young woman whose head was thrown back as, open-mouthed, she gasped in surprise and arousal. Lillian's mouth was on her own in a moment, her tongue exploring Faith's while her hands squeezed again, making Faith feel that her nipples would explode.

When she had released Faith's mouth, Lillian moved over to one side of her, using the oil to lubricate the passage of her hands across Faith's stomach. She could feel the soft flesh hardening beneath her touch and the slight tremors in her belly as Faith's responses met the challenge of the arousal. The trouble with someone as undisciplined as Faith was – like before – keeping her boiling while all the arrangements were made.

Lillian stopped short of Faith's mound, instead, sweeping around her hips, then up her back to her neck to start again, oiling the soft, rib-marked skin. Faith felt the pleasure coming, helpless to prevent its onset, yet knew she should do something.

'Please, Lillian. Please,' she gasped out in a whisper. 'Help me, please, Lillian. Stop it coming. Stop *me* coming.' Her head moved up and down in a frantic movement as she swallowed, her eyes already unfocused. Above her, Lillian smiled at Max and then at Alex, nodding as she broke into a grin. This girl was going to be good. Already she knew that she should delay her pleasure, and she had not been trained at all.

Quickly she put her thumb and forefinger around Faith's nipples, squeezing hard, listening to the little thankful cries from the younger woman as the lust lessened within her liquid belly. But Lillian was still massaging the oil on her back, working it into the skin as she had done for two weeks, familiarising Faith with the procedure. The young woman would soon understand the meaning of all the attention.

She dribbled oil onto her hips, ensuring that a good half of it ran slowly down her 'natal notch' like syrup, whilst the remainder was rubbed into the tissues about the girdle. The pressure there would start to arouse her again, even as Lillian's hand followed the oil down the space between her pale pink buttocks.

Her fingers were quick to smooth the trail of oil up onto the sides of Faith's buttocks, working it into the flesh there long before the oil reached the base of her spine. Then more was added; it ran down past her coccyx to the final destination: Faith's wrinkled, pink and brown anus in its sepia housing.

Faith raised her head in a gasp of familiar pleasure at the liquid sensation on her bottom mouth, clenching her buttocks until Lillian smacked her lightly, telling her to keep still. With her finger liberally coated in the oil, Lillian placed it directly on her anus, pressing until the muscles gave way, and causing Faith to lift her head. Lillian looked at Max, who nodded, smiling. Faith's tongue was sticking out as she felt the pleasure coming on again with the pressure.

Lillian withdrew her finger, scooped up more oil, then began to coat her perineum, pressing and tapping, listening to Faith's ragged breathing as it rose in speed and power. As soon as it changed note, Lillian reached around Faith and, quite deliberately, slapped the sides of her breasts, the sound of oiled flesh striking oiled flesh resonant in its flat crack.

Faith cried out: a short, sharp protest. But she knew that one slap had been necessary, for her pleasure had almost been delivered. If Lillian had been any slower, she would have been too late, which would have been a disgrace in this company. She had seen how Claire had controlled herself, right up to the time when her briefs had been removed and Rupert's mouth had taken possession of her. Surely she could do the same.

Returning to her work with a palm now soaked in oil, Lillian began coating Faith's sex-lips fully; she held her as though this had been the purpose of the embrace, that her oiled hand should measure the heat of her sex. Yet once this had been accomplished, Lillian's fingers separated Faith's lips and her palm pressed upwards, coating the dull red of her cleft with oil.

Faith's natural oil was now seeping from her, mingling with the clear oil Lillian was using; this was brought up to coat her clitoris which was promptly smacked with a fingertip, for her breathing was wrong. She was approaching another climax, which would spoil everything. Faith had to ride the "Three-Horned God" and, if Lillian had anything to do with it, she would. That Faith's pleasure was by now imminent was obvious to all; even Marigold was watching, fascinated at the sight of Lillian playing with this young thing like an expert angler with a good fish.

Simon was beckoned forward by Lillian, who moved back up towards Faith's head; her oily hand ran up the young woman's stomach, between her breasts, then spread out to hold the dangling fruits.

'Simon is here, now,' Lillian whispered softly to the panting young woman, whose eyes were open though she could see very little. The lust that filled her body was causing all other mechanisms to shut down.

'Feel? He's going to lie between your legs, and you must lower yourself onto him. I'll guide him into you, darling, but *you* must move. *You* must sheathe yourself around him.'

Faith could hear her, feel the slippery movement beneath her, yet there seemed to be no reason for Simon to satisfy her wonderful lust.

'Alex. Alex,' she breathed, forming the words with difficulty, for she kept having to withdraw her tongue from her mouth to speak.

'Hush, darling. You belong to the Chosen, not to Alex. Alex is here, watching you. He will be here when you are ready. Simon is beneath you now. Lower yourself onto him.' Lillian's voice was whispering in her ear, urging her almost by the tone of voice alone to comply.

This was one of the tests of the Chosen: whether the applicant would obey. It was an odd fact that only those who could obey were sent for training in obedience: an apparent contradiction in terms. Yet they had found that those unable to obey this instruction were useless to them. To encourage her, Lillian slipped a hand behind Faith, between her legs and, with great care and gentleness, let it slide up the join of her vulva.

Faith's groan of agonised pleasure announced her decision as Lillian's finger reached her love bud, sending another wave of pleasure through her. In Faith's mind, the only way she could obtain release was by complying with Lillian's instruction. Simon had mounted her in the past, and spreading her knees wider, she began to lower herself onto the upright erection of the young man beneath her.

Lillian had seen the tremors flicker across the taut, hard belly, so anticipated the movement by three seconds, just enough time to take Simon's member in her hand and move it slightly. With her other hand, Lillian opened Faith's love lips so that, when the young woman had reached the point where Simon touched her, his hot glans passed smoothly into the heat of her passage. Faith groaned again at the touch, matching Simon's involuntary exclamation.

As soon as she felt herself sheathing him, she drove herself hard downwards until she could go no further. A tortured cry was emitted from her lips as her head was flung back and her vaginal muscles tightened on him. Lillian nodded to Max who approached Faith, both of them meeting beside Faith's face.

'Darling,' Lillian whispered in her left ear, caressing her right hand over Faith's left breast, squeezing it towards the nipple again. Beneath her, Simon was already letting his fingertips run lightly over her right nipple, setting up asynchronous sensations.

'Max is here, darling,' Lillian whispered, glad to see that Faith's mouth was hanging open, her lips almost as swollen as those of her labia. 'He wants your mouth, my darling. He wants to fill your mouth. Open your mouth just a little more. Just a little more, and take in the second horn, darling.'

There was no hesitation this time. Faith's mouth was already opening wider, her lips reaching for him. The sensations from her abdomen were driving her to distraction; yet Simon was holding her legs wide apart with his own legs. His hands had stopped caressing her breasts; now they were pinching her hard nipples, bringing her rising pleasure to within manageable limits. The second horn! Simon was the first, yes. That was a horn stuck within her vagina. As Max's erection entered her mouth, forcing her teeth wider apart, her tongue trying to flicker around it, she realised that this was the second; but what about the third? This was two horns, where was the third? And Lillian, having summoned Alex forward, was speaking again.

'Darling. Lie on Simon. Let your arms go; bring them down to your sides. That's it.' The young woman complied. She had been partly lying on the man, but had not stopped supporting herself. 'Good. Now Alex is here, darling, and he is going to enter your bottom. Yes!' Lillian said quickly as the young woman started, her eyes opening.

Through a kind of haze, Faith could make out only the edge of Lillian's face; yet it was comforting to have her there. What was she saying? Alex? Alex wanted her bottom?

'Put your hands on your buttocks, darling. That's it, grip them,' Lillian crooned, almost ecstatic at her success. 'Now. Pull them gently apart. Gently but firmly, as wide as you can. That's it! Pull them apart so that Alex can enter your bottom. He was the first of us in your cunny, darling, the first in your mouth; he should be the first in your bottom. He's your Master, so he should be the first. There! He's almost there.' She nodded urgently to the tall man as she heard Faith's sob.

As Alex's erection met Faith's palpitating anus, he drove against the muscles, penetrating her to the hilt. Max withdrew his penis from her mouth so that Faith groaned, 'God!' in a voice which only the four of them heard. As soon as she had spoken, Max pressed his penis back against her mouth, finding that she opened it without protest.

'Darling!' Lillian enthused happily. 'You're finally Chosen. You're riding the "Three-Horned God". Now, don't move; don't shake or move your head. Move your hips very, very gently, and squeeze your muscles down there. Squeeze Alex while you're riding Simon. And Max will take care of your mouth.'

There was silence amongst those watching as Faith, after being still for a few moments, began to do as she was told. She was too inexperienced to make much of a job of it – any of the other women could have done better – but all of them had more experience. They had, with only one exception, been in Faith's position; half-kneeling with three erections within her, all of them trying to discharge.

Faith felt almost exhausted, both emotionally and physically. Yet a corner of her mind prompted the familiar blushing, the hot flush which covered a good part of her skin for the shame and degradation she felt. If her mother could see her now, not just taking a man in her sex, but one in her mouth! That would cause her mother to give her a stern lecture on how 'nicely-brought-up' girls behaved. But to be buggered at the same time!

Yet, to Faith's shame, she felt only the lust which Lillian had worked up. She felt the deep, desperate wanting within her, the passion for release she knew she had to satisfy. If she ignored it, if she remained as she was, Faith would never know what it felt like to have three men discharge into her. She would also cry with frustration, for her emotions were being stimulated as much as her body. Lillian knew all the erogenous zones; she had worked on them over the past two weeks. She had massaged Faith carefully, making sure her bottom mouth was well-oiled and pliable. Lillian had tested it with her finger. Faith could remember that happening every day. Lillian had said that if Alex wanted her bottom, she should make sure it was prepared for him; and it had been.

She began to move, feeling Alex move with her. He had taken over control of her breasts from Simon, who laid his hands, palm upwards, flat on his abdomen. As she moved, these palms added to her tactile stimulation and . . . yes! It must be Lillian who was reaching between Alex's legs. Fingers were very lightly rubbing up and down her bare sex-lips, the additional stimulation driving her to near-distraction.

Faith's muscles began to squeeze on the hard rod of Alex's erection within her rectum, though she was unable to see him grimacing as she worked. He had some experience of this sensation – provided by various women over the years – yet he thought that Faith's muscles must be more powerful than most, for it felt very different. Max's expression was almost seraphic as he moved himself in time with this young woman. He had, like the others, to watch for Lillian's signal of Faith's release, though he was listening, too. It was important that they all discharge as closely as possible within her, so that Faith could appreciate the sensation of being completely filled with semen. She would swallow Max's of course, Lillian would make sure of that. Faith would have Simon's in her cervix and Alex's in her back passage; more than enough for anyone.

Faith could feel her own passion rising. Surely, she thought, Lillian would allow her release at last. She was doing as required, riding the 'Three-Horned God'. Yet she had no memory of how this had begun, only that the most wonderful sensations were pulsing through her. Her breasts were on fire. Her vagina felt as though it would burst into flames, and her anus! Her anus felt as though an immovable red-hot poker had been inserted into it. But most of all, the sensations passing between these points were building up to a lubricious climax which positively hurt.

It was as though an ache was turning into an absolute agony of pain. What had once been a pleasurable activity had become a torture. The sooner she relieved these three horns of their cargo, the sooner this pain would be relieved. Yet the pressure was still building, passing the point where she had expected her pleasure to come. Higher it rose, and the higher it went, the tighter grew her grasp on both Alex and Simon, whilst her hands still held her buttocks apart.

With hardly any warning, her release was upon her, her chest jerking; her whole body shook as though animated by a powerful electrical current. Unable to shriek her release due to Max's organ distending her mouth, she was forced to give a long, drawn-out wail which his discharge smothered; his hands held her head still as, his eyes screwed tightly shut, his legs trembling, he waited for his ejaculation to stop.

Beneath her, Simon had been the first to discharge, her stimulation of his erection too much to bear. By tightening up on Alex, Faith had also tightened up on him, so that in addition to the stroking stimulation from her passage, he had also had the stimulation of her vaginal muscles which had devastated him.

Alex was the last to discharge, mostly because Faith had not yet learned to control her muscles to cater for that particular entry. He had remained buried within her, content to stay still while she tried her best. It would damage her anus – even one so liberally oiled – if he began to work his erection back and forth as though filling her vagina. This was not a practice he would adopt too often; her moist sex was more than adequate for his needs; but this was something Faith would have to know, and practise, too. When she returned from the Stables, he would have to test her bottom again; possibly quite severely. If all else failed, he would have to whip her bottom mouth to make it obey, to dilate to receive him, when necessary.

Max withdrew from Faith first, Lillian checking the young woman's mouth for the familiar signs of white fluid before closing it again, then stroking her throat fondly with a finger to induce her to swallow. When she did, licking her dry lips, Lillian asked for water for her while Alex slowly removed himself.

Faith felt this. She was regaining her senses, feeling Alex's soft wetness on her thighs. Then Simon turned her onto her back like a rag doll; he had slipped out in the process of rolling over. Suddenly a pair of strong arms held her, one going round her shoulders, raising her into a sitting position. Something cold and welcome was pressed to her mouth, and liquid trickled down her throat.

Then there was something soft rubbing the chill on her lips, and on her lower lips too, making her jerk.

Her eyes opened. Alex was holding her. Alex, who had introduced her. Alex who had taught her, who had tied her up and spanked her. Alex who had buggered her! She felt as though he was still wedged in her bottom; yet the ache was no longer a pain, the ache had gone, being replaced by a warm, restful feeling. In front of her, Lillian was busy with some water, dipping her finger in a glass, then running her finger around Faith's sex. It was a delicious feeling after the intense heat.

From Lillian, Faith looked up, expecting to see the other two who had penetrated her, but there were no men there at all. Had they left as soon as she had begun her ride? Or at the completion of it? With surprised eyes she looked at the fond expression of Julia, at Prudence's amusement and at Claire's cheerful mien. Even Marigold looked less forbidding, too.

'Why?' she asked, looking up at Alex. 'Why did you . . .?'

'My darling girl,' Lillian answered when he hesitated, 'all of us have to go through that. Each of us has ridden the Three-Horned God in public. You have to rid yourself of all that middle-class morality, Faith. You're one of the Chosen, not the girl who came down from Oxford.'

'Why the "Three-Horned God"?' Faith asked. 'I mean, I can see the "Three-Horned" bit . . .'

'Do you remember Max coming out of your mouth when I entered your bottom?' Alex asked quietly. 'Like almost everyone else, you exclaimed "God".'

'Usually, that's the first time we "receive callers" like that,' Lillian explained quietly, 'though you should expect to have that done again. That's "the Master's right". If your Master wishes, he can insist on it.'

'Even Harry doesn't insist,' Julia said, shaking her head.

'What happens now?' Faith asked. 'Where are the others?'

'They've gone to organise some drinks,' Lillian smiled. 'I don't suppose many of them feel like sex for a while.'

'Rupert came,' Claire said, 'when you were working on Faith. It was lucky he was inside me at the time. If the others were like him . . .' she sighed.

'What should I do?' Faith looked up at Alex, who smiled at her.

Taking both her hands in his, he turned, so that she dropped onto her back again. With no apparent effort he separated her knees, bringing his rising erection close to her, then moving so that his knees separated her thighs wider. He could feel her heat on him, yet it was insufficient to rouse him to penetrate her. Placing himself at her entrance, he held her like that until the pheromones in her musk brought him to excitement, and permitted him to enter.

The women watched with amused expressions as Alex finally lodged himself inside her, correctly interpreting her gasp and jerk as her flesh gave way before him. She was used to being treated with more deference, but the familiar feeling of him soothed away the momentary discomfort.

'This is where you belong, Faith,' Lillian said. 'You're a Pleasure Slave. You function is to satisfy any and all of the Masters, whether with your mouth, your bottom, your cunny or your hands. Your own Master can prevent it, of course. But if he has no objection, then you can be used by another.

'If you disobey, you'll be disciplined. Whipped if need be. You'll be trained in discipline at the Stables and, on your return, your Master will train you in sex and pleasure. He may do this in any way he sees fit. He may want you to obtain your pleasure through pain. That's his decision. You *must* obey him.'

'Are you really my Master?' Faith asked anxiously, breathless, her eyes on the two ice-blue chips above her.

'Your Master is a very shrewd man, Faith,' Lillian said quietly. 'You will meet him after you return from the Stables.'

'I'd like you to be my Master,' Faith said, closing her eyes as the pleasure began building up again.

'Your Master has already claimed you, little one,' Alex said. 'All I am doing is enjoying you for the last few hours before you leave for the Stables.'

'What happens at the Stables?' Faith asked.

'You learn discipline.' He was moving faster within her, matching his own passion to hers.

'How?' Faith asked.

'They have ways.' He looked sad again, but Faith was too aroused to care.

She had Alex's erection in the place she wanted it at last. Tomorrow she would go to the Stables and learn this discipline they spoke so much about. And when she returned, she would demand that Alex be her Master. She was Chosen.

NEW BOOKS

Coming up from Nexus and Black Lace

Nexus

Fallen Angels by Kendal Grahame
July 1994   Price: £4.99   ISBN: 0 352 32934 3
A mysterious stranger sets two young ladies the ultimate lascivious challenge: to engage in as many sexual acts with as many people as possible. Rich rewards await them if they succeed – but the task proves to be its own reward!

The Teaching of Faith by Elizabeth Bruce
July 1994   Price: £4.99   ISBN: 0 352 32936 X
Until she met Alex, Faith had never experienced the full range of pleasures that sex can bring. But after her initiation into his exclusive set of libertines, a whole new realm of prurient possibilities is opened up for her.

The Training Grounds by Sarah Veitch
August 1994   Price: £4.99   ISBN: 0 352 32940 8
Charlotte was expecting to spend her time on the island relaxing and enjoying the sun. But now, having been handed over to the Master, she has discovered the island to be a vast correction centre. She'll soon have a healthy glow anyway ...

Memoirs of a Cornish Governess by Yolanda Celbridge
August 1994   Price: £4.99   ISBN: 0 352 32941 6
As Governess to a Lord and Lady, Miss Constance's chief task is to educate their son Freddie. But word soon gets about of her unusual techniques, and before long, most of the village is popping in for some good old-fashioned correction.

BLACK lace

The Gift of Shame by Sarah Hope-Walker
July 1994   Price: £4.99   ISBN: 0 352 32935 1
Helen had always thought that her fantasies would remain just that – wild and deviant whimsies with no place in everyday life. But Jeffrey soon changes that, helping her overcome her reservations to enjoy their decadent games to the full.

Summer of Enlightenment by Cheryl Mildenhall
July 1994   Price: £4.99   ISBN: 0 352 32937 8
Karin's love life takes a turn for the better when she is introduced to the charming Nicolai. She is drawn to him in spite of his womanising – and the fact that he is married to her friend. As their flirting escalates, further temptations place themselves in her path.

Juliet Rising by Cleo Cordell
August 1994   Price: £4.99   ISBN: 0 352 32938 6
At Madame Nicol's strict academy for young ladies, 18th-century values are by turns enforced with severity and flagrantly scorned. Juliet joins in her lessons enthusiastically; but whether she has learnt them well enough to resist the charms of the devious Reynard is another question.

A Bouquet of Black Orchids by Roxanne Carr
August 1994   Price: £4.99   ISBN: 0 352 32939 4
The luxurious Black Orchid Club once more provides the setting for a modern tale of decadence. Maggie's lustful adventures at the exclusive health spa take an intriguing turn when a charismatic man makes her a tempting offer.

Nexus

NEXUS BACKLIST

Where a month is marked on the right, this book will not be published until that month in 1994. All books are priced £4.99 unless another price is given.

CONTEMPORARY EROTICA

CONTOURS OF DARKNESS	Marco Vassi		
THE DEVIL'S ADVOCATE	Anonymous		
THE DOMINO TATTOO	Cyrian Amberlake	£4.50	
THE DOMINO ENIGMA	Cyrian Amberlake		
THE DOMINO QUEEN	Cyrian Amberlake		
ELAINE	Stephen Ferris		
EMMA'S SECRET WORLD	Hilary James		
EMMA ENSLAVED	Hilary James		
FALLEN ANGELS	Kendal Grahame		
THE FANTASIES OF JOSEPHINE SCOTT	Josephine Scott		
THE GENTLE DEGENERATES	Marco Vassi		
HEART OF DESIRE	Maria del Rey		
HELEN – A MODERN ODALISQUE	Larry Stern		
HIS MISTRESS'S VOICE	G. C. Scott		Nov
THE HOUSE OF MALDONA	Yolanda Celbridge		Dec
THE INSTITUTE	Maria del Rey		
SISTERHOOD OF THE INSTITUTE	Maria del Rey		Sep
JENNIFER'S INSTRUCTION	Cyrian Amberlake		
MELINDA AND THE MASTER	Susanna Hughes		
MELINDA AND ESMERALDA	Susanna Hughes		
MELINDA AND THE COUNTESS	Susanna Hughes		Dec
MIND BLOWER	Marco Vassi		

MS DEEDES AT HOME	Carole Andrews	£4.50	
MS DEEDES ON PARADISE ISLAND	Carole Andrews		
THE NEW STORY OF O	Anonymous		
OBSESSION	Maria del Rey		
ONE WEEK IN THE PRIVATE HOUSE	Esme Ombreux		
THE PALACE OF FANTASIES	Delver Maddingley		
THE PALACE OF HONEYMOONS	Delver Maddingley		
THE PALACE OF EROS	Delver Maddingley		
PARADISE BAY	Maria del Rey		
THE PASSIVE VOICE	G. C. Scott		
THE SALINE SOLUTION	Marco Vassi		
STEPHANIE	Susanna Hughes		
STEPHANIE'S CASTLE	Susanna Hughes		
STEPHANIE'S REVENGE	Susanna Hughes		
STEPHANIE'S DOMAIN	Susanna Hughes		
STEPHANIE'S TRIAL	Susanna Hughes		
STEPHANIE'S PLEASURE	Susanna Hughes		Sep
THE TEACHING OF FAITH	Elizabeth Bruce		
THE TRAINING GROUNDS	Sarah Veitch		

EROTIC SCIENCE FICTION

ADVENTURES IN THE PLEASUREZONE	Delaney Silver	
RETURN TO THE PLEASUREZONE	Delaney Silver	
FANTASYWORLD	Larry Stern	Oct
WANTON	Andrea Arven	

ANCIENT & FANTASY SETTINGS

CHAMPIONS OF LOVE	Anonymous		
CHAMPIONS OF PLEASURE	Anonymous		
CHAMPIONS OF DESIRE	Anonymous		
THE CLOAK OF APHRODITE	Kendal Grahame		Nov
SLAVE OF LIDIR	Aran Ashe	£4.50	
DUNGEONS OF LIDIR	Aran Ashe		
THE FOREST OF BONDAGE	Aran Ashe	£4.50	
PLEASURE ISLAND	Aran Ashe		
WITCH QUEEN OF VIXANIA	Morgana Baron		

EDWARDIAN, VICTORIAN & OLDER EROTICA

ANNIE	Evelyn Culber	
ANNIE AND THE SOCIETY	Evelyn Culber	Oct
BEATRICE	Anonymous	
CHOOSING LOVERS FOR JUSTINE	Aran Ashe	
GARDENS OF DESIRE	Roger Rougiere	
THE LASCIVIOUS MONK	Anonymous	
LURE OF THE MANOR	Barbra Baron	
MAN WITH A MAID 1	Anonymous	
MAN WITH A MAID 2	Anonymous	
MAN WITH A MAID 3	Anonymous	
MEMOIRS OF A CORNISH GOVERNESS	Yolanda Celbridge	
TIME OF HER LIFE	Josephine Scott	
VIOLETTE	Anonymous	

THE JAZZ AGE

BLUE ANGEL DAYS	Margarete von Falkensee	
BLUE ANGEL NIGHTS	Margarete von Falkensee	
BLUE ANGEL SECRETS	Margarete von Falkensee	
CONFESSIONS OF AN ENGLISH MAID	Anonymous	
PLAISIR D'AMOUR	Anne-Marie Villefranche	
FOLIES D'AMOUR	Anne-Marie Villefranche	
JOIE D'AMOUR	Anne-Marie Villefranche	
MYSTERE D'AMOUR	Anne-Marie Villefranche	
SECRETS D'AMOUR	Anne-Marie Villefranche	
SOUVENIR D'AMOUR	Anne-Marie Villefranche	
WAR IN HIGH HEELS	Piers Falconer	

SAMPLERS & COLLECTIONS

EROTICON 1	ed. J-P Spencer	
EROTICON 2	ed. J-P Spencer	
EROTICON 3	ed. J-P Spencer	
EROTICON 4	ed. J-P Spencer	
NEW EROTICA 1	ed. Esme Ombreux	
NEW EROTICA 2	ed. Esme Ombreux	
THE FIESTA LETTERS	ed. Chris Lloyd	£4.50

NON-FICTION

FEMALE SEXUAL AWARENESS	B & E McCarthy	£5.99
HOW TO DRIVE YOUR MAN WILD IN BED	Graham Masterton	
HOW TO DRIVE YOUR WOMAN WILD IN BED	Graham Masterton	
LETTERS TO LINZI	Linzi Drew	
LINZI DREW'S PLEASURE GUIDE	Linzi Drew	

Please send me the books I have ticked above.

Name ....
Address ....
....
.... Post code ....

Send to: **Cash Sales, Nexus Books, 332 Ladbroke Grove, London W10 5AH**

Please enclose a cheque or postal order, made payable to **Nexus Books**, to the value of the books you have ordered plus postage and packing costs as follows:

UK and BFPO – £1.00 for the first book, 50p for the second book, and 30p for each subsequent book to a maximum of £3.00;

Overseas (including Republic of Ireland) – £2.00 for the first book, £1.00 for the second book, and 50p for each subsequent book.

If you would prefer to pay by VISA or ACCESS/MASTERCARD, please write your card number here:

Please allow up to 28 days for delivery

— — — —   — — — —   — — — —   — — — —

Signature: ─────────────────────